OTHER GIL MALLOY MYSTERIES

SHOOTING FOR THE STARS

A Gil Malloy Novel

R. G. Belsky

ATRIA PAPERBACK

New York   London   Toronto   Sydney   New Delhi

ATRIA PARBACK

ATRIA PAPERBACK
An Imprint of Simon & Schuster, Inc.
1230 Avenue of the Americas
New York, NY 10020

First Atria Paperback edition August 2015

ATRIA PAPERBACK and colophon are trademarks of Simon & Schuster, Inc.

For information about special discounts for bulk purchases, please contact Simon & Schuster Special Sales at 1-866-506-1949 or business@simonandschuster.com.

The Simon & Schuster Speakers Bureau can bring authors to your live event. For more information or to book an event, contact the Simon & Schuster Speakers Bureau at 1-866-248-3049 or visit our website at www.simonspeakers.com.

Cover design by James Perales
Cover photos: VINTAGE Theater marquee © SHUTTERSTOCK/Kobby Dagan
BILLBOARD © SHUTTERSTOCK/ESPRIT

Manufactured in the United States of America

10 9 8 7 6 5 4 3 2 1

Library of Congress Cataloging-in-Publication Data

Belsky, Richard.
 Shooting for the stars : a Gil Malloy novel / R. G. Belsky.—First Atria paperback edition.
 pages ; cm.— (The Gil Malloy series)
1. Reporters and reporting—Fiction. 2. Serial murder investigation—Fiction. I. Title.
 PS3552.E53385S55 2015
 813'.54—dc23
2014049242

ISBN 978-1-4767-6236-4
ISBN 978-1-4767-6237-1 (ebook)

For Laura Morgan—the real Laura in my life who reads everything first and thinks Gil Malloy is a lot more interesting than me.

I wish my life was a non-stop Hollywood movie show
A fantasy world of celluloid villains and heroes
Because celluloid heroes never feel any pain
And celluloid heroes never really die

—The Kinks, "Celluloid Heroes"

It's all make believe, isn't it?

—Marilyn Monroe

PART ONE

CELLULOID
HEROES

CHAPTER 1

THE executive producer of *The Prime Time Files* had an office filled with pictures of him posing alongside famous people. George Clooney. Barbra Streisand. Bill and Hillary Clinton. Michael Jordan. Katie Couric. Ted Danson. The message was clear: this guy was plugged-in, powerful, a player with the celebrity elite. I wasn't sure whether to shake his hand or ask for his autograph.

Gary Lang, the executive producer, was telling me now in great detail about all his accomplishments, all the awards he'd won and how much money he'd made in the television and movie business. I'd been listening to him since I walked into his office fifteen minutes earlier. I figured I could last maybe another minute, tops, until my head exploded.

"I'm sure you can understand my concern, Mr. Malloy," Lang said. "I have a reputation to uphold. Abbie Kincaid is an extremely popular television personality and a highly respected journalist. So before I allow you to interview her, I need to make sure you understand that whatever you write about us has to be very classy."

"Classy," I repeated.

"Those are the ground rules we need to agree to before you talk to Abbie. I want to be sure that you or your newspaper won't indulge in any irresponsible journalism here. Abbie's image is very important to me. Whatever you write about her must be done with style and with sophistication. Above all, it must be . . ."

"Classy?"

"Yes."

"I can do classy," I smiled.

Gary Lang was in his midforties. Black curly hair, horn-rimmed glasses, very intense. He was wearing a three-piece pinstriped gray suit, blue shirt, and red tie. The vest and suit jacket were buttoned up and his tie unloosened—even though it was mid-June. Definitely a power suit. Only problem was he had a bit of a paunch that was sticking out between the buttons of the vest and jacket. Hard to impress people when you're sporting a spare tire around your middle.

Me, I had on a pair of washed-out jeans, a blue linen blazer, and a T-shirt underneath with the name and number of third baseman David Wright—the captain of the New York Mets and my favorite New York City athlete at the moment. I should point out that normally I wear the Mets T-shirt hanging out over my pants. But I tucked it in before going to meet Lang. Gil Malloy is the kind of reporter who goes that extra mile for a big story.

"Do you have any questions, Mr. Malloy?" Lang asked me.

"Yeah, do you actually know all these celebrities?" I said, looking around at the famous people in the pictures all around his office.

"Of course I do."

"I mean, you've met George Clooney?"

"Yes."

"Michael Jordan? Bill and Hillary Clinton? Ted Danson . . . ?"

"I met them all. Why else would I be in the pictures?"

"I don't know . . . I thought maybe it was trick photography or something . . . like in *Forrest Gump* when they made it look like Tom Hanks was talking to dead presidents."

"That's ridiculous."

"Actually, I find that easier to believe than you talking to Ted Danson."

"I happen to know Ted Danson very well," Lang snapped. "On my last trip to California, I sat in Ted Danson's living room. I swam in his pool . . ."

"Was he like . . . you know, home at the time?"

Lang frowned.

"I really don't care for your smart mouth, Malloy."

"Yeah, well . . . I get a lot of complaints about it, Mr. Lang. They used to bother me too. I would stay up nights worrying about it. Not so much anymore. So are you going to let me talk to Abbie Kincaid at some point or are you just going to keep trying to dazzle me with your star-studded resume?"

He glared at me. I was beginning to suspect that I had failed his "classy" criteria.

"How much do you know about Abbie?" Lang asked.

"The highlights of her career," I said. "She started out trying to be an actress, but she only had moderate success. Then, a few years ago, she became the star of a daytime TV talk show called *Girl Talk*. One of those programs where women tell how they slept with their lesbian sister-in-law or how they spy into their neighbor's bedroom or how their husband likes to be spanked while wearing diapers. Now she's gone the serious route. She's the host of *The Prime Time Files*. She's now doing investigative reports, interviews with big names in show business and government, lifestyle features, and headline crime stuff. I remember the show starting off as a midseason replacement and now it's on the regular schedule. It ranked number thirteen in the ratings last week."

"Have you ever watched *The Prime Time Files*?" Lang asked.

"Yeah, I caught it the other night."

"What was your reaction?"

"I think Diane Sawyer and Barbara Walters have done it all before, probably a little better too. But Abbie's young, she's cute—she's got great demographics. That's what really counts. Hell," I smiled at him, "I think she'll be a big star."

Lang did not smile back.

"I spoke earlier with someone at your newspaper," he said.

"Stacy Albright."

Stacy Albright was the city editor of the *New York Daily News*, the paper I worked for.

"Yes. Miss Albright seemed very interested when I told her that Abbie was about to break a big exclusive on her TV show and we wanted to do a story promoting Abbie—and this week's show—in your paper."

"Stacy thinks it sounds like something that can get us both a lot of good publicity," I said.

"What do you think?" he asked.

"I think it sounds like a very slow news week. So what's the exclusive about?"

"Laura Marlowe," he said.

"The actress?"

"Yes."

"She's dead."

"Okay."

Laura Marlowe was the hottest young star in the country back in the early '80s. Her first two movies had been smash hits, and she was dubbed America's sweetheart by the press—the young Julia Roberts of her time. But it all ended tragically when an obsessed fan shot and killed her right after a party for her last movie. The fan then committed suicide.

"She's been dead for thirty years," I said to Lang.

"Right."

"So what's your story?"

"What really happened to her."

"Don't I already know that?"

"You only think you do."

The Laura Marlowe murder was not exactly a new topic. Because the killer had committed suicide and the circumstances of her death were shrouded in mystery, it had become popular fodder for sensational TV shows, supermarket tabloids, and even some of the mainstream press over the years. The favorite rumor was that Laura Marlowe—like Jim Morrison or Elvis—was really alive someplace. No one believed it, of course, but it always made for a good story.

"Let me guess," I said. "Laura Marlowe didn't really die."

"No," Lang said, "she's dead."

"Then your big exclusive is that Laura Marlowe is still dead?"

"The bottom line here," he said, "is there's always been a lot of questions about what happened the night Laura Marlowe died. How did the killer get so close to her? What was she doing with him? Where did the killer go after he shot her? What was his motive? Why was her body quickly cremated before the coroner could do a full inquest? Until now, no one's ever been able to provide any of the answers."

"And you've got the answers."

"Enough of them to do a helluva story."

"But you won't tell me exactly what the story is?"

"No."

"Because you're going to break it yourself on your television show."

"That's the deal we worked out with your editor."

I nodded. It didn't seem like much of a story to me, but then I wasn't much of a reporter these days. Oh, I'd had my moments over the years. Front page headlines. A handful of awards. I even got nominated for a Pulitzer Prize by the *Daily News* once. But that all felt like it was in the distant past now.

"Why does anyone even care about Laura Marlowe after all this time?" I asked.

"She was a Hollywood legend."

"How many movies did she make?"

"Three," Lang said.

"That's all?"

"She was only twenty-two when she died."

"And she was that big of a star already?"

"Yeah, can you imagine what might have happened if she'd lived?" he said. "How popular she might have become? It was a real tragedy. A reminder to all of us how fleeting life can be."

Lang looked across the desk at me.

"This is a good story—and Abbie and I are giving you a chance to be a part of it."

"Okay."

"You could use a good story."

"What does that mean?"

"From what I hear, it's been a while since you've done much of anything, Malloy. I asked around about you at the *Daily News*. The people there told me you're terrific when you latch on to a big exclusive. But the rest of the time they say you mostly just sit around the newsroom daydreaming about God knows what and wasting time."

"I prefer to think of it as a creative regrouping," I said.

"Well, just try not to be such a jerk, huh? It would make things a lot easier."

He was right, of course. I sure needed a story. And this, for better or worse, was a story. I knew I had to do everything I could to stay on it. Even if it meant being nice to a guy like Lang. Besides, maybe he could get me Ted Danson's autograph.

"So when do I meet Abbie Kincaid?" I said.

CHAPTER 2

HE meeting with Abbie Kincaid was scheduled for the next morning. After I left Lang's office in midtown, I took a subway downtown to the *Daily News* building in lower Manhattan. I stopped by the entertainment section of the paper and asked one of the movie writers what he could tell me about Laura Marlowe. I was curious.

"Her first movie was *Lucky Lady*, a romantic comedy that became a blockbuster hit," he said. "Very funny, very charming. It did what *Pretty Woman* would later do for Julia Roberts. It turned Laura Marlowe—who was only nineteen at the time—into a Hollywood superstar virtually overnight.

"A year later, she did *The Langley Caper*. A terrific thriller that was another big hit. Sort of like *Lethal Weapon* meets *All The President's Men*. A complete change of pace for her as an actress, but she pulled it off. Every studio head in Hollywood was clamoring to put her in a picture after that. She was the hottest thing in show business.

"Then she made what turned out to be her last film, *Once Upon a Time Forever*. An epic love story—set in the nineteenth century—about a princess who loses her crown and her wealth, but finds the true meaning of happiness." He made a face. "Not a great movie. But it's all we have left of her, so a lot of people look at it as kind of a cult classic."

He clicked on his computer, found a snippet of *Lucky Lady* on YouTube, and played it for me. I watched a few minutes of Laura Marlowe on the screen. She was young and beautiful with jet-black hair, sensual lips and eyes, and a terrific figure. But even more than her looks, it was her charisma and personality that grabbed you right out of the screen. You just knew you were seeing something really special.

Then he played me some Laura Marlowe scenes from *The Langley Caper* and *Once Upon a Time Forever*.

"And those three movies are all she did?" I asked.

"Yes."

"So why is she such a legend?"

"She died young."

"Just like James Dean."

"Right. James Dean only made three movies too, come to think of it. Dying young solves a lot of problems. You never get old, you never do a lot of bad movies at the end of your career, and you never wind up making guest appearances on shows like *Hollywood Squares* or *Celebrity Rehab*."

"It's better to burn out than fade away," I agreed.

———

After that, I read some of the old stories about the Laura Marlowe murder.

It happened when she returned to her New York hotel after a party for *Once Upon a Time Forever*. Witnesses said the guy who shot her had been hanging around the hotel for days, hoping to get a glimpse of her. They thought he was just an enthusiastic fan. They never suspected he was a killer who had somehow made her the target of all his rage and paranoia and obsession.

She was still alive when the first ambulance got there. The paramedics worked on her desperately, trying to stop the bleeding. At first, there was hope she might make it. Thousands of crying and praying people had gathered at the site and outside the hospital where she was taken to recover. But then she took a turn for the worse and the announcement came that there was no more the doctors could do. She was dead.

Two days after she died, the body of the man who'd been stalking her was found in a cheap hotel room near Times Square. His name was Ray Janson. Janson had hung himself.

He left behind a rambling note in which he professed his undying devotion and love for the slain actress and said that he wanted them to be together for eternity. The last line of the note said simply: "Tell Laura I love her." The police ruled it a murder-suicide. The case was closed. And Laura Marlowe faded away into history.

There was a famous picture of Laura Marlowe blowing a kiss to the camera at the party just hours before she died. That memorable, haunting photo of the doomed young actress appeared on the *Daily News* front page with a headline that said simply: ONE LAST KISS. It became one of the most legendary New York City newspaper Page Ones of all time. A huge blowup of it hangs in the *Daily News* lobby—along with front pages on Son of Sam and all the other big crime stories. I probably must have walked past that famous picture of Laura Marlowe more than a thousand times on my way to and from work and never gave it a second thought. Until now.

——

I went online to see if I could find more information about her.

Her real name was Laura Makofsky, and she had come from a broken home in New Jersey. Her father left when she was very young, and her mother worked as a costume designer on several Broadway shows. Laura was an adorable child—and by the time she was a teenager, she was going out on casting calls for TV commercials and stage and movie roles. It was her mother who changed her daughter's name to Laura Marlowe, and—by all accounts—was the catalyst in her career as an actress.

For a long time, nothing happened. There was a bit part here and there, but Laura Marlowe was just one of thousands of pretty young girls trying to break into show business. Then, at the age of nineteen and reportedly so discouraged that she was ready to quit, she somehow got plucked out of obscurity and landed the role in *Lucky Lady* that made her famous. She did her second hit movie by the time she was twenty, and she was only twenty-two when she died shortly after filming that final movie.

Even at the height of her fame, though, there were problems.

During the filming of *The Langley Caper*, she was involved in a serious auto accident that left her in the hospital for six weeks and raised fears that she might be permanently disfigured. There was also a behind-the-scenes legal battle going on between her mother and the agent who had represented her for several years before she hit it big in Hollywood—she'd been fired by Laura's mother. They finally reached an out-of-court settlement, but people around Laura said she seemed very upset over the whole thing.

By the time she began shooting *Once Upon a Time Forever*, she was not in good shape. They had to shut down the production several times when she simply stopped showing up on the set. There was a lot of speculation about the reasons for her disappearance. The most prevalent theory was that she'd suffered some kind of breakdown and was undergoing treatment at a rehab or clinic. Eventually she returned and completed the movie, only weeks before her murder in New York City.

Somewhere along the line she'd gotten married. Her husband's name was Edward Holloway, and he was with her in New York the night she got shot. Looking on in horror as the unthinkable happened, just like Yoko with John Lennon. Kneeling at his wife's side as she lay on the street dying. There was a picture of him delivering the eulogy at her funeral, and descriptions of him breaking down in tears at the gravesite.

Since then he'd dedicated his life to keeping her memory alive. There were Laura Marlowe posters, cups, and other mementos; a Laura Marlowe film seminar and acting school; and even a fan club and newsletter.

"She was the most beautiful person to ever walk this earth," Holloway said in one article. "I think about her every day. And I want everyone else to know her too, even if she is no longer here with us."

The article also pointed out that the Laura Marlowe memorial business still earned about $5 million a year.

Dying young like Laura Marlowe sure did pay off for the living.

———

Stacy Albright, the *Daily News* city editor, walked by my desk.

"Did you get the interview with Abbie Kincaid?" she asked me.

"It's set for tomorrow morning."

"Great."

"Absolutely."

"I think this could be a really important story for you."

"You know, I was just thinking the same thing."

"I'd really like to see you become a big part of the team I'm building here, Gil."

"Hey, Gil Malloy is a team player."

"Let me know how the interview goes tomorrow."

"Sure. Just to be clear, Stacy, the interview is supposed to be about an exclusive story that Abbie is going to break on her TV show this week. About the death of Laura Marlowe, the old movie actress. But they won't tell me what the exclusive is."

"Yes, that's the agreement we worked out."

"So what exactly is my story here?"

"Let me explain again, Gil," she said, as if she was talking to a small child. "I'm trying to set up a marketing partnership with *The Prime Time Files*. The idea is we'd promote their exclusives and they'd do the same with ours. In this case, in return for us doing an advance promo on Abbie's exclusive, they'll mention our article in the show and also let us live stream the segment simultaneously on the *Daily News* website and provide us with video to use afterward. Quid pro quo, if you will. I know this is difficult for someone like you—who is more familiar with the old-fashioned, more traditional ways of journalism—to adapt to the ways we want to do things now. But it is essential for our success in new media to not just be a print newspaper anymore. So let me know as soon as you finish the interview tomorrow. I'll work with you on getting up something very quickly on our website before you write your piece for the next day's paper. I think this could be a positive experience for both of us. Don't you agree, Gil?"

"Right back at you, Stacy," I smiled.

———

She walked back to her office. Stacy Albright personified everything that was wrong with newspapers today. She was twenty-six years old; she'd been named city editor a few months ago after increasing traffic by 250 percent on the *Daily News* website by completely redesigning and relaunching the site. Her background was in social media, multi-media cross-platform management, and digital marketing. I'm not sure if she ever actually covered a news story on her own. But in the wake of layoffs and dismissals and other changes that had turned the *Daily News* upside down in recent times, she had somehow become a rising star while many of the real editors were now gone. Welcome to the world of newspapers in the age of the Internet.

Me, I'd somehow managed to hang on at the *News* through all of the turmoil. Even though I had a pretty checkered career at the paper—filled with lots of high points, but also some infamous low moments too.

When I started some fifteen years ago, it was *all* high points. I was the boy wonder—going from copyboy to reporter to columnist in just a few years. I won awards for my coverage of 9/11, crime in New York City, City Hall investigations, and a bunch of other stuff. It was like I could do no wrong.

But then I did. Something wrong, that is. I wrote a story about an interview I did with a legendary New York hooker named Houston for an investigative series on prostitution in the city. The Houston interview was so good that it won me a lot of awards and even got me nominated for a Pulitzer. Except the interview never really happened. Instead, when I couldn't actually find Houston, I used a bunch of second-hand quotes I'd gotten from people on the street and tried to pass off as a first-person interview with her. I'm still not sure why. I guess I just wanted the story so badly that I was even willing to violate my integrity as a journalist to get it. It's the only time I've ever done that. But once is too much. I crossed over the one line that no journalist can ever compromise. The truth.

I thought my newspaper career was over. But then one day I got a second chance. I wrote another big story—about a corrupt police official who had killed people to hide the secrets of his past in order to further his rise to police commissioner. Later, I broke another big exclusive linking the murder of the Manhattan DA's daughter to a series of unsolved serial killings over the years. I was a star again.

But it turned out not to be that easy for me.

There was the integrity issue, of course. A reporter's integrity—his ability to make people trust him—is the most important thing he has. There was always going to be someone who would bring that up. Oh, Gil Malloy—he's the one that made up that story about the hooker, right? But the truth was that really wasn't so much of a problem for me anymore. In the world of social media and instant journalist online, people tended to forget, forgive, and move on a lot quicker than they used to. You were only as good—or as bad—as your last story.

And that was my real problem.

You see, I'd somehow become more of a celebrity at the *Daily News* than an actual day-to-day reporter. The two big exclusive stories I'd broken had both been high-profile cases that garnered me a lot of attention. There were TV appearances, magazine interviews, book deal offers—all that sort of heady stuff afterward for me both times. So the paper used me as the public face of a *Daily News* reporter whenever they wanted to be noticed or make a big splash in the media. That's how I wound up getting assigned to the Abbie Kincaid story. It was simply a publicity stunt for the paper—or, as Stacy Albright described it, a marketing partnership. So I was a star again these days. Sort of. Except I wanted to be a real reporter. And, to do that, I needed a story. A real story. A big story.

I shut off my computer and walked out of the office. On my way through the *Daily News* lobby, I looked at the picture of Laura Marlowe on the front page from the night she died thirty years ago, blowing a kiss to her adoring crowd at the movie party just before she was murdered. She looked so young, so beautiful, so full of life. Not knowing how little time she had left.

"I think this could be a positive experience for both of us," Stacy Albright had said to me in the newsroom earlier.

I didn't believe her, of course. I figured the Laura Marlowe story would be just a waste of time for me. Another example of how far my career had fallen since the days when I was always on Page One.

In the end though, it turned out Stacy was right—and I was wrong.

CHAPTER 3

THE next morning I woke up early to get ready for my appointment with Abbie Kincaid.

I showered, shaved, and combed my hair; opted for an open-collared white dress shirt instead of the T-shirt along with a pair of khaki slacks; and put on a navy suede sports jacket and black loafers. I picked up a large coffee at a Starbucks and carried it with me as I walked into the lobby of the building where *The Prime Time Files* offices were located. I was clean, coiffured, and caffeine-ready for my big moment with the star. I might have even passed for classy.

A very large security guard wearing a red blazer with the network's emblem on the label wanted to know who I was. I told him I had an appointment with Abbie Kincaid, and I showed him my press card. He stared at it for a moment too long. Then he took down my name and asked me to wait while he called upstairs to check.

I waited.

After several minutes another security guard—almost as big and wearing an identical red blazer—led me to an elevator and rode with me to *The Prime Time Files* studio on the twelfth floor. On the fourth floor a third red-blazered guard got on the elevator when we stopped briefly.

On twelve, I was met by a young, peppy-looking, blond-haired woman. She was wearing a miniskirt, a starched blue blouse, and the same red network blazer as the three security guards.

I wished I had one too.

I was starting to feel left out.

She took me into the reception area for the show. Another big security guard was standing there. This one was well over six feet tall and weighed maybe 225 pounds, all of it muscle. His hair was long, pulled into a ponytail at the back; he had a beard and he was wearing black jeans and a black T-shirt that said: THE PRIME TIME FILES: DON'T MISS IT.

He asked for my press card too. He stared at it almost as long as the guard did downstairs, apparently looking for clues. "Lotsa security here," I said.

He didn't answer me.

"The thing about security," I said to the guy, "is that it can often be counterproductive. You put in all the security so you can operate your business—accomplish the things you need to do—with a feeling of safety. But then the security measures themselves sometimes become a problem, turning out to be so onerous and time-consuming that they prevent you from carrying out the activities you put them in place to protect in the first place. Eventually the security hassles become a bigger impediment to you in the workplace than the safety concerns which led you to implement them."

The big security guard looked at me blankly.

"In other words, the cure turns out to be worse than the original problem," I said. "Do you follow what I'm saying here? Because it really does make a lot of sense."

"Yeah, whatever," he shrugged. The guard said I could sit there while he went to find Abbie. Then he disappeared through a door that led to dressing rooms and a sound stage. While I waited, I took out an iPad I'd brought with me and went through the morning papers—the *Daily News* first, then the *Post* and the *Times*. There was a budget crisis at City Hall, a new threat of war in the Mideast, and a heat wave was headed our way. None of them had any breaking news on Laura Marlowe. Hey, you never know.

At some point from behind the door, I could hear the sounds of people arguing. A man's voice, very loud, and then a woman shouting at about the same level. The shouting went on for several minutes.

Then the door flew open and a man stormed out. He seemed very agitated. He was moving so fast he almost ran into me. I stood up to get out of his way, and we were face-to-face for a second. I could see the fury and the anger there. The guy looked vaguely familiar to me, but I couldn't quite place who he was. He pushed past me without saying a word and walked out.

The bearded guy with the ponytail appeared and gestured for me to come inside.

Abbie was sitting behind a desk in her office. At first glance, she looked like she did on TV. She was a few years younger than me, probably in her late twenties. She had green eyes, long auburn hair, and a striking figure like a model—which came across even better in person than on the screen. She was wearing a brown pants suit and a beige blouse that showed off that figure quite nicely.

But as I got closer, I saw that her makeup was smeared and she looked like she'd been crying. She dabbed at her eyes with a piece of tissue.

"Is this a bad time?" I asked.

Abbie shook her head no.

"I could come back later . . ."

"Just give me a few minutes," she said.

She took a few deep breaths and tried to compose herself.

"I apologize you had to see this," she said finally. "Not a very elegant way to introduce myself to you. So let's start at the top again." She stuck out her hand. "I'm Abbie Kincaid. So glad you could meet with me today."

"I'm Gil Malloy of the *Daily News*."

I shook hands with her and then sat down in a chair across from her.

"So who was that guy?" I asked.

"Just someone I'm dating."

"Uh-huh."

"Actually someone I used to be dating."

"That's an important distinction."

"I told him we had to end the relationship."

"He didn't seem too happy about it."

"Tommy doesn't want to, but I do."

"The course of true love rarely runs smoothly," I told her.

I couldn't think of anything else to say.

"Do you know him?"

"Who?"

"Tommy."

"No, I don't think so. He did look kind of familiar though."

"I'm sure you've heard of his father. Thomas Rizzo."

I stared at her in amazement. Thomas Rizzo was one of the legendary mob figures in New York. Some people called him the boss of all bosses. We'd done a lot of stories about him in the *Daily News* over the years, and I think a few of them mentioned the kid, Thomas Jr. That's why I remembered his face.

"You've been going out with the son of the Godfather?" I said.

"It's not like that," Abbie said. "Tommy's actually a very nice guy."

"Whose father just happens to kill people for a living."

She shrugged. "Tommy told me the stuff they say about his father isn't true. Besides, he isn't involved in his father's business anyway."

"Says who?"

"Tommy. He's really different, you know. Went to Harvard. Made the Dean's List there."

"So what were you two arguing about before I came in? Whether or not he takes you to the big fraternity dance on Friday night?"

"Look, we went out on a few dates, that's all. Nothing serious. It was all very casual. Tommy wanted to pursue the relationship and make it something more. I didn't. I told him that. He came here today to try and get me to change my mind. But I won't. End of story."

"Oh," I said.

She gave me a funny look. "What does that 'oh' mean?"

" 'Oh' as in, how exactly do you go about telling something like that to the son of a man like Thomas Rizzo."

She sighed. "Like I said, Tommy's a great guy. He's going to make some woman a great husband someday. Unfortunately, it's not going to be me. But he's still very hung up on me. That's what that was all about between us in here a few minutes ago."

She smiled across her desk at me.

"I'm sure you've been in messy personal situations like this at some point," she said.

"Not exactly."

"What do you mean?"

"Look, Abbie, I try not to date the offspring of major crime figures. It's just a little idiosyncrasy of mine."

Abbie flashed me her megawatt smile, the smile that had won her millions of viewers on TV. Then she told me she was just going to freshen up a bit before we talked. I said that was fine. She took off the jacket she was wearing, hung it on the back of her desk chair, and then went into an adjoining room where she closed the door.

I sat there waiting some more. I was getting used to waiting at *The Prime Time Files*. It seemed to be the thing to do. At some point, I looked over at the brown jacket hung from her chair. It was a terrific-looking jacket. The only problem was a bulge I noticed in one of the pockets. Hard to look fantastic—even if you are Abbie Kincaid—when you're carrying around something that big.

Several minutes passed. I looked at Abbie's jacket again. The bulge in the pocket was still there. I walked over, leaned down, and stuck my hand in the pocket. There was a gun inside. I didn't know a lot about guns, but I can tell if one is loaded. This one was loaded. I put it back inside the pocket.

I wondered if the gun had any connection to all the security I'd noticed on my visit to the place.

Of course, none of it had anything to do with me.

The heavy security around her.

The fact that she was dating a mob boss's son.

Or that Abbie Kincaid was packing heat.

Nope, it was none of my business at all.

Abbie came out of the bathroom looking more like the woman I knew from television. Her makeup was back in place, her hair was freshly combed.

"Well, I'm sure you didn't plan on coming here to talk about my love life, did you?" she said.

"No, that was just a bit of an added attraction."

"So let's talk about Laura Marlowe," she said.

"That's what I'm here for."

"I understand Gary already told you that I'm about to break a big story about her death on my show this week."

"He did."

"Did he tell you anything about what my exclusive was?"

"Gary was a little vague on the details of that."

"I imagine he was."

"It does present me with somewhat of a problem. You want me to write a story about the story you're going to break. And I can understand why you want to keep the story to yourself. But unless you tell me something about it, I'm not sure what to write. You can see the dilemma I'm in."

"Maybe I can help you," she said.

"With the Laura Marlowe story?"

"Yes."

"How?"

"Let's go to the movies," she said.

CHAPTER 4

THE picture was grainy, and at first I assumed it had been done on a home video camera. But it turned out to be a videotape from a TV news show. I remembered that television was a lot different thirty years ago. Videotapes and VCRs were something brand new back then. The text at the bottom of the screen said: *Laura Marlowe arriving at the Oscars ceremonies—1984.*

Even with the not-so-perfect technology, she looked as beautiful as she did on the movie screen. She was wearing a long flowing red dress, her black hair was pinned up fashionably behind her head, and her eyes seemed wide with excitement. She smiled and waved at the crowd and even stopped to sign a few autographs as she walked up the red carpet that was used for the stars' arrivals.

The screen went dark for a second, and then Laura Marlowe's face came on it again. It looked like the same scene outside the Academy Awards. But everything was different. Her dress. Her hairdo. And, most of all, the expression on her face. She didn't look happy or excited anymore. There was a woman with her this time. A man too, who looked a lot older than her. There were fans again clamoring for her autograph, but she walked right past them without a glance. The bottom of the screen said: *Academy Awards Ceremony—1985.*

"What a difference a year makes, huh?" Abbie said.

We were sitting in a video-screening room next to her office. Abbie clicked on a remote and froze the picture at that second shot of her going into the Oscars in early 1985.

"She looks miserable," I said.

"Yes, she does."

"Why? She's got it all. She's rich, she's famous, and she's beautiful."

"Let's just say there was a lot of things going on in Laura Marlowe's life before she died."

I looked at the screen again. "Who's the woman with her?"

"Her mother."

"She brought her mother to the Oscars?"

"The mother created her. Changed the kid's name, signed her up for acting lessons, sent her out on auditions. She pushed her daughter into show business for years before she finally became a star. The mother is the reason she was there with Hollywood's elite that night."

"What about the father?"

"Long gone."

"Dead?"

"No, just gone. For most of her life anyway. He walked out on the family when Laura was very little. She hardly knew him. But then he showed up again when she became famous. That's him in the picture walking behind her. Probably trying to cut himself in on a piece of the action."

Abbie clicked the remote, and a different picture of Laura Marlowe appeared on the screen.

She was coming out of a plain-looking building and getting into a car. The mother was there again. So was another man who I didn't recognize. Laura Marlowe didn't look beautiful or glamorous now. She was dressed in what appeared to be a hospital gown, she wasn't wearing any makeup, and she seemed to have trouble walking. The mother and the man in the picture were each holding on to one of her arms. There was no cheering crowd this time, just the three of them.

"What's this?" I asked.

"A hospital in California. She was apparently in rehab there. A TV news crew shot this after staking out the place for a few days. It never became public though. Today the Internet and TMZ would have a field day with it. It would go viral. 'Glamorous movie star fights substance abuse.'"

The bottom of the screen said June 21, 1985. Only a few weeks before she was murdered. I remembered reading in the clips that she'd been hospitalized during the filming of her final movie. They'd cleaned her up in rehab, sent her back to finish the film— and then she died. There was no happy ending to this story.

"What was her substance of choice?"

"You name it."

"Who's the guy with her?"

"Her husband."

"Edward Holloway."

"Uh-huh."

"What was that marriage all about?"

"Well, he loved her."

"Did she love him back?"

"Frankly, I don't think she loved anybody at this point."

Abbie shut off the video, and the screen went blank.

"This is all very interesting," I said. "But here we are thirty years later, and what does any of it have to do with anything? More specifically, what does it have to do with me?"

"Can we talk off-the-record?" Abbie asked.

"Meaning you want me to agree not to print anything you're going to tell me?"

"That's my understanding of what off-the-record means."

"I'd rather not."

"Why?"

"Going off-the-record makes things too complicated."

"I know what you mean."

"It's kind of a cop-out for a journalist."

"Definitely."

"I really hate going off-the-record."

"Me too."

"And yet here we are talking about doing it."

"Do we have a deal?"

I didn't really have much of a choice. I knew the only way Abbie was going to talk to me was if I agreed not to print it. If I went off-the-record, I'd at least find out what was on her mind, even if I couldn't do anything about it. If I didn't go off-the-record, I wouldn't know anything. Life is a series of imperfect choices.

I told her we were off-the-record.

Abbie picked up the remote again and clicked another shot on the screen. This one was a montage of four different faces. All four were women.

"Do you know any of them?" she asked.

I looked at the pictures. A couple of them looked vaguely familiar, but I couldn't place them. The only one I knew for sure was Cheryl Carson. She was a country singer. She'd died a while back from a drug overdose during a concert tour somewhere out West.

"Cheryl Carson," I said.

"No one else?"

"I don't think so."

Abbie nodded.

"I did some checking up on you," she said. "It was very interesting. You were pretty famous there for a while."

"Fame is fleeting," I said.

"You've covered a lot of crime stories."

"Yes."

"Do you know much about serial killers?"

"Serial killers?"

I wasn't sure where she was headed with this.

"Yes."

"A little, I suppose. Why?"

"I'm working on a story about a possible serial killer."

"Are we talking about a different story now?"

"How much do you know about serial killers?" Abbie said, ignoring my question.

"I'm not an expert or anything. But I guess I do have some knowledge from stories I've covered in the past."

"Is there always a pattern that links all of the murders?"

"Sure, that's why they call them serial killings."

"Tell me more . . ."

I still wasn't sure where she was going, but I was curious enough to play along until I could find out.

"Look, they're all different," I said. "Every case has unique characteristics. A lot of people have spent a lot of time trying to figure out why serial killers do the terrible things they do. No one has come up with any astounding conclusions yet. But there are common threads that seem to run through most of them."

"Such as?"

"The character flaws or moral aberrations that turn a person into a serial killer usually seem to start in childhood. They come from dysfunctional parents. Or families with histories of drug or alcohol or sexual abuse. They've never known happiness, so they have a compulsion to lash out and make the world around them as unhappy as they are."

"What about the sexual aspect?"

"Yes, sex is a big factor. For most serial killers, the thrill of the kill seems to be the only way they can achieve sexual satisfaction. That's why many of them spend so much time stalking their victims, so they can maximize their pleasure out of the event. The killing itself becomes the equivalent of the sexual orgasm. But there's other factors too besides sex. Some serial killers think of themselves as missionaries—they believe they're doing God's will by ridding society of undesirable elements like prostitutes or homosexuals. Others get off on the power it gives them over their victims. And some are pure thrill killers—who get a high from the act of murder just like from drugs or alcohol. After the actual killing, many of them feel depressed or even remorseful. Like an addict who succumbed to temptation and went on a drug or alcohol binge. They may go weeks, months, or even years before the urge to kill begins to overwhelm them again. It's during this period that some serial killers write letters to newspapers or call the police to confess, hoping they'll be caught. But in the end, they keep on taking lives until they're apprehended. There is no such thing as a reformed serial killer."

"It's always hard to kill the first time, but after that it gets easier," Abbie said. "Isn't that what they say?"

"Exactly."

"Have you ever seen a serial killer case where there is no common thread between the murders?"

"No."

"Never?"

"I've seen a few where I'm not sure what the connection is, but I know there is one."

"In other words, you just haven't found it."

I looked at the pictures of the four women on the screen again.

"Is this about Laura Marlowe?" I asked.

"Maybe."

"You think that the guy who killed her played some role in the deaths of these other women too?"

"I'm not sure."

"That's impossible."

"Why?"

"Because the guy who killed Laura Marlowe has been dead for thirty years. He killed himself in a hotel room a couple of days after her murder. I don't know anything about those other women, but one of them—Cheryl Carson—died well after that. I know that for a fact. So there's no way Laura Marlowe's killer could have killed her too, unless . . ."

That's when it hit me. I suddenly understood. I understood the big story Abbie was working on. She wasn't trying to prove that Laura Marlowe was still alive. She wasn't dredging up old facts or speculation or gossip about the murder just to make a quick hit in the ratings. She had figured out the one thing that could blow the case wide open again even after all these years.

"I think the cops got the wrong guy," Abbie said.

CHAPTER 5

THE article I wrote about Abbie Kincaid's show for the next day's paper stuck pretty close to the basic instructions I'd gotten from Stacy—Abbie was going to break a big exclusive about the long-ago forgotten Laura Marlowe murder on *The Prime Time Files* this week.

I used a bunch of teaser quotes from Abbie about how the story would shock viewers with the disclosures and generate big news about the infamous case.

I also included a lot of the background material on Laura Marlowe and her death that I'd researched since it had all happened so long ago.

I did not write that Abbie would reveal evidence showing authorities might have blamed the wrong man for the murder.

Or that there might have been subsequent murders carried out by the same killer after Laura Marlowe's death.

Or that Abbie had been dating the son of New York City mob boss Thomas Rizzo.

She had shared most of this information with me off-the-record. And I honored that commitment. I didn't even tell Stacy about it. Partly because I take my "off-the-record" vows very seriously as a journalist. But also because . . . well, I liked Abbie Kincaid, and I didn't like Stacy. So I kept all the secrets she had told me that day out of the article.

I sure was looking forward to hearing what more she had to say on the TV show though.

———

That "wrong man" blockbuster was pretty much all I'd gotten out of Abbie on the Laura Marlowe case. I think she probably realized she'd already told me too much after she said it. I wondered if she'd planned to be that open with me before the interview. Maybe she was just in an emotional state because of the fight with the boyfriend, Rizzo. Maybe she'd taken something in the bathroom that relaxed her enough to let her guard down momentarily. Maybe it was because I was such a friendly, likeable guy who people just wanted to pour their hearts out to. Or maybe it was a combination of all of those things.

At one point, I'd asked her about the gun in her jacket.

"How did you know about that?" she asked.

"I'm a hotshot investigative reporter, remember?"

She smiled.

"Why do you need a gun?"

"In case I have to shoot somebody."

"Seriously."

"No reason."

"There's always a reason for a gun."

"It's no big deal. I just have it in case there's ever any trouble."

Abbie talked more about Laura Marlowe's background, expanding on some of the things I'd read in the bio clips. She told me things she'd uncovered about:

Laura's mother and how she'd pushed Laura to become an actress since childhood.

Her father, who ran out on the family when Laura was a little girl and then came back to try and cash in on her success after she became rich and famous.

Laura's first agent, who had stood by her during the struggling early years of trying to make it in show business—a woman who had almost become a surrogate mother to Laura—but then was abruptly fired by the mother as soon as Laura hit it big.

And how Laura—like something out of a real-life Hollywood fairy tale—inexplicably emerged from obscurity to land the part in *Lucky Lady* that made her an overnight sensation and the biggest movie star in America.

Abbie shook her head at the incongruity of it all.

"Did you ever hear the quote from Lauren Bacall about what it takes to become a big star? Bacall said, 'Stardom isn't a profession. It's an accident.' That's what happened to Laura Marlowe. Hell, that's probably the way it happens for most of the people in this business." She shrugged. "Maybe even me."

———

I tried to push her more on the serial killer angle she'd been talking about, and how it might connect to the Laura Marlowe murder. But she didn't divulge any more details. The same when I asked her for more details about why she thought Ray Janson didn't kill Laura and if she had any idea who might have been responsible.

"I'm just curious," I said to her at one point. "Why did you start investigating the Laura Marlowe case again?"

"It's a good story."

"But why now after thirty years?"

"I obtained some new information."

"How?"

"I can't tell you that."

"Will you do it on the show?"

"Not this show. Maybe eventually . . ."

"And you won't tell me who your source was? Even off-the-record?"

"A good reporter never reveals a source, Gil," she said. "You should know that better than anyone."

It wasn't until the end of the interview that she opened up to me again in a genuine way like she did at the beginning.

"I really enjoyed talking with you, Gil," she said as she walked me to the door of her office.

"Me too," I said.

"We should do this again."

"Do what?"

"Talk."

"Do you mean another interview?"

"No, I mean we could just talk sometime. Like over a drink. Or dinner."

"You and me?"

"Yes," she laughed, "that would be the pairing."

I was having trouble grasping all of this. It seemed as if she was asking me out. On a date. Or something like a date. But that couldn't be right. I mean she was Abbie Kincaid, the big TV star. She wouldn't ever want to spend time with a guy like me, would she? Well, apparently she did.

"Why me?" I blurted out.

"I need someone to talk to."

"You must have a lot of people around you that would love to spend time talking with Abbie Kincaid."

"Most of the people I deal with are jerks."

"I know that feeling too."

"I like you, Gil Malloy. You seem like a stand up guy. Someone I can trust. I don't have a lot of people in my life that I can trust right now."

She opened the door, gave me a big hug that lasted for a long time—and then finally turned around and went back into her office.

The big security guard was still there. He glared at me with his arms folded impassively as I walked to the elevator. Dressed from head to toe in black, he reminded me a bit of Darth Vader in the *Star Wars* movies.

"How ya doing?" I said.

He didn't move or say anything.

"Catch any bad guys lately?" I asked.

Still no response.

"Hey, any possibility you could tell me where to get a cool *The Prime Time Files* T-shirt like that?"

My elevator was here now, and I got on. The big security guard watched me intently. He folded his arms again and glared some more. The more I thought about it, he really did look a bit like Darth Vader.

"May the force be with you," I said.

Then the elevator doors closed and I rode back down to the lobby. There was still plenty of heavy security down there too. I thought about it all: the gun in her pocket, the security, the mobster kid boyfriend. Of course, all of this had absolutely nothing to do with me. No connection whatsoever to the story I was supposed to be doing about her and the show.

Nope, whatever was going on in Abbie Kincaid's life, it was none of my business at all.

CHAPTER 6

THE closest police precinct to *The Prime Time Files* studios was the 19th, which is on 67th Street near Third Avenue. I took a cab up there to see if I could find a friendly face to talk to. What I found was Lt. Frank Wohlers. I wasn't sure if he was friendly or not. I'd worked a lot with him a few years back when I was an ace reporter, breaking big crime stories on Page One all the time. Not so much anymore. But I still remembered the way I used to get information out of him.

"I was just in the neighborhood," I said. "I thought I'd drop by and bring you a sandwich to eat."

I handed him a bag of food. He opened it.

"A corned beef sandwich," he said.

"Uh-huh."

"My favorite."

"Yum-yum," I said.

Wohlers was a large man, probably close to 250 pounds, and I knew that food meant more to him than life itself, as the saying goes.

It was a few minutes later—and several bites into the corned beef—before he came up for air.

"So what story are you looking for some information on?"

"What makes you think I'm looking for information on a story?"

"The corned beef cost eighteen dollars."

"You know, this is a pretty sad state of affairs," I said, "when a person can't bring another person something without being accused of having an ulterior motive. Whatever happened to friendship? Whatever happened to brotherhood? Whatever happened to simple acts of human kindness?"

Wohlers took another bite of the sandwich and belched loudly.

"Beats me," he said.

He looked at me across his desk.

"Abbie Kincaid," I told him.

"The TV star?"

"The one and only."

"What about her?"

"I went to her studio this morning and they had more security there than in Times Square on New Year's Eve. A personal security guard who's with her all the time. And the lady keeps a loaded gun in her jacket pocket. Not exactly my idea of the glitzy, carefree life of a big TV star."

"So?"

"I figured if this had anything to do with the police, you'd know about it. Do you?"

Wohlers didn't say anything for a few seconds. I wasn't sure if he was going to or not. In the past, sometimes he told me things and sometimes he didn't. It was hard to tell how much a corned beef sandwich was going to buy me now.

"The Kincaid woman's been getting some threats," he said.

"What kind of threats?"

"Death threats."

"How do they come?"

"Phone calls. Emails. A lot of them recently."

"Any reason the person making the threats says they want her dead?"

"Not specifically. Some of the communications talk about stories she's done or stories she's working on. Some of it sounds personal, like she had some kind of relationship with the person in the past—real or imagined—who is sending the threats. And some of it just sounds like obsessive fan stuff, the crazy rants from the kind of star-struck people who get off on that crazy love-hate worship of a celebrity like Abbie Kincaid. Most of it is gibberish."

Wohlers reached into a drawer of his desk, pulled out a file folder, and slid a couple sheets of paper from it across his desk to me. They were printouts of emails. He said the *Prime Time* security people had sent some of them over as samples of the kind of messages Abbie was getting.

The first one said: "From the world of darkness I will loose demons and devils in the form of scorpions to torment you." Another was: "Death is the greatest form of love, Abbie. And I have chosen to love you." Also: "Don't try to make sense out of your imminent death, Abbie Kincaid. There is no sense to it. But no sense makes sense." And one of the emails simply consisted of a single phrase: "Beware the Z."

"Like you said, they all sound pretty crazy," I told Wohlers.

"Some of them are actually stuff that was once said by Charles Manson. When he and his followers killed that actress Sharon Tate and a bunch of other people back in the '60s. Real quotes from back then, or expanded versions of things he said that have been updated with references to things happening now."

"Isn't Manson in jail for like a million years?"

"Since 1969."

"So this is probably not him then."

"Yeah, we deduced that answer even without your help, Malloy. But thanks anyway for the keen insight."

"Could be one of his followers."

"Most of them are dead or in jail or very old by now."

"What does 'Beware the Z' mean?"

"I have no idea."

"Might be a clue," I pointed out.

Wohlers shrugged. "There's a lot of nuts out there."

I handed the printouts back to him.

"Were there any references to Laura Marlowe, the dead movie actress, in the other stuff you got?"

"Why do you ask that?"

"Because Abbie is working on a big exclusive about Laura Marlowe's murder for her TV show. Plus, the Charles Manson references and the fact that Manson's most famous victim was Sharon Tate, another big Hollywood actress. It just seems likely there might be some kind of crazy connection in the mind of whoever is making these threats."

Wohlers nodded. "There's a bunch of references to Laura Marlowe. Some of them warned the Kincaid woman not to do the Marlowe story. Others say she'll wind up dead the same way. But that still doesn't take us anywhere. We have no idea who's behind all this."

"Can't you track the phone calls or emails some way?"

"Not in this age of social media and disposable cell phones. Everyone's anonymous if they want to be."

"So what are you doing?"

"Not much we can do in this kind of case. Not unless somebody actually does something besides write anonymous threats. Most of the time, that never happens . . . the threats are all bullshit, not real. Besides, as you say, they've got lots of security of their own around her over there."

"Did you meet her personal security guard?"

"The big guy with the ponytail?"

"Yes."

"His name is Vincent D'Nolfo."

"What's his story?"

"Ex-prizefighter. Ex–Army Ranger. Was in both Iraq and Afghanistan, they tell me."

"D'Nolfo sounds like a tough guy."

"I sure wouldn't want to get on the wrong side of him."

"Good advice, albeit a bit too late."

"The two of you didn't get along?"

"I don't think he likes me."

"How could anyone not like you?"

"I made some mild criticisms of his wardrobe, people skills, and overall job demeanor."

Wohlers sighed and finished off the corned beef sandwich. There was something else I wanted to ask him.

"Do you know much about Tommy Rizzo?" I asked.

"Thomas Rizzo's kid."

"I met him this afternoon."

"Lucky you. What did you think?"

"He seemed like a troubled young man."

"His father is a thug, a drug pusher, he traffics in human flesh, he extorts money and—oh, yes—he kills people."

"Maybe that's why his son is so troubled," I suggested.

"Where did you see the kid?"

"At Abbie Kincaid's office."

"What the hell was the Rizzo kid doing there?"

"They had some kind of romantic relationship for a while."

"Well, there's no law against a woman making a mess out of her life by falling in love with the wrong man."

"I certainly hope not," I agreed.

Wohlers belched loudly. I wasn't sure of the exact etiquette on how to respond in a situation like this. Should I assume it to be a *thank you* for my sandwich and tell him *you're welcome*? Did I say *God bless you* like you did when someone sneezed? Did I suggest to him delicately that belching at the meal table was frowned on by Emily Post, Miss Manners, and pretty much everybody in civilized society? Or did I just ignore it and pretend I never heard the belch? I opted for ignoring it.

"C'mon, Malloy, you did alright for yourself," he said. "More than alright. You married that hotshot lady from the DA's office. I've seen her a few times in court. Beauty, brains—she's got everything. How did you ever manage to pull that off?"

"Actually, we got divorced."

"God, that sucks. I'm sorry to hear it."

"Imagine how I felt," I told him.

"Well, these things happen, I guess."

"Yeah, the truth is the marriage has been over for a while now."

"So you're okay about it?"

"Fine."

"You're sure."

"Absolutely."

"Glad to hear it."

"Like you said, these things happen."

"I guess time does have a way of healing this kind of thing, huh?"

"I've moved on with my life," I said.

CHAPTER 7

I WAS living in a new apartment on the West Side of Manhattan. In Chelsea, not far from the Hudson River. I'd moved there from the Upper East Side after I read an article in the *New York Times* real estate section about all the hip, cool, trendy people moving to Chelsea. I wanted to be hip, cool, and trendy too.

When I was married, my wife, Susan, and I lived on East 18th Street, near Gramercy Park. After she moved out, I stayed there for a while, but the memories were too much for me to handle. I moved to a pre-war building in the East 90s. It was okay. But it was really old and falling apart, and I got serenaded to sleep at night by the sound of cars down on Third Avenue.

My new place was a two bedroom in a brand-new high-rise with a view of the Hudson. Well, that's what the ad for it had said anyway. And it was true, I suppose. If you looked out a far window in one of the bedrooms, stood on a chair, and craned your neck in just the right way, you could catch a glimpse of the water.

It was definitely an upgrade for me though. I had a doorman. I had a concierge. I even had a health club and swimming pool in the building. Plus, I was on the thirty-sixth floor, which meant the sounds of the street were no longer a problem. It cost a lot more for me in rent. But I was determined to change my life for the better. This apartment . . . well, it was a start.

I pushed open the door now and went in.

"Hi, honey, I'm home," I said.

There was no answer, of course. No loving wife waiting for me after a hard day at work with a martini and a pair of slippers. No kids running into my arms. Not even a dog or a cat to lick my face. It had taken me a while to get used to living alone after my breakup with Susan. But I had almost come to grips with it now. Almost.

The truth is that when I'd taken the apartment my goal was to one day win Susan back, get her to move back in and marry me again. Well, that's still my long-term goal. The short-term goal is just to get her to take my phone calls and speak to me again. Baby steps. You have to crawl before you can walk.

You see, there'd been an unfortunate incident between us recently.

I was feeling lonely late one night and I called Susan. I told her how much I missed her. How much I needed her. And how much I loved her. I believe I proposed to her over the phone that night. In fact, I proposed to her several times during that ill-fated conversation, as I recall.

Then, from somewhere in the background, I heard the sound of a man's voice.

"Susan, honey, are you coming back to bed?" the male voice said.

"I'll be right there," she told him.

She came back on the line to me.

"Who is he?" I asked.

"That's none of your business, Gil."

"Sure it is."

"I don't quiz you about the women in your life, Gil."

"I don't have any women in my life except you."

"Look, you have no right to . . ."

"I'm your husband, goddammit."

"Ex-husband."

"You and I both know we're going to wind up together again. It's just a matter of time until that happens."

"Why do you keep saying that?"

"Because it's true."

"I gotta go . . ."

"I love you, Susan," I blurted out.

She didn't say anything.

"The appropriate response is to say, 'I love you too,' " I told her.

"Let's not do this anymore, Gil."

"Just tell me you love me. I want to hear it. I don't care if that asshole you're with hears it too."

Things went rapidly downhill from there. After she refused to give me the "I love you" return, I erupted into a tirade of jealous and righteous anger over what I described as her betrayal of me. I said a number of things during that conversation that I wished later I could take back. I had done that in the past when I was afraid I was losing her to someone else, and I had promised myself I would never let it happen again. But the thought of her being in bed with that other man made me so crazy that I just couldn't control myself.

"Please don't call here again," she said when I was finished.

Then she hung up.

Since then, she had remained incommunicado to me no matter how many times I reached out to try to repair the damage I'd done.

I walked into the kitchen, took a bottle of beer from the refrigerator, and brought it back to the living room. I picked up the remote and clicked on the TV. There was a *Gilligan's Island* marathon on one of the cable channels. Gilligan and the Skipper and the Professor were trying to build a ship out of coconuts or something to get off the island. As you can tell, it was a pretty sophisticated plot, so I did my best to concentrate and keep up with it.

Which was good because it stopped me from thinking about all the things I didn't want to think about. Like my ex-wife. My career. My future and my life in general. When I think too much about this stuff I get tense and agitated and feel like the walls of my apartment are closing in on me.

This anxiety had caused me to have a series of what they called "panic attacks." I got shortness of breath, I felt dizzy and became disoriented—I even passed out once in the middle of the newsroom. I've got medicine for it. I've had counseling too. And I tell people I don't have the panic attacks anymore.

But the truth is I do. Not a lot, but they still happen from time to time. Mostly when I'm alone in my apartment, like now.

The health problems had started for me the first time I'd screwed up at the *News* with the fictional Houston interview. All the fallout and disgrace over the revelation about what I'd done led to the onset of the panic attacks. The anxiety and the attacks and these moments of nearly paralyzing panic continued off and on after that, usually in conjunction with the ups and downs of my career at the paper.

I used to see a woman shrink who told me the problem was I measured my worth as Gil Malloy the reporter—not the person. When I was breaking big exclusives on Page One, I was good with myself. But when I wasn't doing big stories, I couldn't handle the down periods of my career. "You use your job, you use being a reporter, as a defense mechanism," the shrink said. "No matter how noble you try to make it—and it is a noble profession—being a reporter allows you to shut out emotion and avoid dealing with what's really inside you. Hence, the panic attacks."

She said the solution was I had to learn to live my life each day without clinging to my reporter persona to shield me from the real issues and emotions I needed to confront. "You have to build a life that's about something more than just being an ace reporter," the shrink told me. "Being a reporter can't be your entire life."

It was good advice, I guess.

But pretty hard for me to follow that advice the way I was feeling right now.

I mean I was working on a story—the Laura Marlowe murder—that wasn't even my story.

I had a twenty-six-year-old boss who cared more about page views and demographics than she did about journalism.

And my wife—okay, my ex-wife—was screwing some friggin' other guy.

Just thinking about all of this was almost enough to push me into another panic attack. But after a few deep breaths and an almost Zenlike effort to remain calm, I was okay again.

I took a swig of beer and tried to put all of these thoughts out of my mind. I focused my attention back on *Gilligan's Island*. No matter how many times I watched these episodes, I always think that maybe this is the one where they'll figure out how to get off the island. They never do, of course. They finally do get rescued in one of the sequel TV movies made years later, but by then I had pretty much lost interest. I hummed the theme song of the show to myself now. A three-hour tour. Three-hour tour.

By the time the episode was over, my beer bottle was empty. I had a couple of options. I could walk into the kitchen, get myself another beer, and keep watching Gilligan while I either fell asleep or simply passed out.

Or I could get out of this lonely apartment for a while.

I looked at the time. Just past ten o'clock. The first edition of the *Daily News* would be hitting the newsstands with my story. I could always read it online, of course. But I still loved the feel of holding an actual newspaper in my hands. I walked over to the window. Even from the thirty-sixth floor, I could tell it was a nice night out there. One of these comfortable early summer evenings in New York City before the heat and humidity settled in for July and August. I decided to go out and buy a copy of the paper.

On my way out through the lobby of my building, the doorman gave me a friendly greeting.

"How are you, Mr. Malloy?" he said.

"I met a TV star today," I told him.

"Good for you."

"Abbie Kincaid."

There was a blank look on his face.

"She has a news program called *The Prime Time Files*. It's a newsmagazine kind of thing. Sort of like Barbara Walters or Diane Sawyer. Take my word for it, Abbie Kincaid is a big star."

"I'm sure she is."

"A big, big star."

"Good for you," he said again as he held the door open for me to go out.

Yep, this was my new life.

High-rise apartment.

High floor.

High rent.

Same old high anxiety.

CHAPTER 8

I WATCHED Abbie Kincaid's show at a place called Headliners. Stacy Albright wanted me to write a follow-up article on whatever Abbie said about Laura Marlowe. She'd invited several of the editors and reporters to watch with her. I was one of them.

For those of us in the newspaper world in New York City, Headliners bar is legendary. There's an old-style printing press in the front. Blowups of famous Page Ones from the city's newspapers—most of them no longer around—hung from behind the bar. There was also something called a *Gallery of Page One Heroes* on another wall, pictures of reporters who had broken memorable stories over the years. One of them was me for a big exclusive I'd done. There was a plaque above the picture, which said: *Gil Malloy, Reporter of the Year.* I was smiling in the picture, standing between Marilyn Staley, who was the *Daily News* city editor then, and Rick Hodges, the managing editor. Hodges died of a heart attack a few years later, and Staley was fired more recently to make room for Stacy Albright. It all seemed like a million years ago now.

When I got to the bar, Stacy and the others were sitting around a table underneath a big wide-screen TV. I pulled up a chair at the end of the table, as far away from Stacy as I could get. Jeff Aronson, a reporter who covered the federal courts for the *News*, was next to me. He was drinking a bourbon on the rocks.

Jeff and I had started out at the paper together as copyboys. My rise had been more rapid, but then so had my flameouts. Aronson, on the other hand, had been a steady contributor for the *Daily News* the whole time. Never a big star, but highly thought of as a federal court reporter.

I'd drunk with Jeff before, and I knew his routine. Always drank bourbon on the rocks. He'd have two of them—no more, no less. Then he'd catch a train to the suburbs in New Rochelle, where he'd go home to his nice house with his nice wife and his four nice little children. He was one of those people who seemed to have it all. He even went to church and visited hospitals on Sunday. Of course, you never really knew for sure about a person. A guy like Jeff Aronson could have bodies of teenaged girls buried in his basement, I suppose. But as far as I could tell, he seemed to be a good reporter, a good husband, and a good father. He had his life in order, everything under control. I never understood how people could deal with all that kind of responsibility. Me, I had trouble just getting to work on time. Maybe it was some sort of a character flaw in me.

"How many stupid things has she said so far?" I asked Aronson.

"Who?"

"Stacy."

He laughed.

"Her record is twelve in one hour," I said. "That was the day she said Joe DiMaggio played for the Brooklyn Dodgers and she couldn't remember if there were four or five Beatles."

"She's young."

"Youth is no excuse for ignorance."

"Weren't you ever young?"

"No," I said, "I was born at the age of thirty-seven and immediately became a cynical, embittered newspaper reporter."

The Laura Marlowe story was the first segment of *The Prime*

Time Files. It started with a montage of pictures showing the movie star at the height of her career. Winning an Oscar for *Lucky Lady*. Arriving at a premiere for *The Langley Caper*. On the set of *Once Upon a Time Forever*. Signing autographs for fans. And finally showing up at the party in New York on the last night of her life.

"Even though Laura Marlowe died thirty years ago, her legend continues to grow," Abbie said. She was standing in front of the New York Regent Hotel where the shooting took place. "One story is that she's still alive somewhere, that she really didn't die that night at this hotel. Like UFOs or Elvis Presley, there are reports of Laura Marlowe sightings in the tabloids and even some of the more legitimate press on a regular basis. Fans have set up websites devoted to the 'Laura isn't really dead' theory. We take a look at this and many other questions about the tragic '80s star in this *Prime Time Files* special report tonight. Some of the answers we found will shock you."

She spent the next several minutes of the segment debunking all those rumors. She said the evidence proved incontrovertibly that Laura Marlowe was indeed dead. Then it started to get interesting.

"The person who police say killed her was a man named Ray Janson. Janson was obsessed with the actress and told people he wanted to marry her. He also said ominously at one point: 'If I can't have her, then no one will.' Janson had stalked her for several days, according to the cops, building up to the final deadly confrontation at this hotel on the night of July 17, 1985. Police say Janson fled the scene, then committed suicide by hanging himself a few days later in a Manhattan hotel. The case was closed. But should it have been?"

Abbie went to an interview with a retired Long Island police sergeant named Greg Birnbaum, who told the following story:

On the night of July 17, 1985, Sgt. Birnbaum had arrested

a man for speeding in Southampton, not far from where Laura Marlowe had a summer beach house. The driver had been going seventy-two miles per hour in a forty-five zone. His license was also expired and he became belligerent with the officers, saying he was in a hurry to get somewhere. The police report said it appeared he was under the influence of drugs or alcohol, although subsequent tests turned up negative.

The suspect was eventually taken to the Suffolk County Court and booked at 9:20 p.m. He spent the night in jail, paid a $150 fine, and was released on his own recognizance in the morning. The name of the suspect, taken from his expired license and his car registration, was James Janson. Which, it turns out, was the Laura Marlowe stalker's real name—James Ray Janson.

He had begun using his middle name of Ray because it was the name of the character Laura marries in the movie *Lucky Lady*. "A check of old police records by *The Prime Time Files* turned up a form that Janson had signed while he was in custody," Abbie said. "We discovered the signature matched that of the Ray Janson who had died in the hotel room days later. It was definitely the same man."

This was followed by an interview with another retired cop, a New York City homicide detective named Bill Erlich. He was one of the detectives who worked on the Laura Marlowe murder case. Erlich said that, contrary to legend and popular lore, no one actually saw Janson shoot the actress. A lot of people saw him hanging around the hotel the day or so before the shooting, asking questions about her and hoping to get a glimpse as she walked through the lobby. Then an eyewitness saw someone running away from the scene that he identified as Janson.

"When he turned up as a suicide in the hotel room a few days later, we just figured it all fit together," Erlich said. "In retrospect, maybe we should have investigated it more."

Then came an interview with Laura's mother and husband. They talked about how shocked they were over these new disclosures. They speculated on how big a Hollywood star the actress would have become if her life hadn't been cut short so tragically. They also threw in a few plugs for the Laura Marlowe museum, memorabilia, and website.

I remembered the two of them shared in the actress's estate. This story would be a bonanza for their business, I thought to myself. Birnbaum and Erlich, the two cops on the program, would be courted for big bucks by all the media. And Abbie's ratings would soar. Everyone was going to make money off this. Everyone except Laura Marlowe.

"The big question this leaves us with, of course," Abbie was saying on the screen, "is who really killed Laura Marlowe? If Ray Janson didn't do it, and it now appears that he was in police custody some seventy-five miles away on Long Island at the time of the shooting, then someone else did. That person has gotten away with murder—one of the most famous murders of all time—for the past thirty years. Next week on *The Prime Time Files*, we'll have even more shocking revelations about this case. Tune in then."

The segment ended with the famous picture of Laura Marlowe, blowing a kiss to her fans just before she died.

———

When it was over, Stacy came and sat with us.

"That's a helluva story," she said.

"Yeah, ain't it?"

"Did she tell you anything about what she was going to say?"

"No."

"You're sure about that?"

"Stacy, you said to write a story about her story without knowing what it was going to be. The whole thing was your idea."

"And she hasn't told you anything about what she's got coming up next week either?"

I thought about our conversation on serial killers.

"No," I said, which was sort of the truth.

"Can you try to talk to her again?"

"Sure."

"This could be a really big exclusive."

"Yeah, but it's her exclusive—not ours."

"Who cares whose story it really is?"

"Well . . ."

"You better get back to the office and write it up right away. I want to get it up on our website as soon as possible. Hell, if we play this right we'll get more traffic from it than *The Prime Times Files'* own webpage does."

On my way out of Headliners, I passed by the picture of myself on the wall again and wondered why the guy in it looked so happy.

CHAPTER 9

I TRIED reaching out to Abbie a couple of times after the telecast, but never got any response from either her or Lang.

I figured whatever connection I'd made with her during that interview in her office was just my imagination.

But then she called me up out of the blue a few days later and asked me to have dinner with her.

We met on a rainy night at a coffee shop near Washington Square Park in Greenwich Village. Abbie was wearing jeans, cowboy boots, a T-shirt, and a baseball cap. She looked comfortable, more relaxed than she had that first day we met. I was expecting a place a bit more glamorous and chic than a coffee shop. But she picked the spot, so it was fine with me.

"I love this place," she said. "I'm sick of all those goddamned pretentious, upscale meat market spots where everybody goes just to show how happening they are. I like the atmosphere here. I like the people. It takes me back to when I first came to New York City as a struggling young actress."

"You ate here then?"

"I worked here."

"As a waitress?"

"That's right."

I looked at one of the waitresses serving food to a family at a booth next to us. I tried to picture a young Abbie wearing a waitress's uniform and dreaming of her big break. I'd eaten here a few times myself over the years. Maybe she even waited on me back then.

"So now you still like to eat here?" I asked.

"Yes."

"To see how far you've come since those days?"

"Something like that."

"I understand."

"Besides," she smiled, "the macaroni and cheese is real good too."

Vincent D'Nolfo, the big security guard I'd seen at *The Prime Time Files* studio, was sitting in a car outside. He'd dropped her off and stayed close by in case she needed him at any point during the evening. That made me a bit uncomfortable. But it was sure better than having him join us inside at the table.

The waitress came over and took our order. She was blond and pretty and very young, probably just out of high school. I wondered if she was an aspiring actress or dancer or TV anchorwoman, like so many waitresses in New York City. I was pretty sure she recognized Abbie, but she didn't say anything. Abbie gave her a warm smile. Maybe she saw herself in the girl a long time ago.

"Did you hate it?" I said to Abbie after the waitress left.

"Waiting on tables here?"

"Yes."

"No, it really wasn't so bad. I mean I was in New York City. I was young. I had all these big dreams. Besides, working in this place was a lot better at the time than the alternative."

"Which was?"

"Being a housewife in Milwaukee."

Abbie told me how she'd grown up in a small town in Wisconsin. She had been her high school homecoming queen, worked summers at the Dairy Queen, and then gotten married at the age of eighteen to her high school boyfriend, a football player named Billy Remesch. He didn't have the grades to get a football scholarship to college, so he took a job in an auto body shop in Milwaukee. It looked like she would settle down there with him for the rest of her life.

Then Abbie won a drawing at a movie theater. The grand prize was an all-expenses-paid trip to New York City. She was having lunch at the Four Seasons as part of the prize package when a Broadway producer saw her, cast her in a small role in a show, and—just like that—she became an actress. She divorced her husband and never went back to Wisconsin.

There were some hard times at first, and that's when she worked as a waitress to pay the bills. After a few years, she became moderately successful—working enough to make a living. Some decent supporting roles in movies, TV commercial work—and even a recurring part in a hit sitcom that lasted for a season and a half.

After that, she did a pilot for a daytime TV talk show, *Girl Talk*, that quickly took off. She signed a multi-year deal with a top syndication company and became a bigger star than she'd ever been as an actress.

The show stressed reality, and nothing was off limits. Abbie wore her emotions on her sleeve. She'd tell the audience about her diets, her sex life, and her innermost secrets. When she was happy, they laughed. When she was sad, they cried. She knew how to push just the right buttons to connect with the viewing public.

Maybe the show's biggest moment came when she revealed on national television how she'd been physically, sexually, and emotionally abused by her husband while they were married. She said she'd kept it a secret for years. She told the TV audience she was coming forward so that other abused women would also find the courage to deal with the problem. She ended the show with a poignant plea to her ex-husband to get professional help before he hurt anyone else. The show set new ratings records.

Later, she got an offer to do her own news-magazine show on nighttime network TV. The little girl who once worked at a Dairy Queen was now interviewing heads of state and some of the biggest names in show business.

"It's a funny thing about fame," she said at one point. "Fame comes and goes very quickly sometimes, like a thief in the night. Take Laura Marlowe, for instance. One minute she's a struggling actress who's going nowhere, the next she's the biggest star in the world. And then she's dead. It all happens so fast. Even if we get lucky like Laura did, we need to be able to enjoy the moment. Because no one ever knows how long it will last. I guess that's the message we can all learn from her life."

As we ate, we talked about the fallout from her story. The cops had reopened the Laura Marlowe investigation. The trail was very cold after thirty years, of course, but they were at least going through the motions of trying to find the real killer. The press had picked up on it in a big way too, with Laura Marlowe's name back in the headlines all over again. And everyone was talking about Abbie and wondering about the blockbuster exclusive she had promised for next week's show.

"Tell me about the serial killer angle," I said.

"I can't."

I stared at her in amazement. "You showed me a picture of a dead singer named Cheryl Carson and three other women. You suggested to me that their deaths were somehow connected. You all but told me you thought they were killed by one person—the same person who killed Laura Marlowe thirty years ago. If it's true, that's one of the greatest serial killer stories of all time. So what else did you find out?"

She shook her head no. "If I told you everything I know right now, you'd think I was paranoid and/or crazy."

"Abbie, I don't think you're paranoid or crazy."

"Well, I guess it's sort of like the old joke about the guy who says: 'Okay, I may be paranoid, but that doesn't mean people aren't following me.' That's kind of the way I feel about my life right now."

"Does this have anything to do with Tommy Rizzo?" I asked.

"Tommy? No, Tommy's the least of my worries. You're wrong about him—he's really a nice guy. Besides, I think he's finally given up on me. We had a long talk. I haven't heard from him since."

"Whatever story you're working on sounds like it could be dangerous," I said. "Maybe you should just walk away from it."

"I can't do that."

"Why?"

"Have you ever walked away from a big story?"

"No."

"My point exactly," she smiled.

It was one of those special New York City moments that don't happen to me too much anymore. The rain falling gently on the streets of the Village. The parade of people—an entire gamut of New York nightlife ranging from funky-looking neighborhood folks to wide-eyed tourists to street hustlers—passing by outside the window.

We talked about some of my notoriety—the good as well as the not-so-good moments I'd had in the public spotlight. Eventually, of course, the conversation got around to the Houston story. The low point of my career. The story that nearly got me fired from the *Daily News* and would remain as an albatross to my career for as long as I was in the newspaper business.

"I've replayed it all over in my mind so many times over the years," I said. "How I ever made the decision to put the imaginary quotes in the story and make it sound like they were really coming from this legendary New York City streetwalker called Houston. I dream about being able to go back in time to undo everything I did wrong on that story. And about how different my life would have been if I hadn't put those fictional words in her mouth. But I did. I'm still not sure why. The only thing I do know for sure is that I will never do anything like that again."

She brought up some of the big stories I'd done at the *Daily News*. The high points. There were plenty of those too. Many of my biggest crime exclusives had involved serial killer cases. Which is probably why Abbie had asked me all those questions that first day on the serial killer angle.

"So how come you're still a newspaper reporter?" she asked me at one point. "You're a talented guy. Don't you want to do something better than that?"

"Some of us think of it as a noble calling."

"Newspapers are dying."

"So I hear."

"TV, the web, social media—that's how people are getting their news these days."

"Gee, you sound like my city editor."

"Have you ever thought about going into television?"

"I don't think it would be a good idea."

"Why not?"

"I've got a big mouth and I annoy people."

"Sounds like you'd be perfect for TV," she laughed.

I wasn't sure if I would ever see her again. I mean I didn't know if this was supposed to be a date or a business meeting or what. But, before we left, she said to me, "We should do this again, Gil."

"Definitely," I said.

"Dinner soon?"

"Sure."

"It's a date then," she said.

On my way home, I couldn't stop thinking about what had happened that evening.

I mean I'd just had dinner with TV celebrity Abbie Kincaid.

And she wanted to see me again.

Me and Abbie Kincaid.

Zowie!

CHAPTER 10

SAW Abbie a few more times after that.

Once, she simply called me up unexpectedly and asked me if I'd like to hang out with her again. I asked her where she wanted to go, and she said nowhere. Told me she just wanted to kick back and relax for a night without being out in public. She asked if she could come over to my place.

We ordered pizza and watched a Laura Marlowe movie on TV. The first one, *Lucky Lady*. I found it on Netflix and thought it might be fun to watch a few minutes of it with Abbie. We wound up watching the whole thing. Neither of us talked a lot during the movie, we just kept watching Laura Marlowe on the screen. She was simply mesmerizing. So young, so beautiful, so talented. She had the whole world, her entire future ahead of her then. Instead, it would end too soon in tragedy.

When the movie was over, Abbie made a call on her cell phone and a few minutes later Vincent showed up. She hugged me and gave me a kiss on the cheek before she left. Vincent stared at me the entire time. I gave him my best hard stare back. I don't think he liked me any better than the first time we met. But that was okay. I was getting used to it.

The next time I saw Abbie was completely different. She took me to some fancy restaurant on the Upper East Side that always

got written up in the gossip columns. There was a constant parade
of fans and other celebrities coming to our table to greet her. She
signed autographs, let people take pictures with her—she was playing the star again. Me, I just watched it all unfold and wondered
how this could be the same Abbie Kincaid I'd eaten pizza with in
my apartment a few nights earlier.

After the restaurant, we went to some private club where she
was again given the star treatment. She exchanged meaningless
chatter with all sorts of beautiful people, drank a lot, and even
put on a show out on the dance floor. She pretty much ignored me
the entire evening. I was just window dressing for her, not anyone
important in her life that night. I understood. I guess. I mean I
never knew why she wanted to spend time with me anyway. I figured she'd just gotten bored with me and this was the real Abbie
Kincaid I was seeing.

At the end of the night, Vincent dropped me off first. He didn't
speak to me during the ride to my apartment. Neither did Abbie.
She just looked out the windows of the limo at the lights of Manhattan buildings and passing cars as we made our way downtown
to my place in Chelsea. When we got there, she gave me a peck
on the cheek, Vincent opened the door of the limo, and I walked
inside my building without looking back, confused and—truth be
told—a little pissed at the way the evening had turned out. I was
pretty sure I'd never see either of them again.

It was a few hours later, and I was asleep, when I woke up to
the buzzing of my intercom. I looked at the clock. Two a.m. The
buzzing continued. Over and over and over again. At first, I wondered if maybe the building was on fire or something. But when I
pushed the intercom button to talk to the doorman, he said there
was someone there who needed to see me. Abbie Kincaid.

I opened the door a few minutes later and saw Abbie standing
there. She looked disoriented, disheveled, and desperate—nothing

like the big arrogant star she'd been when I'd seen her just a few hours ago.

She was crying too.

And—most important of all—she was carrying a gun.

———

I let her into the apartment. She was really sobbing now. I gently took the gun from her hand and laid it on a table. She didn't resist. I wasn't sure she even knew she was holding it. She buried her face in my chest, crying.

"What's going on, Abbie?" I said.

She just kept sobbing uncontrollably.

"Where's your security guard?"

"I sent him home. Then I came here on my own."

"But why . . . ?"

"I just . . . I just want to feel safe with someone."

She held on to me tightly. She had clearly drank a lot more after she left me. I walked her into the bedroom and laid her down on the bed. She kept muttering a lot of stuff, but most of it just sounded like gibberish to me. "Sign of the Z, sign of the Z, please stay away from me," she said at one point. I asked her what she meant, but she just shook her head and wouldn't say any more. I remembered one of the threatening letters sent to her had used the phrase "Beware the Z" and figured it must be about that. But I had no idea what any of it meant.

I walked back out to the kitchen, made some black coffee, and took it to her. She drank some of it and, after a while, began to pull herself together a bit.

I sat on the bed next to her.

She didn't want to talk anymore about what she was afraid of, and I didn't want to push it given her condition. So I just kept talking to her about a lot of other stuff until she sobered up. The show.

Her career. To try to make her feel better, I pointed out how amazing her meteoric rise to stardom had been. How that big break of winning the contest back in Wisconsin had turned her life around. How she'd gone from being an unhappy housewife to an actress and then a big TV star virtually overnight.

"Television is really simple," Abbie said after she'd pulled herself together a bit. "All you have to do is stand out in some way, break away from the pack, do blockbuster things that make people notice you. You can't worry about the consequences. You've got to make news. That's what I do."

"You mean like revealing that your husband abused you in front of the entire nation?" I asked.

"As a matter of fact, yes."

"I'm just curious. What happened to him afterward?"

"He lost his job. His new wife divorced him. I heard he was talking about trying to move away and start a new life where people didn't know him. Not much chance of that. I ran his picture for weeks on my daytime show. He can run, but he can't hide."

"Did you ever have any regrets about doing that?"

"I did a good thing," she said.

"Okay."

"Do you know that after we did that show, calls to battered women hotlines went up three hundred percent?"

"That's great."

"Wives told me they came forward to talk about their husbands just because of what I did."

"Good."

"A lot of lives were turned around by that show."

I wasn't sure if she was talking to me anymore, or simply trying to convince herself.

"I did a good thing," she repeated.

Finally, she fell asleep. I put a blanket over her and turned out the light. Then I went into the living room, lay down on the couch, and tried to figure out what was going on here. Sure, she was beautiful and sexy and exciting. And I sure as hell would love to have some kind of ongoing relationship with her, whatever that turned out to be. But she was clearly a troubled woman. And the last thing I needed in my life right now was someone with that kind of trouble. I knew plenty of troubled people already. Hell, if I wanted to meet a troubled person, all I had to do was look in the mirror.

When I woke up in the morning, she was gone.

So was the gun.

There was a note on the table for me that said:

> Thank you so much, Gil. You're a sweetheart.
> When I'm ready to tell someone my story, you'll be the
> first.
> I promise to tell you all about . . . I owe you that.
>
> xxxx
> Abbie

Except she never did tell me, of course.

That night was the last time I ever saw Abbie Kincaid alive.

CHAPTER 11

T HE police said it happened this way: Abbie Kincaid was found shot to death in a room on the ninth floor of the New York Regent Hotel. That was the same hotel where Laura Marlowe had died some thirty years earlier. Abbie had checked into the hotel at about 7:15 p.m. on the night before her body was found. She appeared to have gone directly there after leaving the TV studio, since people there said they'd seen her until a little after 6:30 p.m. They said she told them she was going to do more research for the story. They assumed she'd gone to the Regent—the place where the actress had been murdered—to get the feel of the story.

She had made a series of phone calls from the hotel room. Most of them were to producers and other people at her show, talking about things she wanted to do the next day. One was to room service for a Caesar salad and a plate of fruit that was made at 8:46. That was the last time anyone heard from her.

Abbie's body was discovered the next morning when the maid let herself in to clean the room. The maid, who spoke very little English, had knocked on the door several times earlier, but had been reluctant to go in because she knew there was a celebrity staying there. When she finally did use her pass key to unlock the door, she discovered Abbie lying on the floor next to the bed in what the papers the next day described as "a pool of blood."

The police said she had been shot three times, twice in the chest and once in the head, in what appeared to be a coup de grace to make sure she was dead. Nothing had been taken from the room, so police quickly ruled out robbery as a motive. They also said there was no evidence of any kind of forced entry. Abbie seemed to have let her killer into the room. The person was either was someone she knew or at least someone she felt wasn't dangerous.

The ballistics report on the gun said it was a .45. It appeared from the trajectory and other evidence in the room that the shooter had been standing only a few feet from her when the gun was fired, another indication that Abbie was probably unaware she was in any danger until it was too late. There were at least a dozen sets of fingerprints in the room, but they proved to be of no help. The ones that had been tracked so far belonged to hotel staff and the others were probably from previous guests. A preliminary medical examiner's report indicated that Abbie had died sometime between 10 p.m. and midnight. But no one heard any shots and no one saw anyone going into or leaving her room.

It turned into a media circus, of course. There were Page One headlines about Abbie's murder. Speculation about a connection to the story she'd just done about Laura Marlowe's death thirty years earlier. Biographies of her life and career. TV reenactments of her death, or at least the likeliest theories on how it happened. And lots of discussion about the price of fame for someone like Abbie Kincaid or Laura Marlowe in our society.

I was part of all this, of course. I did the first news story on the discovery of the body, covered all the press conferences on the status of the investigation, and attended the star-studded funeral they held for Abbie. I also wrote a bylined first-person piece about the time I had spent with her. Everyone told me it was one of the best things I've ever done. But I was doing it all on autopilot. The days were all a blur to me as I tried to deal with Abbie's sudden death.

The most traumatic moment happened when Stacy came up with the idea of me doing a live webcast on the *Daily News* website about my personal relationship with Abbie in the days before her death.

The paper's online audience would email or text or tweet me questions, I'd answer them onscreen for the website, and our internet traffic would soar, Stacy proclaimed proudly.

It didn't seem like that good an idea to me, just crass and sensationalistic. I wanted to be a real journalist, not some gimmick to boost net traffic or newspaper sales by exploiting my relationship with Abbie. But Stacy was insistent. She might not know much about journalism—but she sure as hell knew how to draw a big audience. And I was her star attraction, whether I liked it or not.

The webcast lasted for thirty minutes. I held up pretty well through most of it. I answered questions about Abbie's career, the murder investigation, and how I'd gotten to know her after the interview in her office—as well as a lot of other, straightforward material. But then, just before the end, someone asked me this question: "What will you remember most about Abbie Kincaid?" And all I could think of was that last night at my apartment when she'd come to me in tears, buried her head against my chest, and said, "I just want to feel safe with someone." I teared up as I tried to give an answer; my voice broke with emotion, and I dabbed at my eyes on camera as I tried to regain my composure. Somehow I made it to the end of the webcast.

Afterward, Stacy was ecstatic.

"That was terrific, Gil. We set all kinds of new traffic records with it. Maybe we should do another webcast with you tomorrow."

"Tomorrow?"

"Hell, we can keep doing them all week if there's that much interest out there in the Abbie Kincaid murder."

"I'm sorry about that bit at the end," I said.

"What do you mean?"

"Stacy, I almost cried on camera."

"That was the best part."

"I thought you'd be upset."

"Upset? That video with you wiping tears out of your eyes is already going viral on social media. It was incredibly compelling. You showed real emotion to them. You opened up your heart, you opened up your feelings, and they loved it all."

"Uh, well, I'm glad I was able to put on a good show."

"I just have one request if we do another webcast tomorrow."

"What's that, Stacy?"

"Do you think you can cry on camera like that again?"

———

One night, not long after Abbie was killed, I went back to the coffee shop in Greenwich Village where we'd eaten dinner together that first night. I sat there for a long time, looking at the waitresses and wondering if any of them would ever wind up like Abbie. I tried to imagine Abbie waiting on tables and dreaming of becoming a big star someday. I wondered what would have happened if she hadn't made it big. What if she'd just kept working as a waitress? What if she'd gone back to Wisconsin? What if she'd stayed married to her husband back there? She probably wouldn't be too happy, but she might still be alive.

At some point, I came up with a wild theory that maybe Abbie wasn't really dead. That it could all be a publicity stunt. I mean I thought about what a great ratings bonanza it would be if she had faked her own death. Then Abbie would show up a week or a month later—and say it was all a case of mistaken identity. Claim she had amnesia or was working undercover on a big story or was out of the country—and the girl in the hotel room was really somebody that just looked like her. I actually convinced myself it might be true for a few minutes.

But, of course, it wasn't.

Abbie was dead. There was no doubt about that. She'd been identified by the people she worked with, the medical examiner's office had matched her fingerprints and dental records, and I'd even seen the autopsy photos. They showed Abbie's body, lying on a metal slab in the New York City morgue, with her eyes staring blankly out at me.

I wondered what she thought about during those last few seconds before she was murdered. Was she scared? Was she surprised? Did her life flash before her eyes? Did she think about her television career or working at a Dairy Queen in Wisconsin or maybe even eating pizza with me at my apartment that one night?

I didn't know the answers to any of these questions, and I never would. What I did know about Abbie was this: she'd dug up long-buried secrets about a thirty-year-old celebrity murder case. She'd dumped a boyfriend who was the son of a top underworld boss. And she'd revealed things about her ex-husband on national television that cost him his job, his family, and his reputation.

Abbie Kincaid had done a lot of things to get a lot of people mad at her. Mad enough that she carried a gun for protection. And one of those had gotten her killed.

CHAPTER 12

WANT to do the story," I said to Stacy Albright.

"Of course you do. The search for Abbie Kincaid's killer."

I shook my head no.

"The police are all over that. So is every other reporter in town. I'm not sure how much I could do that everybody else isn't already doing. There are plenty of reporters at this paper who can cover the day-to-day investigation story on the Abbie Kincaid murder. It doesn't have to be me."

"Then what story are you talking about?"

"Laura Marlowe," I said.

She didn't understand at first what I meant.

"There was a lot of stuff going on in Laura Marlowe's life before she died," I said. "I'm not sure if any of it had anything to do with Abbie's murder, but Abbie seemed obsessed with the story. She also told me there was stuff she'd found out she hadn't told anybody yet. Maybe this had something to do with her death, maybe it didn't. But I want to find out the truth about Laura Marlowe."

Stacy still wasn't convinced. But I had come prepared to make my argument with the kind of ammunition I knew would work on her.

"Since the day Abbie Kincaid first broke the news about the real Laura Marlowe killer never being caught, 'Laura Marlowe' has become the highest trending item on social media. Along with '*Lucky Lady*,' '*The Langley Caper*,' and '*Once Upon a Time Forever*'—her three movie titles. My article about *The Prime Time Files* disclosures—plus the speculation about what might come next—produced enough traffic to nearly double our web audience in the days right after Abbie's broadcast. Laura Marlowe became a hot item again. And she still is. Maybe more than ever if I can somehow solve the thirty-year-old unsolved murder of one of Hollywood's most legendary and tragic young stars."

"And if it turns out to be related to the Abbie Kincaid murder . . ."

"Then it's an even better story."

She nodded. I had her now. I figured the traffic numbers would do it.

"I like it, Gil. I like it a lot. I just assumed you'd want to be the lead reporter on the Abbie story since you had a personal relationship with her at the end . . ."

"I can't do anything to bring Abbie back. What I can do is honor her memory in the best way I know how. I'm going to finish the Laura Marlowe story for her."

PART TWO

TRUTH OR MYTH? THE LAURA MARLOWE STORY

CHAPTER 13

I CALLED Susan, my ex-wife, at the DA's office. This time she picked up.

"We need to talk," I said.

"There's nothing more to say, Gil."

"This isn't about us or the guy in your apartment."

"What do you want to discuss then?"

"I need your help on a story."

"The Abbie Kincaid murder?"

"For one."

"What else?"

"The Laura Marlowe case."

There was a silence at the other end.

"Even if I could help you, why should I?"

"For old times' sake," I said. "For all the love we used to have for each other . . . one last thing you can do for me in honor of the marriage vows we once said . . ."

"Jeez, you'll do anything to get a story, won't you?"

"Have we met?"

———

An hour later, I was in her office at Foley Square. She was the deputy district attorney for Manhattan now. She'd moved up when the previous DA resigned and was being touted as possibly the next DA.

It was a corner office with a nice view, the kind of office someone got who was on the way up. She had given me a perfunctory hug as I walked in, then sat behind her big desk and looked at me impassively. As if I was just another appointment on her schedule.

She looked good. Her hair was pulled up in back, and she wore a snug-fitting power suit that hugged her body and must have had guys in the office sneaking peeks every time she walked by. That had all been mine once. And then I let her get away. So being there, sitting in front of her desk, and seeing how great her life was without me was the last thing in the world I wanted to do. But like she said on the phone, I'll do anything for a story.

"So who was the guy in your apartment?" I asked.

"Gil, I thought we weren't going to do this."

"I figured we'd get it out of the way first and then move on to business."

"His name is Michael Garrison."

"What does he do?"

"He's a lawyer."

"Gee, that's original."

She sighed.

"What kind of lawyer?" I asked.

"An estate lawyer."

"Is it serious?"

"What do you mean by serious?"

"How much time do you spend with him?"

"Well, Michael and I are living together."

"That's serious," I said.

There was an awkward silence.

"Do you know the difference between an estate lawyer and a prostitute?" I said.

"Gil . . ."

"A prostitute stops screwing you after you're dead."

Susan didn't laugh. Instead, she just started telling me what the DA's office knew about the Abbie Kincaid murder investigation. No nonsense, all business. Probably why she got the corner office.

"They're looking at Tommy Rizzo. Also at the ex-husband, who showed up from Wisconsin and started harassing her recently. He apparently was still really upset about all the things she said about him on television. He barged into the studio one day and made a big scene. The security people had to kick him out. They're also still checking out all the threatening notes she got to see if it could have been some kind of obsessed fan."

"What about Vincent, the big security guard, and the executive producer, Gary Lang? Are they suspects?"

"Now why would either of them want to kill her?"

"I don't know. I just don't like them. So I hoped they might be suspects."

Eventually we got around to Laura Marlowe. Susan said the cops had technically reopened the case based on Abbie's new evidence, but they were focusing mostly on Abbie's murder. Of course, they were also pursuing the possibility that the two crimes were somehow linked. But the most prevalent theory was that the thirty-year-old Laura Marlowe murder case had nothing to do with Abbie's death. The cops were looking at Abbie as a crime of passion.

"Do you think anyone will ever figure out who killed Laura Marlowe?" I asked.

"Doubtful."

"Why?"

"Because it happened thirty friggin' years ago."

"There's no statute of limitations on murder," I reminded her.

"Let me tell you something," she said. "Most murders are

solved within the first week after they happen. By the second week, that percentage goes down dramatically. By the third week, even more. Once a murder case has been worked on for much longer than that, it goes to the back burner. No law enforcement agency ever officially closes a murder case without an arrest, but the odds of solving it becoming pretty astronomical at that point. When we do catch someone for a decades-old murder, it's generally because the killer screwed up somehow and gave themselves away. And a celebrity cold case like this is even worse because you have the public spotlight on you. You have to be very careful what you say and who you talk to. Take my word for it—it's almost impossible to ever solve a celebrity cold case."

"So do you guys ever catch anyone?" I asked.

Susan made a face. I could tell there was something bothering her about the Laura Marlowe case. I asked her what it was.

"Well, it's not just that the Laura Marlowe case is so old and that she was so famous," she said. "There's something else about it that just doesn't feel right."

"What do you mean?"

"It seems sloppy. The guy gets a traffic ticket on Long Island at the same time she was killed. How come somebody didn't figure that out back then? I know they didn't have all the high-tech systems we do now, but they still checked things out. Everyone seemed to be in such a rush to wrap up this case in a hurry. That bothers me."

"Do you think somebody was trying to cover something up?"

"Maybe not deliberately."

"Then what?"

"It was a high-profile case. Those cops were under a lot of pressure and public scrutiny. Everyone wanted a quick arrest. So I think when this guy Janson, who looked like the killer, turned up dead in the hotel, well . . . they didn't ask a lot of the questions they should have. They went with the flow. They took the easiest route. Everybody talked themselves into believing Janson really did it. So they declared the case solved, closed the books on it, and everybody was happy. I mean they thought they had the right guy. We all did. Until now."

"Did you ever talk to any of the cops who were involved in the investigation?"

"No, most of them are either dead or retired."

"How about Erlich, the one who went on TV to talk about it?"

"I heard he's got an agent now. They're negotiating a book deal about Erlich's role in the case. He's going to make big money off this. Can you believe that? It's like hitting the lottery for him."

I nodded.

"I need a favor," I told her.

"What a surprise."

"I want to see the Laura Marlowe murder file."

"You're kidding, right? That's an official police document. It's not available to the press or the public."

"I understand."

"It's against the rules for me to let anyone show it to you."

"That's why it's called a favor," I smiled.

———

Nothing is ever what it seems to be.

For thirty years, the legend of what happened to Laura Marlowe on the night she died had endured and grown until it achieved nearly mythical proportions.

Everyone thought they knew what happened. Only twenty-two years old and already one of the biggest stars in America, Laura Marlowe stopped to sign an autograph for a fan outside of the Regent Hotel on Fifth Avenue in New York City. The fan shot and killed her in front of a horrified group of people—including her husband, then fled down the street with witnesses yelling for some-one to stop him. He was identified afterward as Ray Janson, who had been stalking the actress for days around the Regent—trying to get a glimpse of her and talk to her and give her presents. A few days later, in an apparent fit of despondency over what he'd done, Janson killed himself in a Times Square hotel after writing a final love note which ended with the phrase: "Tell Laura I love her."

It was a great story. It had everything. Glamour. Drama. Trag-edy. Unrequited love. The only problem was that a lot of it wasn't true.

The official police file that I eventually convinced Susan to let me read said it happened like this:

On the night of the murder, Laura Marlowe dined at the Four Seasons restaurant with her husband from 6:15 to 8 p.m. Then they went to the party for *Once Upon a Time Forever*. The details got a bit sketchy after that. According to the story I'd always heard, she left the party about ten with her husband, returned to the Regent, and was shot when she stopped to sign an autograph for her killer. But that wasn't what the report said. According to this version, Laura disappeared from the party sometime around nine. Which meant her husband spent at least an hour there without her. Ed-ward Holloway eventually returned to the hotel to look for Laura, where he discovered she'd just been shot. The story of Holloway looking on in horror as his wife was gunned down in front of him appeared to be one of those urban legends that people just began to accept as fact after hearing it enough times.

The shooting scene was confusing too. Despite many subse-quent claims from people that they had seen Ray Janson shoot Laura, the police were able to find no actual witnesses to the crime. Various stories about the killer saying "I love you, Laura" or kissing her or leaving flowers by her body all seemed to be bunk too. All anyone knew is that people heard a gunshot at about 10:15 p.m.

Lots of people started converging on the scene then, and witnesses told of the heartbreaking sight of Edward Holloway cradling his wife in his arms and crying as he tried to talk to her. The first ambulance arrived shortly afterward. The medical people worked feverishly on her, thought at first she might survive, and took her to Roosevelt Hospital—where she was pronounced dead on arrival at 11:15 p.m. The cause of death was a gunshot wound to the head.

Even the location of the shooting was different. I'd always assumed she'd been shot right in front of the Regent. But the body was found in an alley alongside the hotel. There was no explanation of why she was in the alley. Did the killer force her there? Or did she know her killer and go with him willingly? No matter how you looked at it, it didn't make sense that she'd died in an alley.

There was another interesting detail. The report noted that neither Laura's mother nor husband were at the hospital where she died. The mother was on a cruise ship with fans promoting a line of Laura Marlowe fashions. She couldn't be reached right away at the time of the tragedy. The husband had collapsed at the shooting scene and was apparently still back at the Regent Hotel. One of the people at the hospital was David Valentine, who identified himself as Laura's father. Also at the hospital that night was Sherry De-Conde, Laura's first agent. I remembered Abbie telling me about her and how big a role she'd played in Laura's early life before she became a big star. Laura's mother had fired her just as Laura's career was breaking wide open. According to the report, Valentine and DeConde had both shown up at the scene around the time of the shooting. I wrote David Valentine and Sherry DeConde's names down in my notebook.

Laura's body was quickly cremated after her death, and there was no public burial service. This helped fuel the rumors that maybe she wasn't really dead and somebody was trying to hide something. But this appears to have all been based on speculation, not fact. Laura's mother was quoted in one article as saying that the family thought it was best to avoid the spectacle of a public funeral—that Laura "had been enough of a public spectacle in her life; we simply wanted her death to be marked with some privacy and dignity." The investigation itself seemed to have been conducted by the Manhattan North homicide squad. The lead investigator was Lt. Jack McPhee. The other two cops were Detectives Luther Wiggins and Bill Erlich, the one from Abbie's TV show. Their conclusion was a simple one. Ray Janson had shot and killed Laura Marlowe because of some sort of deluded love obsession he had about her, then committed suicide a few days later over what he'd done. According to people who knew him, Janson had slipped into some sort of fantasy world about Laura Marlowe, telling people she was his girlfriend, they were going to get married, and that she would have his babies. At first, everyone thought it was just a joke. Then they began to realize how obsessed he'd become over the actress. He told them he'd prove how much Laura loved him. He said they'd read about it in the paper someday soon. So it was an easy leap for the cops to conclude he'd been the shooter. I wrote the cops' names down too.

At least a half-dozen witnesses had seen Janson hanging around the Regent Hotel lobby waiting for the actress during the days leading up to the shooting. He was positively identified at various times by the bellhop, the desk clerk, and a hotel detective. There was no question he was stalking her. But no one could ever definitely put him at the hotel at the time of the murder.

His suicide seemed pretty clear cut too, at least back then. Two days after Laura's murder, Janson checked into the Armitage Hotel, a cheap place in Times Square. He went up to his room, locked the door, and—as near as anyone can figure—hung himself in despair over Laura's death.

The cops put it together pretty quickly, especially after finding the suicide note at the scene he'd written to Laura Marlowe. It did not say "Tell Laura I love her." That phrase—from the tear-jerker song of the early '60s—seemed to have been the product of the imagination of an overzealous reporter trying for a big scoop. But it talked about his undying love for her and concluded by saying: "Laura, we were meant to be together . . . now we will be together forever."

It all seemed so simple to the cops back then. Now, of course, there was a whole different story—and a lot more questions.

By the time I was finished, I had made a lot of notes and written down a lot of names. The major people I wanted to talk to were:

Beverly Makofsky, Laura's mother
Edward Holloway, her husband
David Valentine, Laura's father
Sherry DeConde, the ex-agent
Bill Erlich, Luther Wiggins, and Jack McPhee, the three
    cops who handled the case.

There was one other element to the police file that baffled me. It was a section that had been blacked out. There was a stamp on it that said: *Classified: For CID use only*. CID stood for Criminal Intelligence, which dealt mostly with organized crime cases. It wouldn't have anything to do with the murder of a movie star.

So why was the CID designation in this file?

I had no idea.

Maybe one of the people on my list would know.

CHAPTER 14

BEVERLY Makofsky lived in a penthouse apartment in a fancy building on Fifth Avenue. The place looked like something out of a glossy magazine spread. There were windows on all sides with breathtaking views of the skyscrapers of Manhattan. It had eight bedrooms, leaving plenty of room for both overnight guests and the full-time help—always a pesky problem for me too. The furniture was very expensive; most of it looked like it came from antique stores or museums.

Her name wasn't Beverly Makofsky now, she said. It was Beverly Richmond.

"I've been married three times. First to Laura's father, when I was Beverly Valentine. I didn't want to keep his name, so I went back to my maiden name of Beverly Makofsky when Laura was growing up. Then I was Beverly Maddox. And now I'm Beverly Richmond."

"Richmond is the name of your third husband?"

"Arthur Richmond. A lovely man. The best of my husbands."

"Where is he now?"

"Dead, I'm afraid."

"I'm sorry."

"A heart attack four years ago."

Probably wore himself out walking around this damn apartment, I thought to myself.

She was probably close to seventy by now, but you could see that she'd once been stunningly beautiful, like her daughter, when she was young. I'd told her that I was doing an in-depth feature on Laura for the *Daily News* because there was so much interest after Abbie's TV piece. She seemed eager to help. I remembered the articles I'd read that said how much money she'd made off her dead daughter's memory. On the other hand, maybe she just liked talking about Laura and keeping the memory alive. Sometimes I'm too cynical.

"This has been an incredibly traumatic experience," she said to me. "After all these years, I'd finally come to peace with Laura's death. It was difficult, but at least we knew what happened. Or we thought we did. Now this has opened up all the old wounds again."

"Do you have any thoughts on who might have really killed your daughter?" I asked.

"Some other crazy fan, I suppose."

"Most people are killed by someone they know, not by strangers. All of this time, everyone assumed she was shot by some lone nut. But maybe that's all wrong. We have to at least consider the possibility now there was some other motive behind her murder."

"Who did Laura know that would want her dead? She was such a lovely person."

She talked for a long time about her daughter's career. The struggles, the rejections, and then the glory days when *Lucky Lady* made Laura an overnight superstar. She dropped in names along the way like Jack Nicholson and Robert Redford and Marlon Brando. She made it sound like a fairy tale where everything was magical and nothing ever went wrong. Whenever I asked about something that had gone wrong—Laura's disappearance from the set of her last movie, rumors of substance abuse problems, other personal problems she might have been having—she deflected the question and changed the topic. She didn't want to talk about any of those things. Or maybe she just wanted to remember the good times.

She didn't have any reluctance to talk about Laura's father.

"That son of a bitch," she said. "I married him right out of high school because I was pregnant with Laura. It was a disaster right from the very start. I had ambitions of my own as an actress, but I had to put them all on hold, which was fine with Davy because he had absolutely no ambition of any kind. All he wanted to do was drink and go out on some boat and fish all day. I thought my life couldn't get any worse. But then it did. After I found out what he did to Laura."

"What did he do?"

"He abused her."

"You mean physically? He hit her?"

"That too."

"Sexually?"

She nodded.

"How did you react?"

"I told him I would kill him if he ever laid a hand on her again. I meant it too. My God, she was four years old! But I got lucky. He left on his own. One day he just never came home from a fishing trip. That was the way Davy did things. No goodbyes, no money, no nothing—he just disappeared. Good riddance, as far as I was concerned."

"And that's the last you ever saw of him?"

"Yes."

"Did Laura ever ask about him when she was growing up?"

"A few times. I told her the truth."

"How did she take it?"

"She hated him. Laura was suspicious of all men for a long time. In fact, she never really dated or had a romantic relationship with anyone until she met Edward Holloway. Eddie was so different from her father. Eddie was gentle and kind and he loved her so much. He was just devastated when she died. He's never remarried, you know. I asked him why once. He said to me that once you've been married to Laura Marlowe, no other woman could ever take her place."

"I'm going to try to talk to Holloway later," I said. "Tell me a little more about him."

"Eddie's a good boy. He's a producer. Raises money to put on Broadway plays and he works with theater groups. He's very involved in the whole New York City cultural community."

"And you still work with him on the Laura Marlowe enterprises?"

"Yes, we share that fifty-fifty."

"And everyone's happy with that arrangement?"

"Absolutely," she smiled.

I'll bet you are, I thought to myself as I looked around the lavish apartment.

———

Eddie wasn't a boy anymore. He was in his fifties and waging a valiant battle against the ravages of Father Time. He'd had several plastic surgeries, he told me proudly—showing off the changes that had been done to his nose, cheekbones, eyelids, and even his ears. He wore a toupee that he said cost $10,000 and was made out of real hair. He took a handful of pills every day to keep his weight down; they gave him enough energy and stamina to run in last year's New York City Marathon.

"If you look young, you feel young too," Holloway said to me. "I'm fifty-six years old and I feel like I'm twenty-six."

"I'm thirty-seven and I feel like I'm fifty-seven."

"Have you ever had plastic surgery?"

"Not yet."

He studied my face. "You'll need some in a few years."

"Thank you."

"It's nothing to be ashamed about."

"Didn't God create us all in his or her own image?"

"God didn't count on double chins and crow's-feet."

We were sitting in Sardi's, the legendary Broadway celebrity hangout in New York City. Edward Holloway seemed to really rate there. We had the best table in the place, in the front of the restaurant. I'd been there before on my own and wound up sitting near the kitchen. I was impressed.

All sorts of people stopped by to say hello or chat for a few minutes. There was a TV anchorwoman, a bestselling author, a Broadway actor, and even a couple of baseball players from the Yankees.

"Let me guess," I said to Holloway in between people. "You've been here before."

"Yes," he laughed.

"What do you do for a living again?"

"I do a lot of things."

"Like running the Laura Marlowe memorial business with her mother?"

"Yes."

"And you invest in Broadway plays?"

"Sometimes."

"Such as?"

He gave me a few names that I'd never heard of.

"And you're a producer?"

"That's right."

"So what are you producing right now?"

"I've got several things in development."

"How far developed are they?"

"Various stages."

"You know, I'm still having a hard time figuring out exactly what it is you do," I said.

He smiled. "So what do you want to know about Laura?"

Holloway gave me the same version of the story that her mother had. The sanitized one. Laura was a beautiful person. Laura was so happy. Laura was a saint. Laura had so much to look forward to. Nothing about drugs or depression or any imperfections in the little fairytale world they'd created about her.

"How did you meet her?" I asked.

"She hit me."

"She hit you?"

He laughed. "I know it sounds kind of strange, but that's what happened. I was crossing the street on Rodeo Drive in Los Angeles when a car hit me. I was knocked to the ground, but not really hurt. When I looked up, the driver was standing over me. It was Laura Marlowe. I thought I was dreaming. Once she knew I was all right, she was so grateful she offered to buy me lunch. I guess it was just fate, because we really hit it off—and, of course, we fell in love."

"How long after that were you married?"

"Very soon."

"Were you happy together?"

"Deliriously so."

Laura Marlowe didn't sound too happy to me at the end, but I didn't say anything.

"We had such wonderful plans together," he said, his eyes tearing up now. "For her career, for a family, for a real life outside Hollywood. But she never got the chance. That bastard—whoever it was, Ray Janson or someone else—killed her. For me, it was like the JFK assassination. Those few seconds changed history and changed me forever. I've had a lot of good things happen to me since then, but I'd trade them all to spend just a few seconds with Laura again. She was so special. But she was gone so quickly. And nothing can ever change that now."

I asked him about the shooting. He gave me an account that

was similar to the one I'd read in the police report. "I'd left the party and gone back to the hotel to look for Laura," he said. "I just got out of my cab when I heard the gunshot and saw Laura lying on the ground. Someone—I always assumed it was Janson, but I never got a good look at the face—was standing over her with a gun in their hand, then ran away. I went to Laura's side, and held her and tried to comfort her until the ambulance arrived. She couldn't speak, she just looked up at me with these sad eyes. She died shortly afterward."

I checked my notes from the interview with the mother to see if there was anything else I needed to ask him.

"Did you know Laura's father?" I asked.

He made a face. "Yes, I sure did."

"You didn't like him?"

"He abandoned Laura when she was just a little girl. Ran off and left her and Beverly on their own. Then he shows up after she becomes a big star and tries to act like he's her father again. Trying to get his hands on some of her money, I'm sure."

"What did Laura say about him?"

"She never talked to me about her father. I guess it was too painful. He apparently did things to her when she was a child. Things that, well . . . bad things. Maybe she still remembered them, maybe they were in her subconscious somewhere. That guy was bad news."

"So why was he still in her life at the end? Even at the hospital on the night Laura died?"

Holloway looked pained. "That was such a terrible night. Beverly wasn't there and I was . . . well, I don't remember a lot. I was pretty shaken up by what happened. But when Beverly came back, she made sure Valentine was out of the picture for good."

"Is he still alive?"

"I don't know."

"Got any idea where I might go looking for him?"

Holloway suddenly realized where I was headed with this.

"My God, do you think he might have killed her?" he asked.

"You said he was very angry. Maybe he was angry enough at her and her mother to shoot her as some sort of twisted revenge for cutting him out of all her money."

"I've never thought about it, but it could have happened that way."

"It's just a theory," I shrugged.

"I've spent thirty years hating Ray Janson for what I thought he did," Holloway said. "I guess I can't hate him anymore. But I want someone to blame for what happened to Laura. If it turns out to be Davy Valentine, her father, that would be great. I'd love to hate that bastard Valentine for the next thirty years."

CHAPTER 15

S HERRY DeConde, Laura Marlowe's first agent, had an office on the second floor of a townhouse in Greenwich Village.

"I remember the first day I met Laura," she told me. "I was just starting out then, barely out of college and trying to break into the business of being an agent. She came up to see me with her mother. I knew right away she could be a star. Even at that young age you could tell. She had something special. You spend a lifetime in this business looking for someone like Laura. And she just walked into my office that day."

Doing the math, I knew that Sherry DeConde had to be close to sixty. But she looked a lot younger than that. She had long, blond, straight hair that hung halfway down her back and made her look a bit like like a '60s hippie. She was wearing blue jeans, brown leather boots, and a T-shirt underneath a checkered flannel shirt on top. It wasn't exactly sexy attire, but somehow it made her look sexy. Not in a young girl way, but that "been there, done that . . . this is the real me, take it or leave it" look.

"People talk about overnight stars, but there really aren't any," she said. "Sure, stardom is about luck and opportunity and sometimes even talent too. But most of all, you can't give up. That's what I always told Laura and her mother. I put her up for everything— teen shows, commercials, movie roles. But she was just another face in the crowd. Then suddenly, when she was nineteen, she exploded into this incredible superstar. I've been in this business a long time, and I've never seen anything like it. It was amazing."

"How did Laura handle the early rejections?"

"She was fine, but it really bothered her mother. Beverly is not what you would call a patient woman. She was, to put it bluntly, the stage mother from hell. Always second guessing, always criticizing, always giving me a hard time over everything I did. Look, I know Beverly wanted to be an actress herself once so there was a lot of frustration on her part. Unfortunately, she took it out on everybody around her—me, producers and, worst of all, on Laura. I felt sorry for that girl. I took care of her. Somebody had to."

"Didn't her mother take care of her?"

She shrugged. "I'm sure Beverly loved her daughter. But she showed it in funny ways. It was like she wanted to turn Laura into what she always wanted to be. She said she was doing it all for Laura, but I think she was really doing it for herself. Maybe it would have been different if Laura's father was around. But he left when she was just a little girl. Laura had no one to rely on but Beverly and me. I think she was very lonely. So I wound up spending a lot of time with her. I was more than Laura's agent. She became kind of like a daughter to me."

That's what Abbie had said. Sherry DeConde had been almost like a "surrogate mother" to the struggling young actress.

"But you were probably only a few years older than her back then, right?" I pointed out.

"Okay, maybe I was more like a big sister," she laughed.

It was a nice laugh. A helluva laugh actually. I looked around the office. There were photos of celebrities on her desk and walls. Some I knew, some I didn't. But no sign of any pictures that looked like a husband or children. I glanced down at her left hand. There was no ring there. I'm a reporter. I notice stuff like that.

"What about her husband?"

"Holloway?"

"He was her husband, wasn't he?"

"In a manner of speaking, I suppose."

"What are we talking about here?"

"People tell me that marriage was arranged by Beverly, the same way she tried to arrange everything in Laura's life."

"Why would Laura's mother want her to marry Holloway?"

"I don't know, but Beverly had a reason for everything she did."

She talked more about how surprised she was when Laura suddenly became an overnight star after struggling for so many years.

"I kept sending her up for every part I could think of, but nothing ever happened," she said. "She got very depressed. At one point, I think she dropped out of the business altogether—I didn't hear from her for nearly a year. Then one day she calls me up out of the blue. She said she was in Hollywood, there was a movie project called *Lucky Lady*, and they were looking for a teenage ingénue with a new face to play the lead. They thought she was perfect for the role. The rest, as they say, is history. She became a star."

"So what happened to you?" I asked.

"As soon as Laura hit it big and got the offer, Beverly decided she wanted a big-name agent. Now you have to understand, I never had anything in writing with them. It was always a handshake deal, right from the very start. I never thought I needed anything else. I thought I was their friend as well as their agent. Like I said, I really cared about Laura as a person. I tried to tell Beverly that. But she didn't care, she just told me that my services were no longer needed. She fired me."

"Did you fight it?"

"I did for a while. I consulted a lawyer. He said I had a pretty good case if I got in front of a jury. At the very least, I could walk away with a big cash settlement for the *Lucky Lady* deal, since I was still her agent when she got the offer to star in the film. But, in the end, I just thought it would be too painful to go through all that."

"So you simply walked away from probably millions of dollars in agent's fees?"

"Easy come, easy go," she smiled.

"Does it bother you a lot?"

"What do you think? Laura was the star client of a lifetime. America's sweetheart. And, just when she hit it big after all the early struggles, I lost out on all that fame and money."

"Which raises the question, Ms. DeConde . . ."

"Did I kill Laura Marlowe out of rage and for revenge after being fired? It's a viable scenario, I must admit. I mean I've got a good little thing going here with my agency business, but my life is nothing like it would have been if I had hit it big with Laura when she became a superstar. So maybe I arranged a meeting with her that night at the hotel, brought along a gun, and shot her to death as payback. Was that going to be your question, Mr. Malloy?"

"Well," I smiled, "I wasn't going to put it quite that bluntly."

"I was mad about losing Laura. But I wasn't mad at her. What made me feel really bad was that I'd let Laura down. Maybe I could have helped her if I'd stayed around and fought her mother. Maybe I could have protected her somehow. Now we'll never know."

DeConde said she tried to maintain a relationship with Laura, although she was no longer her agent. But even though she agreed to drop the legal action, she received a lawyer's letter from Laura's mother ordering her to stay away from Laura.

"I was too heartsick over everything that had happened to fight anymore. I just gave up."

"Did you ever see Laura again?"

"Yes."

"When was that?"

"Not long before she died."

"What happened?"

"She came to see me in my office. She said she wanted to talk. She said she missed the talks we used to have. And so we sat and talked. She was a mess. She'd been crying, she had no makeup on, and her hair was all over the place. She said everything was going wrong in her life. She talked about taking drugs, drinking, and being unhappy all the time. I think she just wanted to get away from it for a short time. This was the only place she thought she could do that. Before she left, she hugged me and told me how much she missed me. I thought I would see her again. I wanted to help her. But then she was dead."

"You were at the hotel that night, right? You saw her before the ambulance took her to the hospital?"

"Yes."

"Why were you there?"

"To try to talk to her again."

"Did you?"

"No," she said sadly. "I was too late."

———

The big-time agent Laura's mother had hired after Sherry DeConde was named Glenn Charlton. Charlton had died a few years earlier. But I was able to track down his wife, who still lived in Beverly Hills. I called her up, told her about the Laura Marlowe piece I was working on, and asked her to share any recollections.

Her account of Laura's troubled life was similar to what Sherry DeConde had said.

So was her description of Laura's mother.

"Glenn, my husband, told me the mother was impossible to work for. She constantly wanted to micromanage everything. He actually didn't stay on as Laura's agent very long. He was very successful in Hollywood, you know, and he didn't want to be told how to do his job by some frustrated, failed actress. That's how he used to describe Laura's mother. After Glenn severed ties with Laura, the mother and her husband pretty much managed her career on their own. Glenn hated that woman. Called her 'the stage mother from hell.' But he always said he felt sorry Laura had to grow up with a parent like that."

"I understand the father was a real bad guy too."

"That's what we heard."

"But you never met him, huh?"

"No. He wasn't around."

There was something missing from the story. Something that had been bothering me right from the start.

"How did Laura get the part?" I asked. "The big break in *Lucky Lady* that made her an overnight star?"

"Glenn and I wondered about that too," Mrs. Charlton said. "It seemed like dumb luck. But Glenn told me once maybe she got some help."

"What kind of help?"

"Laura was a very beautiful girl. But she was also very naive and trusting and innocent of the effect she had on a man. Glenn thought maybe she finally realized that and used it to her advantage. He told me she became close to someone who was extremely powerful in Hollywood circles."

"She slept her way to the top?"

"Yes, something like that."

"Did your husband tell you who this Hollywood big shot was? Was he a producer or director or what?"

"He was more in the business end of things."

"A financier."

"In a manner of speaking, you might say."

"I don't understand . . ."

"He was involved in lots of things."

"Such as . . ."

"He was a mob guy. A very famous one. He was a lot younger then, of course. He was just starting to build his crime empire. He spent a lot of time in Hollywood, and had really begun to wield some influence behind the scenes in the movie business. And, they say, he was totally enamored of Laura. She had that effect on men. This guy would have done anything for her. Glenn suspected he used his influence to get Laura the part in *Lucky Lady*."

"What was his name?" I asked.

"Thomas Rizzo."

CHAPTER **16**

BACK in the newsroom, I sat at my desk trying to figure out what I had here.

I knew now that Thomas Rizzo had been romantically involved with Laura Marlowe at some point before she died. I also knew that Rizzo's son was romantically involved with Abbie Kincaid before she died. I knew that Abbie had been investigating Laura Marlowe's murder, and I knew that Laura's police file had an entire section that was blacked out by the agency that dealt with mob-related activities. Thomas Rizzo was one of the most prominent members of the mob. There was a thread running through all this that even I could follow.

So what did it all mean?

I had a theory. What if Thomas Rizzo either knew something or had something to do with Laura's long-ago murder? What if he told this information to his son Tommy? What if Tommy had passed it on to Abbie? What if that was why she started looking into the Laura Marlowe murder? What if the Rizzo family then had to kill her—to prevent her from revealing what she found out?

It was a pretty good theory, and I sat there for a long time congratulating myself on my brilliance. I decided I deserved some kind of reward. So I went downstairs to a deli and bought myself a cup of coffee and a sugar-glazed donut. I came back to my desk, ate the donut, drank the coffee, and continued to marvel at how smart I was.

There were a couple of things still bothering me though.

Beverly Richmond told me she'd never seen Laura's father, David Valentine, again after he ran off and left them when Laura was a little girl. Except he did come back. I'd seen his picture with them at the Oscars ceremonies a few months before Laura died. And Edward Holloway had talked about the father showing up to try to get his hands on some of Laura's money after she hit it big.

Plus, Valentine was at the scene the night Laura was shot. So Valentine seemed to be much more of a part of Laura's life at the end than Beverly Richmond wanted to admit.

That brought up a possible alternative scenario for the murder. The father she hates suddenly turns up, tries to get back into her life and climb aboard the Laura Marlowe gravy train once she becomes a Hollywood superstar. She rejects him; he gets angry and he kills her. Except that still doesn't explain why the mother would lie about seeing him again. Was she trying to protect him? Of course not—she clearly detested him. So why not point out that he could be a potential suspect in her death?

Which led to another problem. Beverly Richmond never asked me anything about who really killed her daughter. I had to bring it up to her. With Ray Janson now out of the picture, it was the obvious question. Who did it? Maybe she didn't ask because she already knew who did it. Maybe she was hiding the truth. On the other hand, maybe she just forgot to bring it up.

There was one other thing too. The story of how Laura Marlowe and Edward Holloway met. I'd actually read that account in one of the articles I'd read while I was researching her. It told the story the same way that Holloway did, right down to the tiniest details of what her first words were. His memory of the incident was perfect. Too perfect. Almost like something that was rehearsed or could be recited from memory after so much time. What did that have to do with anything? I didn't have the slightest idea, but it bothered me.

———

Mostly though, I was intrigued by the Rizzo connection to both Laura Marlowe and Abbie Kincaid.

If I just pulled on that string some more, maybe I'd find some answers.

I saw Jeff Aronson—the reporter I'd been hanging out with at Headliners—in the office. His beat was the federal courts, which included the U.S. Attorney's office. The U.S. Attorney, like the police, had a special strike force that investigated organized crime. I walked over to his desk.

"What do you know about Thomas Rizzo?" I asked.

"Too much. Why?"

"I'm thinking of joining up. I figure 'made man' would look good on my resume."

"Very funny. Rizzo's a bad guy. He's into racketeering, loan-sharking, extortion, prostitution, drugs, and murder. Lots of murders. He's killed at least fifty or sixty people over the years that we know about—probably a lot more that we don't."

"Haven't the cops ever convicted him for any of this?"

"Not yet. No case the cops or feds bring against him ever sticks. Witnesses change their stories, evidence disappears—he's got a lot of clout. But, sooner or later, someone will probably get him. He's getting pretty old now anyway. I hear he's almost retired."

"What about the son, Tommy?"

"I don't know much about him. He went away to college a few years ago, then set himself up in some sort of real estate business. I'm not sure if it's a front for the mob or what. The word is he and his father don't exactly see eye-to-eye on everything, but I guess he'll inherit the whole rotten empire one day. There are no other kids around, and Rizzo's wife died a few years ago."

"So how do I find Thomas Rizzo?" I asked.

"Have you heard anything I've been saying here? This guy is really bad news."

"I need to talk to him."

Aronson sighed. "The last I heard Rizzo and his cronies hang out at a place called Florentine's in Little Italy. Whenever he shows up, there's maybe ten to fifteen people with him, most of them bodyguards, and they take a banquet room in the back. Rizzo sits in the same seat every time—head of the table, back to the wall and facing the door. Anybody walks into that room unannounced, there's gonna be fireworks."

CHAPTER 17

FLORENTINE'S was only moderately busy when I got there. I walked over to the bar and sat down where I could get a good view of the whole room. I was wearing a pair of charcoal gray jeans, a black turtleneck, and a dark jacket. My basic James Bond spying attire. I hoped it helped me blend in and go unnoticed.

Maybe a dozen tables in the place were filled. I checked them all closely. The only thing I deduced was that nobody in the place was dressed as cool as I was. I'd brought along a photo of Thomas Rizzo; I checked it now and then looked around the room again. No one looked like him. No Tommy Jr. either.

The bartender came over.

"Can I help you, sir?" he asked.

Behind me, I heard a wine steward explaining some of the choices to a table of eight.

"I'll take a beer," I said. "Amstel."

He left to get my order. While he was gone, I looked around the restaurant some more. The banquet room was in the back. If you twisted your neck back to one side, you could see inside it. I twisted my neck and looked. There was no one inside.

The bartender brought my beer. He poured some into a tall glass, waited for the foam to go down a bit, and then filled it to the top. Very professional. It was certainly a pleasure to watch a true craftsman at his job.

"I'm looking for Thomas Rizzo," I told him.

"Who's that?" he smiled.

"How about Tommy Jr., his son?"

"Never heard of either of them."

Behind me, the people at the table were still trying to figure out which wine to order. Indecisive. Not like me. I sipped on my beer and waited for something to happen. It didn't take long.

A few minutes later, a guy quietly slipped onto the stool next to me. I glanced at him out of the corner of my eye. He was big, maybe six-foot-five, and muscular. There was also a bulge under his jacket that was probably a gun. He was watching me carefully. The bartender had disappeared down to the other end of the bar and was trying hard to ignore us.

"Hi," the guy said.

"Hi."

"What are you doing?"

"Drinking a beer."

"By yourself?"

"I didn't know I needed help to drink it."

I looked at the bulge under his coat.

"Say, is that a gun under there?" I said. "I should point out to you that New York City gun laws are quite stringent and anyone found with an unauthorized firearm in their possession—"

"Who the hell are you?" he asked with an exasperated tone.

I showed him my card. The one that says: Gil Malloy, *New York Daily News* reporter, and has a drawing of the *Daily News* building in the corner.

"A newspaper reporter," he muttered.

"What gave me away? Was it the picture of the *Daily News* building or the word 'reporter'?"

"What do you want?"

I took a deep breath and plunged ahead with the reason I was there. "Look, let's save a lot of time here," I said. "I know Thomas Rizzo eats in this restaurant. I know you know him—and I suspect you are in his employment. I want to talk to him. Tell him it's about Laura Marlowe. Tell him I want to know more about their relationship and how he helped her get her start in Hollywood."

The guy looked at my card for a second, then slipped it into his pocket. He got up from the stool.

"Have a nice night," he said, "and stay out of trouble."

I made an imaginary gun with my forefinger and thumb, pointed it at him, and pretended to pull the trigger.

"You too," I said.

He shook his head and walked away, leaving me alone again. I nursed the beer for another ten minutes or so. No one else came over to talk to me. No one pulled a gun on me. No one went into the banquet room. No one broke out in any Mafia fight songs. Even the bartender seemed to have lost interest in me.

I left the restaurant and walked down the street to a newsstand. I bought the early editions of the other papers. I read through them. There were lots of stories about Abbie's murder, but none of them told me anything I didn't know. On the way back, I took one more look into Florentine's.

Thomas Rizzo wasn't there.

Tommy Jr. either.

The banquet room was still empty.

And there was no sign of my friend at the bar.

Probably so excited about meeting a real-life newspaper reporter that he ran right off to tell someone.

———

They came for me the next day. A Lincoln Town Car pulled up to the curb next to me as I approached the *Daily News* building. The driver got out. He didn't look like a mob guy, more like a TV game show host. He was young, good looking, dressed in a leisure suit with an open-collared shirt. He flashed me a big smile.

"We'd like to have a word with you," he said, gesturing to a man sitting in the back seat of the car.

"What about?"

"Thomas Rizzo. You've been asking some questions about him."

"Do you have some answers?"

"Maybe we can help you."

He opened the back door of the car and gestured for me to get in. He smiled again. I smiled back. I didn't figure they were going to kidnap me in broad daylight right off the street, and I was interested to find out what they had to say. I got in the car.

There was a guy in the back seat smoking a cigarette. It wasn't Thomas Rizzo. The inside of the Lincoln was filled with smoke. I sat down in the back next to him. The first guy got in too, sitting in the front seat and turning around to face us. I started to cough from the smoke.

"Have you ever read the surgeon general's report?" I asked.

He looked down at the cigarette in his hand.

"Yeah, I know. These things are going to kill me one day."

"To say nothing of the dangers of second-hand smoke to your family and loved ones."

"Life's a bitch, isn't it?"

He took another drag on the cigarette.

"You've been asking around for Mr. Rizzo?" he said. "Why?"

"What's it to you?"

"He's our employer."

"Thomas Sr. or Jr.?"

The man with the cigarette looked at the guy in the front seat and laughed at that. The other guy laughed too. I wasn't sure what the joke was, but I laughed along with them. I just wanted to be part of the group. "No, we don't work for Tommy Jr.," the one next to me smiled. "We work for Mr. Rizzo. Now why are you so interested in talking to him?"

"I'm working on a story about Laura Marlowe's murder thirty years ago."

"What does that have to do with him?"

"Laura was having a love affair with Rizzo before she died," I said as matter-of-factly as I could.

Both men in the car looked at each other. The first guy wasn't smiling anymore.

"Who told you that?" he asked.

"I can't say."

"That's not the answer we want to hear, Malloy."

"Look," I said, "it's not that I don't want to tell you; I can't. It came from what we newspaper types call a confidential source. I can't disclose that kind of thing any more than you can talk about your secret Mafia handshake. I'm sure you understand."

The man with the cigarette looked over at the guy in the front seat and frowned. He frowned back. I was pretty sure they didn't understand.

"Well, it's not really a rule," I said quickly. "I mean it's just sort of a journalistic guideline. I never even agreed with it, to tell you the truth. Besides, who's ever going to know if I accidentally let slip to you who my source was just this one time, huh?"

"Who told you, Malloy?" the guy with the cigarette asked.

"I read it in the police report."

"The police report."

"Yes, there's a secret classified section in there from the organized-crime task force."

"And it talks about Mr. Rizzo having a relationship with Laura Marlowe?"

"Page eighteen, Section C of the appendix," I said, which I thought was a nice touch.

I figured I was safe enough because there was no way they could check out my story.

"So can I talk to Rizzo?" I asked.

"He doesn't talk to the press."

"Yeah, but now you can tell him what a nice guy I am."

"Sorry, but Mr. Rizzo is a very busy man."

He made a gesture to the driver to let me out.

"Let me ask you one more question," I said. "How does the kid Tommy fit into all this? I find it a heck of a coincidence that he was dating Abbie Kincaid, who was investigating the death of Laura Marlowe and then was murdered herself. What do you guys make of that?"

The guy with the cigarette shrugged. "Do you have any children, Malloy?"

"No."

"I have seven. I love them all dearly, but sometimes they're a disappointment. Do you know one of my boys actually came home the other day wearing an earring? An earring!" He shook his head sadly. "They don't always turn out the way you thought they would."

"Like Tommy?" I asked.

"Tommy has caused his father some anguish. But Mr. Rizzo loves him very much. He would do anything for him. Do you understand what I'm saying?"

I nodded sympathetically.

"Kids." I smiled. "You can't live with 'em, you can't live without 'em."

They opened the door and let me out of the car. The one in the back seat with the cigarette smiled at me one more time through the open window.

"Laura Marlowe died a long time ago," he said. "Let her rest in peace."

CHAPTER 18

I WAS on a journalistic high now. I felt the adrenaline rushing through me. The way it always did when I had a breakthrough on a big story. I'd pulled the thread on the Rizzo connection, and I'd gotten a nibble back. I knew now that Rizzo was somehow involved in all of this. I didn't know how or why yet. But I was determined to find out, no matter what it took.

Sitting at my desk in the newsroom that evening after my meeting with the Rizzo guys, I realized I was too excited to go home right away. I didn't want to be in that lonely apartment right now. I wanted some kind of companionship. More specifically, I craved female companionship. For a long time, I'd held on to the hope that I could get back with Susan. But that clearly wasn't going to happen. It was time for me to move on. Just like Susan had moved on.

My brief time with Abbie—whatever that relationship had been—proved to me that I could be attracted to another woman besides Susan. All I had to do was find one. I thought about all the women I knew, all the women I'd met recently. I ranked them in the order of sexual attraction I felt toward them and wrote the names down on a sheet of paper. I stared for a long time at the top name on my list.

Then I took out my cell phone, found a number, and dialed it.

"Sherry DeConde Agency," the voice at the other end said. "Sherry DeConde speaking."

"Hi, this is Gil Malloy. Remember me?"

"Of course. Do you have more questions about Laura?"

"Not really."

"What can I do for you then?"

"Well, that depends. Would your answer be 'yes' to any of the following questions: A) Are you married? B) Are you in a serious relationship? C) Are you gay, asexual, or otherwise not interested in men?"

"Uh, my answer to all those would be 'no.'"

"Then I have another question."

"Really?"

"Bear with me."

"Okay."

"Do you find me physically repugnant for any reason?"

"I actually thought you were kind of cute."

She laughed. Still a nice laugh.

"So would you like to have dinner with me tonight?" I asked.

"C'mon, I'm old enough to be your mother."

"But you're not my mother. That's an important distinction."

"I'm still too old for you."

"Is that a yes or a no?"

"Maybe."

"Maybe yes?"

She laughed again.

"Where do you want to meet?" she asked.

We met at a place in Little Italy. They knew her there, and she got us a nice booth where we could talk without being bothered too much. We talked a lot about a lot of things. Mostly about Laura Marlowe, of course.

"Laura was such a troubled girl," she said. "Booze, drugs, mental breakdowns—all in just twenty-two years. The mother pushed her to become a star all her life. I believe that was at the root of many of Laura's problems. She had all this fame and stardom and money, but she didn't care about any of it. It was what her mother wanted, not her. She was on a course for disaster long before someone shot her that night outside the Regent.

"People didn't write about stars' personal lives so much back then. A lot of stuff was off-limits. Today the sad story of Laura Marlowe and her mother, and her struggles with stardom, would be big news. But thirty years ago, people just talked about it privately. To most people, she *was* America's sweetheart. But there was a tremendous price she had to pay for that.

"It was a lot like Marilyn Monroe. I heard that Marilyn never really believed she was pretty. She always thought of herself as plain, poor little Norma Jean Baker. She was convinced that everything she had would fall apart one day. In the end, I guess it did. That's what happened to Laura Marlowe too. We idolize our stars, we put them on a pedestal and worship them. Maybe we should feel sorry for them."

I asked her about Thomas Rizzo. She said she didn't know anything about Rizzo or any connection with Laura.

Then I told her about my meeting with Edward Holloway.

"The luckiest guy in the world," she said. "A real nobody who managed to marry the princess and get rich from her too."

"Do you believe that story about the way they met?" I asked.

She chuckled. "The famous actress hits the ordinary Joe with her car. And right in the heart of Beverly Hills—on Rodeo Drive, no less. She looks down at him lying in the street, their eyes meet, they fall in love—and they wind up getting married. It's a magical story, don't you think? It's got that whole Hollywood fairytale mystique to it. Dreams do come true in Tinseltown."

"I don't think it's true."

"No. But so what? Do you really think Lana Turner was discovered sitting at the counter of a drugstore? People make up stories like this all the time in Hollywood. They want to make the stars' lives seem glamorous. What does it have to do with anything?"

Eventually we got around to talking about my life. I told her everything. About my career ups and downs. About Susan. About my anxiety attacks. I know you're not supposed to be that open and candid about yourself on a first date. But I wanted her to know the real me. I didn't want to hold any secrets back from this woman. Somehow that seemed very important to me.

"What about you?" I asked at one point. "Marriages? Children?"

She took her fork and played with the pasta on her plate. I had a feeling she was trying to decide how candid to be with me.

"I've been married," she said finally. "A few times. None of them lasted. No children. I never made a conscious decision not to have children. It just didn't seem that compelling to me while I was concentrating on my career. You don't think about stuff like that when you're young. Maybe some people do, but I didn't. And then one day you wake up and you're sixty years old, and you wonder how you got to where you were. No husband, no kids, no family. You've got your job and not much else. The only people you have any kind of relationships with are people you know profession-ally—and most of them are just trying to get something out of you."

"Like a newspaper reporter, huh?"

"I didn't mean that, Gil."

"Anyway, this isn't a relationship."

"No, we're just having dinner."

"So let's enjoy it."

"I am enjoying it," she said.

Then she reached over and put her hand on top of mine.

———

We were headed in separate directions after we left, so we waited on the street for separate cabs.

"What do you think would have happened if Laura Marlowe had lived?" she asked.

"She would have had a great career," I said automatically.

"Maybe," she said. "Or maybe not. I was thinking about Laura the other day when I saw an obit on a pop singer who died. She was sixty-one years old, and her last hit had been in 1975. Everyone thought she had a long career ahead of her too. She had it all back then, just like Laura did—beauty, a great voice, and she was a terrific performer. But there were some problems at her record company, she changed managers, and the public just forgot about her. She tried to make a comeback for years, but it never took. Eventually she went back to gospel singing in churches, which is where she started out. That's what she was still doing when she died. She was sixty-one years old, and she was a long time away from being a star. She was a trivia item when she died. Who was the singer who was the one-hit wonder back in 1975?

"You never know how it's going to work out for any of them. It all seems so easy at the beginning when they're young and new and the whole world seems to be there for the taking. But eventually the beauty fades, the talent gets corrupted, the public turns its attention to new stars—and one day they find no one is returning their phone calls anymore. It's sad.

"Laura Marlowe never had to go through any of that. She's frozen in perpetual immortality. She'll always be beautiful, she'll always be a star, she'll always be young in our memory."

"Just like Buddy Holly or Selena or James Dean," I said.

"Who knows what would have become of any of them? We'll never know because they're legends now."

I nodded. "Laura Marlowe achieved immortality by dying at the age of twenty-two. But she lost out on a life."

Her cab pulled up now. She turned to me before she got in and put her hand out. I didn't shake it. I kissed her instead. She kissed me back. It was a nice kiss. A damn fine kiss. I decided I liked Sherry DeConde's kisses even better than her laugh.

CHAPTER 19

O F the three main police investigators on the Laura Marlowe case, two of them were dead. McPhee collapsed of a heart attack in the squad room in 1988. Wiggins died in a car crash in 1996. The only one still around to talk to was Bill Erlich, the one I'd seen on TV. He was the junior investigator on the case, only thirty at the time of Laura's murder. He retired from the force in 2005 and now was the head of security for an armored car service. I tracked him down at his office in Queens.

"By the time McPhee, Wiggins, and I showed up, the place was a circus," Erlich said. "Cops, press, weeping fans everywhere. The initial report over the police radio had just said there was a woman down with gunshot wounds at the Regent Hotel. The first uniformed cops who showed up in a black and white found out it was Laura Marlowe, and they put it out on the radio. That's when all hell broke loose. One of the local radio stations picked it up, and everyone knew. The place was crawling with people within minutes. I've seen a lot of bad crime scenes since then, but that one was the worst. The integrity of the investigation was compromised right there from the very start, and we were never able to get it back. The ambulance was already gone by the time we got there. They'd taken her to the hospital."

"What did you do at the scene?"

"I tried to find witnesses."

"Did you?"

"Oh, I found lots of witnesses."

"What did they tell you?"

"Anything you wanted to hear. Some of them claimed she signed an autograph for the guy before she was shot. Some claimed he kissed her as she lay there on the ground. One girl told me the killer left a dozen roses on the body. It was like everyone wanted to be a part of history, and they saw what they wanted to see or just made it up. We never found a witness who actually saw the shooting. Like I said on TV, there were people who saw this Janson guy hounding her—maybe even stalking her—but no one can definitely place him there at the time of the murder. We got people who heard the gunshot, we got people who saw someone running away, we got people who identified Janson at the hotel earlier on the day of the shooting. We just added it all up, and it seemed pretty obvious that Ray Janson did it. But now it looks like we were wrong."

I thought about what Susan had said. How the investigation somehow felt wrong, like the cops were racing to wrap it up in a hurry. I asked Erlich about it.

"Yeah, we made a lot of mistakes," he said.

"It almost looks like you went out of your way to make sure Ray Janson got blamed for the murder. He made a good scapegoat. Especially if someone didn't want the real killer caught."

Erlich snorted in disgust. "Oh, sure, the fix was in. Somebody paid off all of us—me, Wiggins, McPhee, our captain, the police commissioner, even the mayor—to cover up one of the biggest crimes of our careers. And if we got all this money, how come Wiggins and McPhee were still working as cops until the day they died. And I'm coming in here fifty hours a week so I can pay off the rest of my kid's college tuition. Does that really make any sense to you?"

"Actually it doesn't," I admitted.

"Everyone's always looking for a conspiracy when something like this happens because they don't want to accept the simple truth. The truth is we did rush to judgment a bit, but it wasn't because we were corrupt. There was a lot of pressure to solve this case quickly. When Janson offed himself in the hotel room and everything pointed to him doing Laura Marlowe, we were relieved. No one wanted to keep looking for any other suspect. This was nice and neat. No trial, no lawyers, no appeals. Everyone was happy. So we closed the book on the case and went on to the next one. That's what we do."

Erlich was right, of course. I'd covered the police for a number of years, and that was the procedure. If they had a suspect, they went out and gathered evidence that pointed to that guy so they could make their case. They didn't go out and look for evidence that took them in different directions. If they did, they'd never solve any cases. Being a cop was like doing triage in an emergency room. You did what you had to do to get the job done.

We talked for maybe an hour about the case. Then he told me about his career and some of the cases he'd worked on later. He said the security job was okay, but he missed the excitement of being a cop.

"They tell me I can probably make a lot of money now off this Laura Marlowe stuff," he said. "Somebody hooked me up with an agent who's talking about a book deal and maybe even a made-for-TV movie. He says I'm a hot commodity. He'd probably be very unhappy if he knew I was talking to you here for nothing. But I don't really care that much about the money. It was never about money for me, it was always about the job. I loved the job. I just wish I'd done this one right. We screwed it up—all of us did—and the real killer got away. That's going to haunt me all the rest of my life."

I believed him. I didn't think he was a bad cop or a dirty one or an inept one. He just got caught up in a strange set of circumstances that propelled everyone—the police, the press, and the public—into the wrong direction. Now I hoped it wasn't too late to make it right.

"Do you have any idea who might have really killed her?" I asked.

"This all happened thirty years ago. Until now, everyone was sure Janson did it. I haven't really given it a lot of thought over the years. God knows who might have killed Laura Marlowe. And even if you found out, how could you prove it after all this time? Damn, I'd sure like to try though. This one's always going to bother me unless I find out some answers."

"Any hunches?" I asked.

He thought about it for a second.

"If I had to bet, I'd put my money on the father."

"Laura's father?"

"Yes, Valentine. David Valentine. There was something strange about him."

"They say he abused Laura when she was a little girl, abandoned the family when she was just four or five, and then showed up at the end to try to cash in on her fame and fortune. Maybe she turned him down."

"I guess that could be a motive."

"Why didn't you like Valentine?"

"I thought he was lying to me."

"About what?"

"I was never sure."

"Any idea if he's still alive?"

"Who knows? I haven't thought about him in years."

"Do you remember anything else about him?"

"He was in the Marines, I remember. He liked fishing too. I happened to remark that I'd been on a fishing trip, and he wanted to know all about it. He said he hoped to start a charter fishing business."

Erlich looked over at me. "Are you going to try to find Valentine?"

"I think so."

"If you do, give me a call."

"Why?"

"Maybe I can help you nail the bastard."

CHAPTER 20

DAVID Valentine, Laura's father, was alive. I tracked him down to a trailer park in New Jersey.

It was on the Jersey Shore in the fishing town of Barnegat. There were lots of nice houses in the area, but Valentine's place wasn't one of them. The trailer park consisted of about twenty-five mobile homes clustered together in a wooded area about a mile from the beach. Valentine's trailer wasn't the worst looking of them, but it was pretty bad. There was a large dent on one side of it, a window was broken, and it badly needed a paint job.

I sat in my car at the entrance to the road leading into the trailer park and tried to figure out the best way to handle this.

It was possible that Valentine was the person who murdered Laura Marlowe thirty years ago and got away with it until now. He sure seemed like he could be a suspect, although I still couldn't figure out how the Rizzo family fit into all of this.

At the very least, Valentine was a despicable human being who beat his daughter, sexually abused her, and then abandoned both his wife and child, coming back only when he thought he could get some money from them. No matter how you looked at it, this was not a very nice guy.

I decided I needed a plan. If I just barged in on Valentine now without any real plan of action, I might blow the whole thing. With a plan, I could milk this guy for information until I got what I wanted. With a plan, I could maybe gather enough evidence to point the finger of guilt at him. With the right plan, I could break this case wide open. I knew from experience that a good plan was often the difference between success and failure in situations like this. So I sat there in my car trying to come up with the best possible plan for approaching David Valentine. I weighed a number of options. At the end of all this, I was only sure of one thing. I had no plan.

I got out of the car, walked up to Valentine's trailer, and knocked on the door. There was no answer. I knocked again.

After a few minutes, the door opened about an inch and a man peered out. I didn't know exactly what Valentine looked like now, but he had to be nearly seventy years old. This guy seemed younger, although it was hard to tell while peering into the darkness of the trailer.

"What do you want?" the guy asked.

"I'm looking for David Valentine."

"Why?"

"I want to talk to him."

"About what?"

"Who are you?"

"Who are you?"

"I asked first."

"Goodbye," he said, and slammed the door in my face.

I stood there on the step of the trailer trying to figure out what to do next. It was the first really hot day of summer, and the sun hung large in the sky. I'd only been outside the air conditioning of the car for a few minutes, but there was already sweat trickling down my face and the back of my neck. I'd passed by a beachside bar a mile or so back on the road. I thought about how nice it would be to go back there, drink a cold beer on the beach, and forget all about David Valentine.

I knocked on the door again. The same guy opened it.

"How about we go back to square one and start over again?" I asked.

He eyed me warily. "Okay," he said.

"My name is Gil Malloy. I work for the *New York Daily News*. I'm a newspaper reporter."

"What are you doing here?"

"I want to talk to David Valentine. The father of Laura Marlowe, the old movie actress. I'm doing a story about her life and death. I thought Mr. Valentine might be able to provide me with some valuable insight and information on the subject."

He didn't say anything.

"Are you David Valentine?" I asked.

"Yes, I am."

"Mr. Valentine, I'd be extremely grateful if you'd let me step inside."

He thought about it for a second, then opened up the door wide enough to let me in.

"Why didn't you just say that in the first place?" he said.

"I came without any plan," I admitted.

———

The inside of the trailer was a surprise. It was clean and neat and very tastefully furnished. There was a large comfortable couch, an easy chair, and a big-screen TV tuned to a sports channel. There were bookshelves along every wall and several large paintings. One of them was Laura Marlowe. She was standing by the sea, looking out in the distance as if she was searching for something.

"I found that picture at a place on Hollywood Boulevard," Valentine said to me. "I thought it captured the essence of her better than anything else I'd ever seen. That's why I keep it there."

I looked at some of the books on the shelves. There was stuff on philosophy, history, the arts.

"Do you read these?" I asked.

I knew it came out badly as soon as I said it.

"Yeah, but I move my lips while I'm doing it."

"I'm sorry, I didn't mean it that way."

"Sure you did, but that's okay."

Valentine was not what I expected at all. Inside the trailer, I could see him better. He looked like he was still in his fifties, even though I knew he had to be at least twenty years older. He had short, cropped, gray hair. He seemed trim and in good shape, and you could still see some of the good looks Laura had inherited from him. He gestured for me to sit down. I plopped onto the couch. He sat in the easy chair across from me.

"Why a mobile home?" I asked.

"Because I like to move around."

"So you just hook the thing up to a car and go wherever you want?"

"Something like that."

"What do you do for a living?"

"Fishing mostly. I've got a boat. I do charter fishing trips and catch some fish on my own too, to sell at the markets. I've also got another job on the boardwalk over in Seaside Heights. I run the tilt-a-whirl a couple of days a week, sometimes help out at the concession stands. I was in the Marines for a long time and got a pension out of that. I don't need a lot of money. I just like to keep busy." He smiled. "Of course, you didn't come here to talk about me, did you? All you care about is Laura."

"Like I said, I'm working on a story about her."

I went through some of it. Especially my conversations with Beverly Richmond and Edward Holloway.

"What did you think of Beverly?" he asked.

"She's a real grande dame of New York society now," I said.

"She was a grande dame even before she was a grande dame, if you know what I mean. What about Eddie?"

"He seems to be enjoying his life too."

"They don't like me very much, do they?"

"No, they don't, Mr. Valentine. Actually everyone I met had only bad things to say about you. They all seemed to hate you for some reason."

"I don't hate them. I don't hate anyone anymore . . ."

There was a problem here. I had expected to meet a monster in David Valentine, maybe even a killer. But he didn't seem like that. He seemed like a nice, easy-going, interesting guy. I didn't want to like him, but I did. Frankly, I liked him a lot better than anyone else I'd met in Laura's family.

Valentine looked down at his watch. It was a little after twelve.

"Have you had lunch yet?"

"No, I'm starving."

"Let's get something to eat. Do you like seafood?"

"Love it."

"So let's go catch some."

———

We took Valentine's fishing boat out about a mile from the marina.

"Do you know how to fish?" he asked.

"Not one of my skills," I told him.

He brought out two fishing poles and showed me the basics. How to bait the line. How to put it in the water. What to do if I got a bite. I'm going to be perfectly honest here, I had no desire to actually catch anything. I didn't know what happened after you caught a fish, but it conjured up images of cutting that sucker open and doing other unpleasant things. My feeling was that God made restaurants to do that, and then serve tartar sauce on the side.

I didn't have to ask him too many questions about Laura. He seemed to want to talk about her.

"Beverly and I got married when we were still in high school," Valentine said. "I was only seventeen, and she'd just turned eighteen. The pregnancy was an accident. We didn't know much about protection or birth control. We were both stunned when we found out she was pregnant. Abortions weren't such an easy option back then. So she had the baby, and I did the honorable thing and married her.

"My God, that was a recipe for disaster right there. Two teenagers who barely knew each other, rushing into marriage with a baby and no money; there was no way it was ever going to work. Beverly was miserable right from the very start. She had dreamed of being an actress herself, and now she was stuck with a baby and a husband instead of a career in show business. I guess that's why she pushed Laura so hard to be a star. She wanted to make Laura achieve everything she'd missed out on herself. Laura was her only way out.

"We got this little place in New Jersey where we could live cheaply. I was working at a factory there. The pay wasn't terrible, but it was never enough for Beverly. She was always talking about making it big and wondering why I didn't care about being more successful. She'd go into the city all the time, looking for work as a production assistant or a gofer or whatever she could find in hopes of breaking into show business. But that wasn't enough for her. I guess that's when she first got the idea of using Laura to make all her own dreams come true. I wanted a wife. I wanted a daughter. I wanted to come home to them at night and be a real family. But Beverly . . . well, she never was interested in that. She wanted to be somebody."

I took a deep breath before asking the question I had to ask.

"She says you did things to your daughter," I said. "She says you beat Laura. She says you sexually abused her. She says that when she made you stop, you abandoned them and never cared about Laura again. Other people say that you only came back into Laura's life at the end, after she hit it big. That you were looking to cash in on her fame and fortune. That's what they say anyway."

"All lies."

"What's the truth then?"

Valentine looked out at the water.

"First off," he said, "I didn't leave Beverly. She left me. I came home from work one day and she was gone. She took Laura, all her stuff, and whatever money we had. There was nothing. I finally tracked her down to a place in Manhattan. She'd started seeing some movie director, and she and Laura moved in with him. She hired a lawyer to go to court and get a restraining order that prevented me from going anywhere near Laura. That's when all the lies about me started. She needed a reason for the court order, so she just made stuff up. Then she kept telling the story over and over again, until it just got a life of its own. By the time we got to divorce court, the judge refused to allow me any custody rights involving Laura. I tried to defend myself, but no one believed me. Besides, I didn't want to put Laura through the trauma of a long custody battle. So I just gave up. I walked away from it all and I never looked back."

"What did you do then?"

"I joined the Marines. I spent time as a paratrooper. And when I left, I got a pension that allowed me to start this fishing business. I don't have to answer to anybody now. I like that."

It was a nice story, but there was something wrong.

"Did you ever miss your daughter and wonder how she was growing up?" I asked.

"Sure I did. But there was nothing I could do."

"Except you did go back and see her just before she died. Why?"

"She needed me."

"How did you know that?"

"She told me so."

I stared at him. "Laura herself asked you to come back?"

He nodded. "She called me up one day out of the blue. A few months before she died. I knew she was a big movie star now, so I was shocked to hear from her. She said she'd heard all the stories about the terrible things I'd done, and she wanted to know if they were true. I said they weren't. She believed me. She said she had memories of me still from the time she was a little girl, and they were happy memories. They were the same kind of memories I had. Beverly had done everything to turn her against me, but she couldn't erase those memories of a father's love.

"After a while, Laura told me how unhappy she was. She said everybody wanted something from her, but nobody cared what she wanted. She said she was tired and worn out and scared about the future. She said she needed somebody she could trust. I told her I'd always be there for her, and I tried to do just that. I began spending time with her again in those last few months of her life. I'll always be grateful that I at least had that time with my daughter.

"Of course, it wasn't easy. Beverly was furious that I was there, but she couldn't do anything about it because Laura wanted me. The husband, Edward Holloway, he always sided with Beverly. They were both using Laura to get what they wanted, as far as I was concerned. I told them that too. I said I was the only one that cared about her.

"That last night, Laura and I were supposed to meet after the party at her hotel. I was going to try to convince her she needed a long rest. She was only twenty-two years old, but it was as if she'd already lived a lifetime. I don't know if she would have listened to me, but I like to think she might have. Of course, we'll never know now, will we?

"I got to the Regent just a few minutes after the shooting. I ran to her side as she lay there on the ground. I prayed for a miracle just like everyone else. I was holding her hand when they put her into the ambulance. I'd promised I'd always be there for her until the very end, and I was."

We'd been out on the ocean for more than an hour now and still hadn't caught anything. I was hungry. I told this to Valentine. He said you never could predict when the fish would be biting, so you always came prepared. He went down below again and came up in a little while with a platter of sandwiches. Ham, turkey, tuna fish. I took a tuna fish sandwich and devoured it ravenously. It had lots of mayonnaise in it, bits of onion and celery, and a fresh tomato on top. It was very good. I decided this fishing business was okay as long as you ate them out of the can, not directly from the ocean.

"Have you ever told this story to anyone else?" I asked.

"You mean to another reporter?"

"Yes."

"No, you're the first."

"How come?"

"No other reporter ever asked me about it."

———

The article appeared on Page One of the Sunday *Daily News*. The headline said:

THE BAFFLING CASE OF LAURA MARLOWE

New details emerge
In actress's murder
After thirty years

BY GIL MALLOY

We all know the legend. Laura Marlowe, a beautiful, gifted young actress who had become America's sweetheart, was taken from us in a tragic few seconds by a crazed fan who gunned her down outside the Regent Hotel on July 17, 1985.

There's only one problem with the legend.

It's not true.

A wide-ranging *Daily News* investigation—in the wake of the clearing of the long-dead man thought to have killed Laura Marlowe—has revealed a series of disturbing questions about what happened to her that night and in the final weeks of her life.

There are also indications that her murder could be linked to the killing of television personality Abbie Kincaid, who was shot to death recently after revealing secrets about the Marlowe case—and promising more revelations in the future.

The article started on Page One and jumped to an entire page in the back. I detailed all the differences between the widely accepted version of how Laura Marlowe died and the real account from the police files. I talked about my interviews with her mother, father, husband, and ex-agent, Sherry DeConde. And I raised the specter of Thomas Rizzo's apparent involvement in her life during that period leading up to her death.

There were pictures of Laura at the height of her career, as a little girl, of her mother and husband, and of the vigil outside the hospital where she died thirty years ago.

More importantly, there was a picture of me next to my byline. I got the real star treatment for this one.

I was back on the front page. I was a real reporter again. Not just a public relations stunt to take advantage of my name and big-story background. Not working on multi-platform projects for Stacy like the one she'd had me do on *The Prime Time Files*.

Not worrying about going viral on the Internet, doing webcasts, or establishing my social media presence.

This was all about a story. A real, old-fashioned story. My story. Which is really all I've ever cared about in this business. The stories.

CHAPTER 21

I WAS sitting with my feet up on my desk, drinking black coffee, and waiting for the Pulitzer people to call when Tommy Rizzo Jr. showed up at the *Daily News*.

I almost didn't recognize him at first. I'd only seen him in person that one time at Abbie's TV studio. It all happened so quickly that it didn't make much of an impression. He didn't seem angry this time. He was wearing a brightly colored pullover golf shirt, khaki slacks, and open-toed sandals. He was a young guy, maybe thirty at the most, with a friendly smile and nice eyes. He didn't look like the son of the Godfather. He looked . . . well, he looked sort of normal.

He put the Sunday *Daily News* down on my desk in front of me and pointed to my article.

"I'm Tommy Rizzo."

"I know."

"We need to talk about this," he said.

"Sure."

He looked around the crowded newsroom. Some people had already noticed him there and begun to stare.

"Not in here."

"Where?"

"Let's take a walk."

131

We rode the elevator down to the street. It was nearly lunch-time, and the sidewalks were crowded with people. I remembered reading somewhere how Thomas Rizzo Sr. held meetings all the time on the sidewalk because he was afraid of offices being bugged. Maybe his son had the same worry.

I also thought about how I might be taking a bit of a chance by leaving the office with this guy. In addition to seeming upset up about the article, he had been in love with Abbie Kincaid. I wondered if he knew about me and Abbie. I mean I'd gone out with her after she dumped him. I sure hoped Thomas Rizzo Jr. wasn't the jealous type.

He seemed nice enough on the surface, but that's what they said about his father too. Thomas Rizzo was supposed to be the kind of person who gave a pat on the back and a friendly smile just before he put an ice pick in your head. If his kid put an ice pick in my head, I wouldn't be able to finish the Laura Marlowe story. On the bright side though, I wouldn't ever have to listen to Stacy again. I always like to maintain an optimistic outlook.

"You wrote about my father in your story," he said as we walked through the crowds. "Why did you have to do that?"

"Because he turned out to be part of the story."

"I wish you hadn't."

"Is that what he sent you to tell me?"

"I'm not here as an emissary of my father."

"Then why are you here?"

"Because I'm concerned about where all of this is heading. My father became very upset when he read your article—especially the part linking him with Laura Marlowe."

"Upset? How upset? Upset like he wants to have me thrown in the East River with a pair of cement overshoes?"

Rizzo smiled weakly, like a guy who's had to deal with those kinds of jokes all his life.

"As I told you, my father doesn't even know I'm here. He'd be very upset with me if he found out. My father and me, we don't get along too well."

"Why is that?"

"I guess I'm sort of a disappointment to him."

I remembered the guy in the car who worked for Thomas Rizzo telling me the same thing. "Children can be a great disappointment," he said to me that day. "But Mr. Rizzo still loves his son very much." According to Abbie though, Tommy Rizzo Jr. had graduated with honors from Harvard Business School. Aronson said he had started his own real estate company. So what was the problem? I asked Rizzo that question.

"Let's just say my father and I have different priorities in life," he shrugged. "I have a real estate business on the Lower East Side near Tompkins Square. It's not the best neighborhood and I don't get rich there. But there is a great deal of satisfaction for me in helping poor people get affordable housing. Making money isn't important to me. I want to help people. I buy buildings that nobody else wants, renovate them, and make them available to tenants at a rate they can pay. I'm helping make this city a better place to live. That's what's really important to me. My father doesn't understand that."

"He wanted you to grow up and be a chip off the old Mafia block just like him?"

"My father's way doesn't work anymore. The world is changing. I think even he realizes that now. But it's been a long struggle. You see, my father always wanted me to follow in his footsteps. Instead, I have my own ambitions and dreams. My father doesn't always agree with them. That happens a lot between fathers and sons, I suppose. But it's worse when your father is Thomas Rizzo."

"Growing up as his son must have been very difficult."

"Let me tell you a story about my father," Tommy Rizzo said. "A story he likes to tell himself. When he was twelve years old, someone robbed his house. My father's family was very poor, but his mother had some jewelry that had been handed down from our ancestors over the years—dating back to when the Rizzos were still in Italy. She was home alone and the jewelry was very sentimental to her, and she was heartsick over it. One day, the man who stole it tried to sell it in the neighborhood. He didn't know who my father was, but my father recognized the jewelry right away. The guy was wearing a watch that had been in my father's family for years on his left wrist. A few days later, the man turned up stabbed to death on top of a vacant building. His left hand—the hand that the watch had been on—was cut off. No one ever talked about exactly what happened, but everyone in the neighborhood knew my father had carried out his own justice. It was all about family honor, he told me once. And being a real man who stood up for your family. Honor, family, being a real man—those things have always been very, very important to my father."

"And he doesn't think that working in real estate is particularly honorable or manly?"

"My father and I have very different ideas about what being a real man is all about."

He talked about the real estate business. How he had restored landmark buildings on the Lower East Side, saved people from eviction, and built a lot of affordable housing in neighborhoods that needed it. It all sounded very impressive. Of course, it could all be a big front like one of his father's businesses. Tommy Rizzo might be ripping off the contractors, ripping off the tenants, and maybe even burying bodies at construction sites. But he seemed sincere. It all seemed very important to him.

The truth was he seemed like a nice guy. I liked him. I could see why Abbie had liked him.

"What happened between you and Abbie?" I asked.

"We went out for a while. It didn't work out. But there was

never anything really serious between us. I realize that now. I'm very sorry about what happened to her. She was a good person."

"She told me that you wanted to keep seeing her."

"Abbie and I weren't really right for each other."

"But she was the one who broke up with you, right?"

"I guess so."

"Didn't that make you mad?"

"At first."

"And later?"

"I got over it."

"Just out of curiosity, where were you the night Abbie was killed?"

"I didn't kill Abbie, Mr. Malloy. I told that to the police. I'm pretty sure they believed me too, because they haven't come back since then. I think they're looking at her ex-husband as the most likely suspect in the murder."

Eventually we got back to Laura Marlowe.

"My father is a very strong man," Rizzo told me, "but he becomes very emotional about the subject of Laura Marlowe. I don't know exactly what happened, but I can guess. My father met her when she was a struggling young actress. He was married to my mother at the time, and I believe he always took the bond of marriage very seriously. He never played around. Except maybe this time. I believe he fell in love with Laura, and he helped her to become a star and then she died. It was only a fleeting time in my father's life, but he's never forgotten about it. She's a very special memory to him. He wants her to rest in peace. That's why I'd like you to stop writing about my father and her."

"Maybe your father was afraid thirty years ago that someone would find out about the affair with Laura Marlowe," I said. "Maybe he was afraid she would go public or tell his wife or post it on the mob bulletin board for all his friends to see. Maybe he had to shut her up. Maybe he had her killed, then set it up to make it look like a patsy—this guy Janson—did it. That's why he—and you—don't want me looking into it any deeper. It kind of all makes sense when you think about it."

"That's ridiculous."

"Why?"

"My father never would have killed Laura Marlowe."

"Because he's such a sweetheart who wouldn't hurt a fly?"

"No, he's no angel. I don't kid myself about that."

"So why won't you at least consider the possibility that he might have been responsible for her death and now wants to keep that hidden?"

"Because he loved her."

Of course he did.

Everyone loved Laura Marlowe.

Except the person who killed her.

PART THREE

SHOOTING FOR THE STARS

THERE was another angle I needed to pursue. Before she died, Abbie had indicated to me she'd found some sort of connection between Laura Marlowe's murder and several other killings. I wasn't sure what she was talking about at the time, and I still didn't know. But if there really was any link between Laura and those other deaths, then I needed to be looking at them too.

Abbie had shown me pictures of four other women that first day in her office when she asked me questions about serial killer cases. I didn't recognize any of them at the time except Cheryl Carson. But Abbie might have left behind more information about them in her office. I decided to check it out at *The Prime Time Files* studios.

There was no bodyguard to meet me this time. Just Gary Lang. He didn't seem any happier with me than he did that first day we met in his office.

"Everything's such a mess here now," he said, shaking his head. "We don't know whether the show's going to be canceled or they're going to try to make it work with a new host. It's all being decided over the next few days. I still can't believe it. Everything was going so great. The show was a big hit. Me and Abbie were on our way. Now she's gone, and I'm screwed."

"Yeah, it was awfully inconsiderate of Abbie to get herself murdered."

"It sure was," he said, either ignoring or completely missing the sarcasm.

"Abbie was working on the Laura Marlowe story when she died," I said. "But she seemed to think it might be connected to a series of other killings of women over the years. She showed me their pictures. One of them was Cheryl Carson, the country singer that died of a drug overdose a while back. Can you tell me any more about this?"

"I don't know what you're talking about."

"She never told you any of this?"

"No."

"What did Abbie tell you she had found out for the next show on the Laura Marlowe story?"

"Just that it was some sort of big secret she'd been working on for a while. She kept saying it was going to be something really great, but that's all. She said I'd find out more when she was ready to go on the air with it. And that I—and everyone else—was going to be really shocked by the next Laura Marlowe exclusive."

"Did she leave any video or notes or anything about it?"

"Not that I know of."

"Doesn't that seem unusual for her not to tell you anything about a big story she was working on for the next show?"

"Sure, but I was used to it. Abbie had been acting strangely for a while before that. She was stressed out, kept going on crying jags—and was very secretive about what she was doing. She was also drinking heavily at times, and I'm pretty sure she was abusing a few drugs. Prescription and otherwise. I just figured that all the threats she was getting from some crazy stalker or whatever had really gotten to her. She was kind of a mess."

I thought about the way Abbie was that last night she showed up at my apartment. I couldn't disagree with Lang that something was bothering her.

"Would you mind if I looked around her office myself?"

"Whatever," he shrugged.

I got the feeling he just wanted to get rid of me, and that he figured this was the easiest way to do it. He walked me down the hall to the office where I'd met with Abbie that first day I'd been here.

"Who do you think killed Abbie?" I asked, just for something to say.

"My money's on Tommy Rizzo," Lang said. "I didn't like Abbie getting involved with him. The Rizzos are scary people."

"What about Abbie's ex-husband, Bill Remesch?" I asked. "Did you ever meet him?"

"The one from Wisconsin. Yeah, he showed up here. He was really mad at her because of what she did on TV about their marriage. He kept saying she'd ruined his life. He thought he was a tough guy. Some kind of ex–football player. But he wasn't so tough. Vincent took care of him, and I never saw him again."

"Vincent? The big guy with the ponytail?"

"Yeah, Vincent D'Nolfo used to work here."

"Used to?"

"His job was to protect Abbie."

"And now she's dead."

"Like I said, there's no job for him anymore."

———

There was no new video on Laura Marlowe that I could find in Abbie's office. There also were no messages written in invisible ink on the wall, no secret compartments filled with clues in Abbie's desk, and no signed confessions from Laura Marlowe's real killer. I spent about thirty minutes poking around drawers and file cabinets before I found something. It was a file filled with newspaper clippings, computer printouts, and notes—in what looked like Abbie's handwriting—on yellow lined legal paper.

I went through the newspaper clips and printouts first. They were about a series of deaths. Five different people. The names were:

Cheryl Carson
Stephanie Lee
Susan Fairmont
Deborah Ditmar
Laura Marlowe

I read about all four deaths besides Laura Marlowe, writing stuff down in my notebook and trying to figure out what it all meant.

The story about Cheryl Carson was pretty much the way I remembered it. She'd been an up-and-coming country singer who'd just broken through with her first Top Ten hit when she died of a heroin overdose in a Seattle hotel room while on tour with her band back in the late '80s. She'd had an ongoing drug problem, she'd suffered a few close calls with overdoses in the past, and the medical examiner's report said it appeared she simply injected too much of an especially powerful batch of heroin bought earlier that day.

Stephanie Lee was a young TV news anchor in Santa Fe, New Mexico, who'd disappeared one night after doing her 11 p.m. news show in 1988. Police found her car, keys, and purse in the parking lot of the station the next day. They said there appeared to be signs of a struggle and shell casings were found nearby. Several days later, her body turned up in a cage at the local zoo. She had been shot to death, then her body was mutilated by animals in the cage. No motive was ever found for the grisly murder and no one was ever arrested.

Susan Fairmont, an emerging new political media star, was a controversial young TV host in Denver who had made a big name for herself in just a few years of work. An outspoken liberal, she made a lot of enemies with her nightly broadcasts, during which she was a tireless advocate for abortion, school busing, legalizing of drugs, and unlimited welfare for the poor. She was shot to death in front of her home one morning in 1989 after a particularly acrimonious on-air debate with an anti-abortion leader the night before. The anti-abortionist was questioned, but never charged. The case was still unsolved.

Perhaps the most intriguing victim was Deborah Ditmar, a young actress found murdered in 1982—three years before Laura died. The two killings bore some remarkable similarities. Deborah Ditmar had done commercials, small stage plays, and finally scored her biggest role with a recurring part as a sexy next-door neighbor on a TV sitcom. At some point, she began receiving disturbing letters from a fan. They started out talking about how much he loved her, but then became progressively more violent and possessive. One day she opened the front door of her house in Los Angeles, and he was standing there. Then he shot her to death and fled. He was never found.

Five names of dead women. All of them famous to a certain degree. Laura Marlowe and Cheryl Carson were major celebrities. The other three were considered up-and-coming stars.

I paged through the notes that accompanied the newspaper clippings. Much of it appeared to be stuff Abbie had written down as she read through them. The names of the five women. The details of their deaths. She'd also put down questions beside the names such as *job description?* and *time frame of murder?* At one point, she had written *it's all about the stars.* Sometimes she'd even drawn arrows between different aspects of the murders that seemed similar. Abbie had been doing the same thing I was doing. She was looking for a link between the five celebrity deaths.

On the last page of the file, there were no notes. It was just a single sheet of paper with a verse of some kind on it, written in a different handwriting from Abbie's. It looked like the threatening emails that Lt. Wohlers, the detective at the 19th Precinct, had shown me, except this message had been hand-delivered somehow instead of being sent by email. The verse said:

> Sign of the Z.
> Sign of the Z.
> Where or where
> Can you be?
>
> Sign of the Z,
> Sign of the Z,
> Please stay
> Away from me.
>
> Sign of the Z,
> Sign of the Z,
> Now coming
> After Abbie.

There was a date at the top of the page. It was the same date that Abbie had showed up at my apartment, babbling something about "sign of the Z" and carrying a gun. Now I knew why she was so scared that night.

Below all this, written in big block letters—again not Abbie's handwriting—were the names of the dead women celebrities.

Plus one more name.

Abbie Kincaid.

CHAPTER 23

V INCENT D'Nolfo had a new job. He was working security at a nightclub off of Union Square. It was one of those trendy places with loud music, flashing lights, and beautiful people all over the place.

"This is just temporary," D'Nolfo told me. "Until I get something else."

"What happened at *The Prime Time Files*?"

"I screwed up."

"It wasn't your fault."

"Abbie's dead. I was supposed to protect her."

"You couldn't have known something was going to happen that night."

"That was my job—to know."

We were sitting in front of the club. It was nearly 11 at night, but the streets were crowded with people on a balmy summer night. Some of them going in and out of the place where he worked, others heading for other nightspots in the area. Many of the women were wearing extremely skimpy outfits. Short skirts, short shorts, tight-fitting and revealing tops. As a reporter, I have a keen instinct for observing stuff like this.

I studied several of the women carefully, especially a young blonde who passed by us with a swivel-hipped walk in what must have been six-inch-high platform heels. Just getting detail for my story, of course. All part of the job of being a professional journalist. Sure, it's tough work, but somebody's gotta do it.

As for D'Nolfo, he didn't seem so scary to me now. He didn't give me a hard time either like he did before. I think he might have even been glad to see me. He'd been really shaken up by Abbie's death, he said, and I got the feeling he wanted to share that grief with someone.

"Do you remember in the movie *The Godfather* when Don Corleone—Brando's character—is shot? His bodyguard had taken the day off. The family kills him later. Partly because they figure he must have known something in advance. But also because they wanted to blame somebody. You always blame the bodyguard when the client gets killed. That's just the way it is."

"And the show blamed you."

"Lang did. He said I'd gotten his star killed. He said I'd screwed up his career. He said she was his meal ticket and now she was gone. That's when he fired me. Can you believe that guy?"

"Bereavement takes many forms," I said.

"Huh?"

"Sometimes we say things like that to hide our true feelings."

"Lang's only true feelings are for himself. He doesn't give a damn about Abbie."

"How did you feel about her?"

"I liked her. I really did. She was the real deal. It wasn't just about the job, she was a friend too. I feel bad enough already about what happened. I don't need that jerk Lang telling me how I should have saved her. I beat myself up enough over it without anyone else's help."

"How long did you do security for her?"

"Since she came to *Prime Time*."

He said he'd been working for another show at the network that got canceled. He told me about being in the Army. After that, he was an ex–Housing Authority cop. He'd spent eight years patrolling the city's projects and then left to go into private security work where he could make more money. He said he and Abbie hit it off right away, and things had been great. Until that last night.

"She told me not to come," he said. "She said she had to do something personal. She said she wanted to be alone and I could take the night off."

"Did you know she'd been carrying a gun for protection?"

"Of course I did. She said it was no big deal. Just a precaution."

"Did you believe her?"

"I wasn't sure what to think. There was that period just before she died when we became aware of all the scary emails and threats she was getting. And the show put all the extra security on her. That's when she started carrying the gun too. But she told me that last day before she went to the hotel that there was nothing to worry about. That she knew where the threats had come from and that they weren't real. I don't think she was even carrying the gun anymore on the night she died. She thought she was in no danger. She was wrong."

I explained to him how I was doing a story about Laura Marlowe, the last story Abbie was working on when she died.

"Do you think this Laura thing had something to do with what happened to her?" he asked.

"It's possible."

"Well, the cops don't agree with you. They came to talk to me the other day. They asked me a lot of questions about that last day, enemies Abbie might have had, arguments I remember—stuff like that. I mentioned the Laura Marlowe story, but they weren't very interested. They're focusing more on the present. I got the feeling they think it was Tommy Rizzo or that kid from Wisconsin she was married to."

"What did you tell them about Rizzo?" I asked.

"I said they went out for a little while, and then they broke up. I thought it might get ugly. I was worried about that because I wasn't sure how to handle the situation. I mean the kid is Thomas Rizzo's son, so I didn't want to have to rough him up if things got out of hand. But it never came to that. He was always very polite to me. We got along okay."

"What about her ex-husband?"

"He showed up on the set one day. He was still upset over the piece she'd done about him on her old daytime show. About how he'd abused her and beaten her and been pretty much of an all-around jerk. He was furious. He kept ranting about how she'd ruined his life and made a fool out of him. I had to throw him out of the building. He thought he was a tough guy—some kind of a big football player back in high school, Abbie said—but he was out of shape and not much of a fighter. He came back again a few days before she died. I guess that's why the police are so interested in him. Abbie didn't want to see him, so I just escorted him out of the building. I had no trouble with him."

I tried to return the conversation back to the Laura Marlowe story. He didn't know a lot about that. Abbie had been incredibly secretive about what she was doing, not telling him much more than she'd told Lang. He did say that she'd asked him for help in tracking down information on a couple of things though.

"The first was about a month ago. She asked me if I knew any law enforcement people in Los Angeles. I said I had an ex-partner who'd moved out there and was now with the LAPD. I called him up and got her some information."

"What was she looking for?"

"She wanted to know about some old movie company that used

to be around years ago. I'm not sure if it had anything to do with the Laura Marlowe business. But I just assumed so because of the Hollywood connection and all."

"Do you remember the name of the company?"

He thought for a second. "Glow worm, glitter . . . something like that . . . wait a minute, glimmer. Yeah, that was it. Glimmer Productions."

"What else did she ask you?"

"She was also looking for information on some kind of cult or radical group."

"What was the name of the group?"

"It didn't actually have a name—just a letter from the alphabet."

"The letter *Z*?" I asked.

"Yeah, that's right."

"Did she ever say 'Sign of the Z'?"

"That sounds familiar."

I told him about the verse I'd found in Abbie's office about a "Sign of the Z." About her talking to me about it at my apartment. And about the threatening note to her I'd seen in Wohlers' office, which included the phrase: "Beware the Z."

"What does it mean?" D'Nolfo asked.

"I'm not sure."

———

Glimmer Productions wasn't listed anywhere. It wasn't registered with the Hollywood Writers Guild or any other group in the film-making industry. I couldn't find anything about it on the Internet or in the *Daily News* library or anywhere else I looked. As far as I could tell, Glimmer Productions didn't exist.

But it did once. Of course, that was thirty years ago. Even the big movie studios had changed a lot since then. Some of them weren't around anymore. No reason to expect something like

Glimmer Productions—which was probably much more of a second-tier operation—to still be there.

I started making calls at random to some movie studios and productions companies and agents. I wasn't sure what I was looking for. I wasn't sure what else to do though. So I just decided to throw a bunch of stuff up against the wall and see if anything stuck. Sometimes that worked, sometimes it didn't.

When I was a young reporter, I sat next to a rewrite-man from the night shift who said he was the best telephone guy on the paper. He boasted he could get more over the phone than most people could get at the scene. I watched him one night while he got an exclusive interview with the parents of an NYU coed who'd been brutally slain in her dorm room. No one else could get them to talk, but he did. I asked him later how he pulled it off. He said he'd called them the first time, and they hung up. They kept doing this every time he called. So how did he get the interview? I asked. On the fifteenth call, they broke down and told him everything. I was the only reporter willing to make fifteen calls, he told me. I never forgot that lesson.

It only took me nine calls to find someone who remembered Glimmer Productions. The guy was an executive now with one of the major studios, but he said he'd started out working in the same specialty area as Glimmer.

"What specialty are we talking about here?" I asked.

"Pornography."

"Real X-rated stuff?"

"Softcore."

"Did people take their clothes off?"

"Frequently."

"I think I've got the picture."

I asked him if he remembered the name of the head person at Glimmer Productions.

"No, but it wouldn't matter anyway."

"Why not?"

"An outfit like that never was upfront with you. The nominal head of the company wasn't really in charge. There were people that pulled the strings. People who had a lot of money and a lot of clout. But they didn't stand too well in the eyes of the law. So they stayed in the background and let somebody be up front and pretend to be in charge."

"Are we talking about the underworld here?"

"Yes, we are."

"Any names?"

"Hey, I'm just talking out loud here."

"How about Thomas Rizzo?"

"Sure, I've heard of him. I can't really say though."

"So what do you think became of Glimmer Productions?"

"My God, the whole market's different now. Now you can just get instant access to the porn site of your choice from your computer. Something like Glimmer Productions would be long gone."

"Who were the girls who acted in these films?"

"Who knows? No one cared that much. Basically, you just got attractive-looking people and turned the camera on them. There's always plenty of candidates around for that sort of stuff. They come in by the busloads every week looking for their big break in Hollywood. If they're lucky, maybe they wind up in something like what Glimmer Productions used to be. The rest go back home again on the bus."

———

The Sign of the Z was easier to track down. I found some old articles about it online and more buried deep in the *Daily News* library.

The leader of the group was a man named Russell Zorn, a kind of Charlie Manson wannabe. It was back in 1969 when Manson and his band of crazed hippies murdered actress Sharon Tate and a bunch of other people in Los Angeles. That cold-blooded killing spree sent shock waves through the nation, symbolizing somehow once and for all that by the end of the '60s the days of the flower children and the good vibes were definitely over.

Zorn had tried to set up a cult family too, just like Manson did. He attracted a handful of zealots to a remote ranch in the California desert near Barstow. There was a picture of him in one of the newspaper clippings. In it he even seemed to have tried to emulate Manson's look. Long shoulder-length hair, piercing eyes, and a tattoo on his forehead. There were several women looking at him adoringly in the picture. Just like the Manson women used to.

The idea of the Charles Manson wannabe group was intriguing. You could float a theory, I suppose, that they'd murdered Laura Marlowe as some sort of Sharon Tate–type ritual killing. Except Zorn had been arrested for another murder the year before Laura's death, and he was executed in 1988. His followers died or went to jail along with him. So what about all the names on Abbie's list? Most of them happened after Zorn was dead and the Sign of the Z gone. Why did Abbie think there was a common thread between all of the killings?

And what about Abbie? Did some renegade member of the Sign of the Z come back and murder her after all this time just because she was looking into Laura Marlowe's death all over again? That scenario was so unlikely it would test the credulity of even the most ardent Kennedy conspiracy advocate.

I didn't have the answers to a lot of these questions, but I knew where I might find them. California. California was where Laura Marlowe had been a big movie star. California was where Thomas Rizzo spent a lot of time back then. California was where Glimmer Productions had been. And California was the home of the group called Sign of the Z.

If I wanted the answers to these things, I knew I had to get to California.

CHAPTER 24

O N the night before I left for Los Angeles, I hooked up with Sherry DeConde again. I'd been thinking about her a lot. I tried telling myself my interest was at least partly because she was a potential source of more information for my story. But I sure wasn't thinking about Laura Marlowe when I remembered that first night with her. I was thinking about the kiss we shared on the street.

Sherry met me at my office this time. She was wearing a denim jacket, gingham blouse, tan jeans, and moccasins. Her blond hair was combed straight back and hung down almost to her jeans. She looked good. She sure as hell didn't look sixty.

"I still haven't gotten used to the way a newspaper office looks these days," she said. "It's so much different than the newsrooms I remember when I was starting out and visited a few. There were a lot of grizzled old men back then smoking cigarettes, banging away on typewriters, and wearing those green visor hats you always see in all the old newspaper movies."

"This place is a bit more like an insurance office," I said. "Nice neat little work cubicles. Computer terminals at each desk. No smoking allowed in the building. As for the grizzled old men, fifty-five percent of our staff is now women and thirty-one percent is under the age of thirty. We've even got a daycare center on the first floor."

I gave her a brief tour of the building. Told her how we'd moved downtown from our previous location on West 33rd Street. Before that, (and before I came to the *News*), the paper was on East 42nd Street in the building where they shot some of the exterior scenes for the Superman movies. This wasn't nearly as romantic as the building on 42nd Street, but it was still a newspaper office. That was what really mattered.

"It looks like an exciting place to work," Sherry said.

"Yeah, sometimes I still yell 'stop the presses' when I walk in the city room."

She looked around. "Where are the presses?"

"Actually, they're in New Jersey now."

"So saying 'stop the presses' really doesn't make much sense."

"I know, but it makes me feel like Perry White at the *Daily Planet*."

We went to a steak restaurant on 47th Street. It was the kind of place where New York celebrities sometimes dropped in. I once saw Regis Philbin there. I wasn't sure if Sherry would be impressed by Regis Philbin, but the steaks were pretty good. Besides, I was going to let Stacy and the *Daily News* pick up the check. Hey, Sherry was a source. Anyway, I didn't figure Stacy would complain much. She didn't bat an eye when I told her I wanted to go to California. I was the golden boy again, riding high with my stories about Abbie Kincaid and Laura Marlowe. And one thing I'd learned over the years was that when you're on a roll, stay with it.

The only problem with Sherry being a source though is it presented me with a bit of an ethical dilemma. What if I got lucky with her tonight? The rule is that reporters aren't supposed to sleep with sources. Of course, I have a somewhat more flexible interpretation of this rule. Yes, I think it's wrong for a reporter to sleep with a source to get a story. On the other hand, if you're going to sleep with the source anyway, and you just happen to get the story along the way . . . well, then that's okay.

I think.

We talked about ourselves some more, asking each other questions and filling in a few of the blanks left over from our first conversation.

I wanted to know more about her three marriages.

"Well, the first one was to a TV soap star. I was very young then, in my early twenties. Then I married a movie producer. That lasted a couple of years. After that, I tried one more time. With another entertainment agent. We stayed together for more than ten years, although the marriage itself pretty much self-destructed before that. And that's pretty much the whole story. Since that last divorce, I've been on my own."

"You sure seem to like show-business people, huh?"

"Actually, I prefer anyone besides show business at this point."

"Then why did you marry so many?"

"I just go where my libido takes me," she smiled.

"Do you want to get married again?"

"I don't think that's going to happen at my age. But you—you can bounce back from the failed marriage with this woman Susan you told me about. Find someone new, live happily ever after—all that stuff."

"You think?"

"Sure, you've got a lot of good qualities that any woman would find attractive."

"Such as?"

"Well, for one thing, you're cute."

"Be still my heart."

"You're funny too. Not always as funny as you think you are, but still funny."

"That's good, I guess."

"You're smart."

"Good again."

"And you're not afraid to speak your mind."

"Is that good?"

"It's an admirable quality, I think. Of course, maybe not all women would agree with me on that."

"Let's put it down then as a maybe," I said.

"All in all, there are lots of reasons for a woman to be attracted to you."

"How about you?" I said. "Do you find me attractive?"

"Like I told you before, I'm too old for you."

"That's not the question."

"You should be looking for someone your own age."

"Okay, do you find me attractive in a boy-toy kind of way?"

"Yes," she smiled, "I do."

"Well, I'm glad we got that out of the way," I told her. "Now we can eat."

Over steaks, baked potatoes, and salad, we eventually got around to Laura Marlowe again. Sherry repeated the account of how troubled Laura was—and how she regretted not being able to help Laura when she came to her office so distraught just before she died.

"It wasn't just the overnight stardom that messed up Laura," Sherry said. "She was unhappy long before that because of the way her mother kept pushing her in the entertainment business, even though Laura just wanted to live some kind of normal life for a young girl. I understand she broke with the mother at one point. More than once, or so I'm told. There was a period of a year or so before she became a big star where Laura just dropped out of sight. The mother couldn't find her, no one knew what happened. When she finally did turn up, she was getting work in Hollywood.

Somehow the mother got herself back in the picture then. I'm not sure how, but the mother was a very strong-willed woman, and Laura wasn't able to stand up to her. But she tried."

"How?"

"Not long before she died, while she was making her last movie, Laura dropped out of sight again. No one realized it, but she simply disappeared for a while. Everyone thinks it was a mental breakdown, but I suspect it was more than that. I think she was trying to break her mother's hold on her again. And, when that failed, maybe that put her in the hospital. Anyway, it was a very troubled time. I always think that when she came to me at the end, it was one last try to break away from her mother. But it was too late."

"She just ran out of time at the age of twenty-two," I said.

Sherry nodded.

"There was something else going on too. The money. After her first two big hits, Laura was worth a lot of money. The contract for *Once Upon a Time Forever*, her third movie, was for $5 million—a tremendous amount in those days. There were at least a half-dozen other pending multi-million-dollar deals out there waiting for her to sign. For her mother and the people around her, it was the big payday they'd been dreaming about. But Laura threw a big monkey wrench into all of that. In the months before she died, she filed a lawsuit to gain access to her own money. It turned out the mother had control over it until Laura was thirty. The money stayed in a kind of trust fund or something until then. Laura wanted an accounting of what her mother had done with the money she'd made so far and wanted the agreement ended so the money was in her name. She probably would have won the suit too. If she had lived."

"Didn't anybody ever look at the mother as a suspect?"

"No reason to. They had this guy Janson."

"And now that it's turned out he didn't do it? I mean the money business does become a pretty good motive for murder for someone else."

"For her mother?"

"Or somebody else who stood to lose a fortune. Like maybe the husband. And you said the movie company had millions at stake too."

She laughed. "Beverly's a lot of things, but she's no murderer. And she certainly wouldn't kill her own daughter. Laura meant everything to Beverly; she lived out her own life and fantasies through her. As for Holloway, he was a wormy little guy, but he really did love her. And movie studios play hard ball with their stars, but they don't murder them."

"Okay, maybe none of them are murderers, but I know one person in Laura's life who was."

"Who?"

"Thomas Rizzo."

I asked her again if she'd ever heard anything about Rizzo's involvement with Laura. She said all she knew was what I'd printed in the paper.

I told her about my encounters with the Rizzo men in the car. And about the visit I had from Tommy Jr. after my article appeared. That seemed to shake her up a bit. She said she didn't want to talk anymore about Thomas Rizzo. She seemed scared of him. A lot of people were scared of Rizzo. Maybe I should be too.

———

After dinner, we took a cab to her place. She lived in a two-story brownstone building in the West Village. It sure looked like a nice place. I hoped she would invite me to see the inside. We got out of the cab and I walked her to the door. I wasn't sure what to do at this point. Finally I made the first move.

"Can I come in?" I asked.

"It's late," she said.

"Not that late."

"I have to get up early."

I leaned over and kissed her.

"Are you sure?" I asked.

She didn't kiss me back. Instead, she pulled away and put out her hand to me to say goodnight.

"I have to get up early," she repeated.

I shook her hand. I didn't know what else to do. I felt foolish.

"Thanks, I had a great time," she said.

"It doesn't seem like it."

"I really did."

She looked at me sadly now.

"You're a good one, Gil Malloy," she said.

"So are you," I told her.

"No," she said, "I used to be. A long time ago."

Then she turned around and went inside.

CHAPTER 25

My plane landed at LAX in Los Angeles a little after 11 a.m. local time the next day. I picked up my baggage, rented a car, and bought a copy of the *Los Angeles Times*, which had not put the story of my arrival on Page One. By noon, I was headed north up the I-405 freeway toward Hollywood.

Despite all the glamour attached to Hollywood, it looked remarkably ordinary. People walking around in short-sleeve shirts and shorts and casual clothes. Brand new office buildings, health food stores, and fast food places. I did pass some famous spots I recognized. Grauman's Chinese Theater. The Wax Museum. Frederick's of Hollywood. I kept going until I got to Hollywood and Vine, then parked the car and got out.

This was the legendary cross street in the heart of Hollywood, the place where dreams were supposed to come true. The Hollywood Walk of Fame was on the sidewalk here, with its roster of all the famous movie stars immortalized in cement. But for every one that made it, there were thousands more who didn't. They sometimes called it the Boulevard of Broken Dreams. I wondered if Laura Marlowe had stood here once, more than three decades ago, and dreamed about being a star. Off in the distance, I could see the hills of Hollywood with the famed *Hollywood* sign sitting there like a beacon, calling all the starry-eyed dreamers to this town to have their hearts broken. Laura Marlowe followed her dream here, and it got her killed.

I got back in my car. It took me nearly an hour until I found an address in Santa Monica where the movie executive told me Glimmer Productions used to be. There was an office supply store there now. I parked in front and got out. It was a modern, one-story building that looked like it had been built within the past few years. I pushed open the front door and went inside.

"Can I help you?" a young woman behind the counter said.

"I'm looking for some information," I said, flashing her my friendliest smile. "I'm a newspaper reporter from New York."

I took out my press card and showed it to her. She was probably about twenty years old. She was wearing a T-shirt with the name of a band on the front that I'd never heard of. She had a ring through her nose. I suddenly felt very old talking to her.

"There used to be a place called Glimmer Productions at this address," I said. "Did you ever hear of it?"

"No, but I've only worked here four months."

"How long has this store been here?"

"About a year or two, I think."

"What was it before?"

"A phone store."

"And before that."

"I have no idea. We're talking maybe five or six years ago."

"The place I'm looking for was here thirty years ago."

"Thirty years! Wow, I wasn't even born then. You might try the manager. He'll be in later. He's been here a lot longer than me."

"How old is he?"

"Oh, very old."

"Like what?"

"Maybe thirty-five, thirty-six."

"Which would make him about five or six years old at the time we're talking about."

She thought about that for a second. "Yeah, you're right," she said. "No good, huh?"

"No good," I smiled. "But thanks for trying to help."

I went outside. I'd hoped it would be easier than this, but it never was. I looked up and down the street. There were lots of stores. A deli. A drugstore. A couple of restaurants. A dry cleaning store. A car wash. Maybe someone at one of them had been around thirty years ago.

It took me nearly an hour before I finally found what I was looking for. The owner of the dry cleaners proudly told me that his family had run the business there for nearly half a century. There was even a wall behind him filled with framed newspaper clippings about many of the celebrities that had come in there over the years.

"My father, his father before him, and now me at this very same spot," he said. "There's not too many family businesses around these days. But we're one. My name is Louis Balducci. The third generation of the Balducci family to run this dry cleaning business."

I told him what I was looking for.

"Oh, the movie place that used to be down the street," he said.

"You remember it?"

"Sure. Of course, I was just a kid then. Working in my father's store. But I used to see all the pretty girls going in and out of that place. Let me tell you—I still remember some of them. It was like a young boy's fantasy, watching that parade of beautiful women."

"I'm trying to track down someone who might have worked there. Hopefully, one of the people who ran it if they're still alive. I know it's a long shot, but . . ."

"Oh, I know who ran it."

"You do?"

"Sure, she did."

He pointed to the wall of framed newspaper clippings behind him. Then he reached up and took one down. He placed it on the counter in front of me. The headline said: CALL HER MISS OR MS., BUT DON'T CALL HER MADAME. There was a picture of an attractive older woman posing in front of a mansion. The caption identified her as "Jackie Sinclair—businesswoman, entrepreneur, and legendary Hollywood party giver."

The article said she'd been the queen of the porn movie business once, turning out large numbers of them—first for second-rate movie houses and home projector use in the days before home video came along, then stuff for the VCR market. She published her own magazine, opened up a nightclub on Sunset Strip, and became known for the wild parties she hosted in the Hollywood Hills. It all came crashing down for her in the 1980s, when she was busted by the cops for running a ring of high-priced prostitutes. According to the charges, she catered to movie stars, executives of the major studios, and politicians. She was the Heidi Fleiss of her time, the original Hollywood Madame. But then, as quickly as the charges were brought, they were suddenly dropped. Since then, the article said she had made a fortune by investing shrewdly in the Los Angeles real estate market. She lived in a big house on Mulholland Drive that used to belong to Bobby Darin.

"She was the head of Glimmer Productions?" I asked.

"That's right," Balducci said.

"And you knew her?"

"She came in here all the time. She even kept coming for a while after the movie place closed. That's why I put this up when I saw it in the paper. I hadn't seen her in a long time, but I sure remembered her. She's a part of the history of this store, of this block—just like all the other famous people that came in here."

"I wonder if she's still alive?"

He shrugged. "Probably. That article wasn't written that long ago."

I looked down at the newspaper clipping again. He was right. It was from five years ago.

"You wouldn't know how to find her now, would you?"

"God, no."

I looked at the newspaper picture of Jackie Sinclair one more time, especially the house on Mulholland Drive behind her.

"That's okay, you've been a big help."

I checked the map in my car for Mulholland Drive, then drove over there. It was a street filled with beautiful homes. I looked for one that resembled the one in the picture in the paper. I couldn't be sure, of course, she would still live there—but it was a place to start. It turned out to be a tougher job than I expected. There were too many houses, and a lot of them were set back from the road so far I couldn't see them very well. Finally, I stopped and asked a man on the street if he knew where Bobby Darin used to live. I asked it like I was a tourist on a tour of the stars' homes. He gave me directions to an address about a mile away. When I got there, I recognized the house as the same one in the picture. But there was a problem. A security fence surrounded the property. There was an intercom at the front gate. I pushed the button.

"State your business, please," a deep voice said at the other end.

"Does Jackie Sinclair live here?"

"Who's asking?"

"My name is Gil Malloy, and I'm an attorney from New York City," I said, giving him the little speech I'd rehearsed on the ride over. "A client of mine recently died, leaving a large amount of money to Ms. Sinclair. We're trying to track her down to make her aware of this inheritance."

There was a long silence on the other end.

"Are you there?" I asked finally.

Still nothing. Then I saw someone walking down the driveway toward me. A security guard.

"You'll have to leave," he said when he got to the gate.

"Why?"

"This is private property."

"Is there any way I can reach her?" I asked.

"You can leave a number, if you want."

"Will she call me?"

"You've got thirty seconds to do whatever you're going to do before I call the police," he said.

I took out a piece of paper and scribbled down my name and phone number and the hotel where I was staying. I handed it through the fence to him.

"Tell her it's really important," I said.

"Have a nice day," he said as he began walking back toward the house.

CHAPTER 26

I DROVE into downtown Los Angeles and found Parker Center, where the police headquarters is located. I told them who I was and asked to speak to somebody who handled cult cases. Eventually, I wound up in the office of a lieutenant named Marty Dahlstrom. Dahlstrom said he was part of a special unit that had been set up to deal with cults and other violent groups.

"Did you ever hear of a group called Sign of the Z?" I asked.

"Yeah, it was a long time ago though."

"They might have killed someone in New York."

"Who?"

"Laura Marlowe."

"The movie star? The one that's been dead for thirty years?"

"Yes."

"Didn't they catch somebody for that?"

"They did, but it looks now like they got the wrong man."

"Right, I heard about that."

"There may be more murders too."

"Who?"

"Abbie Kincaid."

"The TV reporter who got shot?"

"Yes."

"That was just a few weeks ago."

"I know."

"Anyone else?"

I took out a sheet of paper with the names Abbie had listed. I put it down on the desk in front of Dahlstrom. He read through the names.

"Okay, let me get this straight," he said when he was finished. "You think that this Sign of the Z group killed Laura Marlowe thirty years ago and then killed this Kincaid woman last month? And along the way over the past three decades they may just have killed these other people too. Is that right?"

"It's possible."

"Do you have any proof of that?"

"No."

"Any evidence of any kind?"

"Not really."

"So this is all just a theory of yours?"

"I'm kind of winging it here," I admitted.

I told him everything I knew. About my conversation with Abbie, the one where she told me about her serial killer theory. About finding the Sign of the Z verses. About how Abbie seemed afraid of something and was carrying a gun for protection.

"She apparently thought there was a connection between the deaths of Laura Marlowe and all of the other people on that list. She was trying to find out what that connection was. Now she's dead. Ergo, maybe she was killed by whoever murdered all those other people. There is a certain symmetry to it all, don't you think?"

Dahlstrom stared at me blankly. He was probably about my age, but he looked a lot older—with a quickly receding hairline, a bit of a paunch that probably came from sitting behind a desk too much, and a colorless wardrobe. I figured him for a guy who was very cautious. Not the type to make a lot of waves in the department or play a hunch. But he was all I had to work with.

"Let me tell you about Sign of the Z," he said. "First off, we're talking about ancient history here. They haven't even been around since the early '80s. Like you said, the leader—this weirdo, Russell Zorn—was a Charles Manson wannabe. After the Sharon Tate killings and all the publicity over the Manson family, we got a lot of people who tried to be like Manson. Zorn called his group Sign of the Z—which fits nicely with his last name, huh?—and set himself up on an abandoned ranch out in the desert. People drifted in and out, but there was a hard core of regulars. Zorn; his sidekick, some guy named Bobby Mesa he hung out with; Zorn's girlfriend, a spaced-out chick named Sally Easton; and about a half-dozen other men and women followers. He seemed to have some sort of hypnotic power over them, I have no idea why. Maybe because they were all strung out on drugs most of the time. But like I said, this was a long time ago."

"What happened to all of them?"

"Sometime back in '83 or '84, I think, they robbed a convenience store in the valley. When the guy behind the counter didn't open the cash register fast enough, Zorn shot him dead. Another worker hiding in the back of the store identified him to authorities.

"A whole SWAT team swooped down on their ranch. It turns out they were armed pretty heavily. They held off the cops for a couple of hours. When the SWAT guys did go in, they found them all dead except for Zorn, Mesa, and Zorn's girlfriend. Two of them had been shot by police bullets, and the rest did some kind of weird mass suicide so they wouldn't be arrested. Zorn and the girl surrendered. Some leaders, huh? Mesa somehow got away. But they eventually caught up with him too.

"Anyway, Zorn was convicted of first-degree murder, and he died in the gas chamber later. Mesa got a life sentence as an accomplice to murder. He was stabbed to death in prison a few years after that. The only one still alive is the girl. Her name's Sally Easton. It came out at the trial that she was waiting outside in the car during the robbery, so they gave her a twenty-year sentence. She got out a while back, and now she's a born-again Christian affiliated with some kind of church up in Barstow. It sounds kooky to me. Once a kook, always a kook, I guess. But at least she's not killing people anymore.

"My point in all this is that it's pretty hard to imagine people from this group carrying out a whole series of murders over the past thirty years, including the one that just happened in New York. They're either all dead or in jail. When most of these other murders you're talking about happened. Including Laura Marlowe's death."

"There could be another member of the group still out there," I said.

"Unlikely."

"But it is possible."

"Anything's possible."

"So will you look into it for me?"

"Look into what?"

"The group. The other killings on this list. Just see if there's any possible link between any of them."

"Why?"

"Sometimes when you're looking for something specific like this, you see things everybody else might have missed."

"After thirty years?"

"Sure, why not?"

I handed him my card with my cell phone number as well as the name of the hotel where I was staying in Los Angeles written in the corner.

"Get in touch with me if you find out anything, lieutenant."

"Now why would I do that?"

"The exchange of information is crucial to a free democracy," I said.

Dahlstom made a face and looked down at my card.

"Does that charming personality of yours usually get the cops back in New York City to help you, Malloy?"

"Well . . ."

"It won't here either," he said.

———

When I got back to my hotel, I tried to figure out what to do next. There was a small balcony outside my room. I stood on it for a long time, thinking about Laura Marlowe. Below me, the evening traffic was starting to pick up on Wilshire Boulevard. Maybe the next Steven Spielberg was in one of those cars. Or a young Jennifer Lawrence, Bradley Cooper, or Brad Pitt. The southern California sky was calm and still—and off in the distance I could see the hills of Hollywood. The Boulevard of Broken Dreams. Laura Marlowe had followed her dream here, and she wound up dead.

My phone rang. There was no caller ID visible, but I answered it anyway. What the hell did I have to lose?

"Is this Gil Malloy?" a woman's voice at the other end said.

"Yes."

"My name is Jackie Sinclair."

Aha!

"I understand you have some business you'd like to discuss with me, Mr. Malloy."

"Yes, I'm an attorney here from New York and I . . ."

"Meet me at the bar of the Beverly Wilshire hotel in an hour," she said.

Then she hung up.

CHAPTER 27

T HE bar at the Beverly Wilshire was everything a bar should
be. The lounge was dark and spacious with a long mahogany
bar running alongside one wall and a handful of small tables next
to a window overlooking the entrance to the hotel. Soft jazz music
was playing on a stereo system. There were about a dozen people
in the place, most of them scattered around the tables and a few
at the bar.

There was only one woman sitting by herself in the place. She
was at a table by the window. I walked over to her.

"I'm Jackie Sinclair," she said.

"Gil Malloy. As I said on the phone, I represent a lawyer in New
York who . . ."

"So I heard."

I sat down. She looked pretty much like she did in the newspaper picture that had been taken a few years ago. Like most of
the people in Laura Marlowe's life, she had to be well into her
sixties by now. But she had a nice face with a deep California tan,
she'd clearly had plastic surgery done over the years, and her body
looked in good shape too. She was wearing a beige miniskirt, a
Los Angeles Lakers T-shirt with cut-off sleeves, and high-heeled
sandals. Her arms were tanned too, and there was a tiny tattoo
on one of them. She looked like she'd been around. Even though

I couldn't make it into bed with Sherry DeConde, maybe I could score with this senior citizen. Here's to you, Mrs. Robinson.

She was drinking a tequila. She asked me if I wanted one. I said sure. I figured I'd just go with the flow and see what happened.

"You said something about a lot of money I was going to get," she said.

"Well, actually . . ."

"Actually, that's all bullshit, isn't it? Just a story you made up to meet with me. Not a very good one, to be honest with you. I'd have to be pretty stupid to believe it, and I'm not stupid. You might have come up with something a bit more original."

"I kind of had to improvise in a hurry," I said.

"The truth is your name is Gil Malloy, but that's about the only honest thing you've told me so far. You don't work for a law firm and there is no inheritance from a long lost relative. You're a newspaper reporter for the *New York Daily News*."

"How did you know that?" I asked.

"There's a video security camera outside my house. It took a picture of your car. I ran the license plates with a friend of mine in the state government, and it came back as a rental that had billed to the *New York Daily News*. So I called the *Daily News* and asked for Gil Malloy. They said you were out of town working on a story." She shrugged. "Like I said, I'm not stupid. It wasn't exactly brain surgery to figure all that out."

She took a drink of her tequila. "So what's this all about anyway?"

"Glimmer Productions."

"My God, I'd forgotten all about that. 'Artistic videos for the serious connoisseur of the human body.' That's how we billed the stuff we sold. The times were different back then. But every society has its own brand of pornography. People never change."

"So you owned Glimmer Productions?"

"That's right."

"Did you have any partners? Any silent owners who didn't want to bear the public scrutiny of being upfront about their involvement in the business?"

"I'm not sure what you're talking about," she said.

"Sure you are. From what I understand, Glimmer Productions was probably bankrolled by the mob. They called the shots. You were the front person. The person who made the operation look at least semi-legitimate."

"What's your point?"

"I want to know who the money man was."

"I'm not talking to you about this."

"Was it Thomas Rizzo?" I asked.

"I'm certainly not talking to you about Rizzo."

"Why not?"

"It's not a healthy thing to do."

"So you're saying it was Rizzo?"

"No, I'm not. But even if it was, so what? More to the point, why does a reporter from New York come all the way out here to ask me about a company that I ran thirty years ago?"

"I think it's connected to a story I'm working on."

"What story?"

"The death of Laura Marlowe."

"The movie star?"

"Yes. Did you know her?"

"I may have run into her a couple of times at parties."

"That's all?"

"Why are you asking me these questions?"

I shook my head. "I'm not sure why you agreed to see me. Maybe you wanted to find out what I knew. Maybe you were just curious or bored or wanted to see where it all went. But you are a smart lady. If you called the *Daily News* and found out where I was, you probably also checked and discovered I'd written a big story this past Sunday for the *News* on Laura Marlowe. You and I both know why I came here. So, at this point, let's not waste any more time. I'm saying to you what you said to me when I sat down here. Let's cut out the bullshit, huh?"

Jackie Sinclair stared at me.

"Well, well," she said, "you've got quite the mouth on you, haven't you?"

"Everybody I meet out here keeps telling me that."

"And in New York everyone just accepts it?"

"Actually they say it there too."

She smiled, finished off her tequila, and ordered another one. She was drinking a lot faster now. My kind of girl.

"So what is it you want to know?" she asked.

"Tell me everything you know about Laura Marlowe," I said.

CHAPTER 28

S HE talked about herself first. There is a pace to any interview, a rhythm that you need to follow to get the subject to open up to you. It is a dance of sorts, a series of steps that culminate—if a reporter does it right—in a good story. It was a dance I had done many times before. I knew the steps.

"I came out here to try to make it as an actress," Sinclair said. "From Birmingham, Alabama, if you can believe that. I had a nice little southern drawl back then. It's pretty much gone now. But it used to drive the guys wild, they told me. So I really laid it on thick when I went on auditions. Back then, I was like thousands of other girls here. I had such big dreams. I was just a couple of months past my eighteenth birthday, and I was young and naive. I thought I'd get discovered right away, become a big movie star, and all the people back in Birmingham would see my picture on the cover of magazines very soon. The funny thing is it almost happened that way. Almost.

"I got parts right away. Like I said, they loved that southern accent. My first part in a movie was small, I only had one line—but I delivered it like I was going for an Oscar. The parts got bigger after that. I did about a half-dozen pictures, a few TV episodes, and some commercials. Then I got my big break. A co-starring role in one of those beach party movies. I was going to be the lead actress's best friend. It was a juicy role, which might have catapulted me into being a real star. But there was one catch. I had to sleep with the producer."

"I've heard about the Hollywood casting couch," I said. "Is that what we're talking about here?"

She nodded. "Oh, I'd done it before. I'd slept with producers to get as far as I had. I knew it was just a reality of life out here then. I knew it was all part of the game you had to play to make it in Hollywood. And I was willing to play the game to get what I wanted."

"So what went wrong?"

"This guy—the producer—took me to a house up in the Hollywood Hills. He was really nice at first. He took out champagne, and we drank it and talked about all sorts of things. The movie. My career. How beautiful he thought I was. He promised me wonderful things. Then he started to kiss me. Well, he'd had quite a bit to drink by this point and he couldn't perform in the bedroom. That made him mad. He had to blame somebody, so he blamed me. He started calling me all sorts of terrible things. I decided I better leave. That's when things got rough.

"He grabbed me, pulled me away from the door, and shoved me back onto the bed. He tried to force himself on me, but he still couldn't do anything. That made him even madder. So he started to hit me. I remember his fist hitting my face over and over. Then I lost consciousness. When I woke up, I was in a hospital bed. I found out later he'd panicked and dumped me off at the emergency room. One of my eyes was swollen shut, but I managed to get it open enough to look at myself in the mirror. I was a mess. Bruises, scars, bandages. There was no way I was going to be able to go in front of a camera for a long time until it all healed.

"The next day the producer came to my room. He said they were going to begin shooting the picture in a few days, and he'd have to give the part to someone else. He said there'd be other parts for me in the future though if I just stayed cool. Staying cool meant not going to the police or telling anybody what happened. When he left, there was a wad of cash on the table next to my bed. He never said he was sorry though. Not once. If he'd just said he was sorry, maybe I wouldn't have done what I did."

"What did you do?"

"I told the police everything. I swore out a complaint for his arrest on assault and battery charges. I didn't want what happened to me to happen to anybody else. I didn't want him to get away with it."

"Did they arrest him?"

She shook her head no. "The cops came back to me the next day. They said there was insufficient evidence to proceed. They said he claimed I'd shown up at his door, offering to have sex with him in exchange for a part in his picture. He said I'd attacked him when he said no. He said he knew nothing about the bruises on my face, that I must have gotten them later from a pimp or someone else. He even threatened to file a counter police complaint against me for harassment."

"And he had enough clout with the cops to pull that off?"

"This guy was one of the most powerful people in Hollywood. What do you think?"

"What happened then?"

"I tried to get on with my life. I healed, got my good looks back, and tried to get other parts. But suddenly there weren't any more parts. Everything my agent tried to put me up for they said no. 'What's going on here,' my agent finally asked me. So I told him what happened. When I finished the story, he just shook his head sadly. He said I'd really screwed myself. He said I'd never get hired in Hollywood again. The next day, he sent me a letter saying he was no longer my agent. The producer had blackballed me all around Hollywood. If I wanted to live here, I was going to have to do something else besides being a movie star."

She looked down at her tequila, picked it up, and took another gulp. She seemed a long ways away. Maybe she was thinking about those long-ago days. About how scared and confused she was back then. But then she smiled across the table at me. She didn't seem scared or confused at all. There was a look of satisfaction on her face.

"So I decided that I was tired of being the victim," she said. "If someone had that much power in Hollywood to be able to do what he did to me, then I wanted to have that kind of power too. That's what I did. First in the porn industry. Then in real estate. I became a player in this town. Money, power, influence—that's what it's all about. I became one of the hunters, not the hunted."

She looked around the stately bar. "And so here I am today, sitting in the Beverly Wilshire and looking like I belong," she said.

I nodded. I figured this was a good time to make my move.

"Let's talk about Laura Marlowe."

"What do you want to know?"

"Did she work for you?"

"You know she did."

"Tell me about it."

"The stuff we made was what you called soft porn, I guess. There was nudity, and a lot of foreplay—but no actual sex. We got in a lot more stores that way, and we didn't have to worry so much about getting in trouble with the postal service. But everyone knew what they really were. Porn is an old story. It's been around forever, you know.

"The girls that came to me were an old story too. Some of them just arrived in Hollywood and were still dreaming they'd find their big break. Others had been beaten down and chewed up already by the Hollywood machine. But they didn't want to go back to wherever they came from. Or maybe they couldn't. Or maybe they still had a fantasy that a talent scout or producer would discover them one day if they just didn't quit. Sometimes the dream dies hard.

"Laura was different though. You could tell that from the first moment you met her. She was beautiful, of course, but it was more than that. She had this aura about her, something that just made her stand out from all the other gorgeous women in this town. She was in pretty bad psychological shape by the time she got to me. She'd been working in show business her entire life, she said, and she was discouraged and depressed. She'd never had any kind of a real life. She was nineteen years old, but she was like a child. She told me that she never really knew her father, and that her mother was very overbearing and demanding. She was a mess."

"Where was the mother?"

"Back in New York. There'd been some kind of a falling out between them. She'd left New York, drifted around the country for six months or so, and finally wound up in Los Angeles. Laura didn't even know if she wanted to be in show business anymore at that point. She was very confused. I think she was just looking for some kind of peace in her life. She told me she'd never had a chance to be happy. Maybe I felt sorry for her. Maybe it was some kind of motherly instinct in me. Maybe I saw something of myself in Laura, and I wanted to help her have the career I never had. But I decided to help her become a movie star. And that's just what I did."

"The question is: How did she go from being in porn films to becoming America's sweetheart?"

"Not exactly the most common route to stardom, is it? But not that uncommon either," she said. "You'd be surprised."

I thought about asking her who else had followed that same route. But I resisted the temptation. She was talking about Laura Marlowe, telling me things I didn't know. I didn't want to do anything to interrupt that.

"In addition to making the films, my girls used to perform other services too. There were many wealthy, powerful men in this town who were eager to pay big money for a chance to spend an hour or two of pleasure with one of these young lovelies. The funny thing is some of them were producers and directors, the same ones who had rejected them at casting calls. But they didn't seem to object to going to bed with them. I used to think there was a certain irony to that. Which I guess is what gave me the idea.

"One of the men Laura was seeing was a big-time producer—the same producer who had beaten me up years earlier. When I found out, I got mad at first. But then I decided to get even. I set up a hidden camera in the hotel room where they had their trysts—and I filmed it all. The producer was still having trouble in the sack, which came across in his performance—or lack of performance, I guess. Besides, I knew he had a big house now in Beverly Hills with a wife who would take him to the cleaners if she ever found out he was playing around. One way or another, this film would have ruined him in Hollywood if it ever got out.

"So I went to his office and told him what I did. I even showed him the film. I especially enjoyed watching his embarrassment as he watched it. At first, he thought I was there to blackmail him. Which I guess I was. But not in the way he thought. He asked me how much money I wanted. No money, I said. He looked confused. Then I told him my price. He was starting a new movie in a few weeks. I wanted Laura to have a part in it. He had no choice, of course. It wasn't a big part, but it got her started. And the rest, as they say, is history."

There was something missing. She had told me a lot of the story, but she'd left out one big piece of the puzzle.

"What about Thomas Rizzo?" I asked.

"Who?" she smiled.

"He was the money man for your operation, right?"

"I guess that's as good a way as any to put it."

"And one of your clients too?"

"I'd hardly call him a client."

"But he sometimes slept with the girls."

"Only one. Laura."

She told me that Rizzo had always treated her well. No rough stuff, no threats—it was always business. And despite his reputation, she said he was a very moral, almost puritanical man. She believed it made him uncomfortable to be involved in a pornography business, but that's all it was to him—a business. He never messed with the merchandise. He talked about his wife, he talked about his young son, he went to church regularly. He'd told her once that he had never broken his marital vows.

"But then he met Laura," she said. "And Rizzo fell in love with Laura."

"What kind of love are we talking about here?"

"Head over heels. Passionate. Schoolboy crush. Whatever you wanted to call it. He had it bad. He wanted to marry her and live happily ever after."

"Except he was already married. How did he deal with that dilemma?"

"Laura was the love of his life, he told me. She cared about him too. Oh, I don't know if she loved him in the same way he loved her. He was kind of like a friend and a lover and a father figure all rolled into one. She'd been confused and scared and lost for so long. Rizzo protected her."

"What else did he do for her?"

"He really made her a big movie star. I got her started that day with the producer, but Rizzo was the one who catapulted her to fame. He was a silent partner then in one of the big studios. It was off the books, of course. But the mob was very involved in Hollywood. Rizzo used all his clout and all his money and all his powers of intimidation to get her the lead role in *Lucky Lady*, which made her an overnight star. The fantasy is that Laura got that part through a lucky break. Well, she got a break, alright. But there was more than luck involved. There always is in Hollywood. It's all about who you know. Laura knew Rizzo."

"What happened to the two of them?" I asked.

"I talked to Laura at the end before she died. She was very confused at that point. Being a big star hadn't solved all the problems in her life. I was never sure what they all were. She didn't talk about them a lot. But she did talk that day about Rizzo. She told me he had gone back to his wife and family. He was a stand-up guy, she said. She knew that sounded funny, because of all the terrible things that they said he'd done. But he'd always treated her well. She spoke of him with great affection. She cared about him very much.

"Anyway, he went back to New York. Laura became a big star, then she died—and she became a legend. They were like two ships passing in the night, I guess. People tell me Rizzo never forgot her though. They say he gets very emotional if anyone ever mentions her name or one of her movies comes on TV. I heard a story that he sends a dozen roses to the cemetery where her ashes are buried every year on the anniversary of her death and on her birthday." She shook her head. "The mobster and the movie star. Love works in strange ways, huh? You never know what it does to people."

After Glimmer Productions went out of business, Jackie Sinclair said she'd gotten involved in real estate, buying up a lot of properties in Beverly Hills and in the Valley just before prices started to skyrocket. She was a wealthy woman now. She threw lavish parties, she knew the rich and famous, and she moved in all the right circles. She'd taken Hollywood on at its own game, and she'd beaten it.

But, sitting there in that dark bar, she looked wistful as she talked about it all. Maybe it was the memories of Laura Marlowe. Maybe it was memories of her long-ago death. Or maybe it was the memories of herself back then, the young girl with the southern accent who came to Hollywood with dreams of becoming a famous movie star.

Sure, she'd made it in Hollywood in a different way.

She was a player.

But she wasn't a star.

Sometimes the dream dies hard.

CHAPTER 29

I DROVE up to Barstow the next day to see Sally Easton, the surviving member of Sign of the Z. I took the freeway out of Los Angeles, then headed north up into the mountains and through the desert until I got there. Barstow was like another world compared to Hollywood. A sleepy little place surrounded by sand, sagebrush, and cactus. Easton lived about thirty minutes beyond the town, at the end of a long gravel road with no other houses around. If she was trying to get away from it all, she'd picked the right spot.

I'd called her the night before and said I was coming. I went through several scenarios in my head beforehand about how to play this. I thought about telling her I was interested in buying her property. I thought about posing as some sort of federal law enforcement official and bluffing her into talking to me. In the end though, I wound up just telling her the truth. Or at least most of it. I said I was a journalist who wanted to do a story about her new life after prison. She was fine with that. She told me to come up.

Sally Easton was in her early fifties now. She had gray hair and lines in her face, and looked a lot different than she did in the newspaper picture taken when she was arrested. But she still had that lost little girl quality to her. It was as if she'd never found what she was looking for so she buried herself in whatever life she was in at the moment—whether it be a cult like Sign of the Z or a lonely farm in the middle of the desert.

She met me at the front door holding a bible in her hand. Inside there were several pictures of Jesus in the living room and a large cross hung over the fireplace.

"I discovered Jesus in jail," she said. "He gave me the peace that I'd been seeking. All my problems, all my worries, all my anxieties disappeared as soon as I accepted Jesus as my savior. Have you accepted him, Mr. Malloy?"

"Actually, I have," I said.

I told her I'd been baptized as a young boy growing up in Ohio.

"Have you continued to accept him as your friend and savior since then?"

"We've drifted apart a bit over the years."

"You should reaffirm those vows," she said.

"Maybe you're right."

"Jesus can change your life."

"My life could use some changing," I said.

She told me she'd bought the farm after she got out of jail with money her parents left her. She raised chickens, sold eggs and vegetables she grew, and lived a quiet life here. She was a member of the local church and taught Sunday School. I pretended to be interested, waiting for a chance to ask her about her days with Zorn and the cult.

"How much do you remember about Sign of the Z?" I asked.

"That was a long time ago."

"But it's part of the story of your life."

"Yes, of course it is."

"What was Russell Zorn like?" I asked.

I thought it might be difficult to get her to talk about Zorn and the cult, but it wasn't. She seemed almost eager to relive those days. Like they were happy times, not a nightmare of blood and violence and insanity that had put her in jail for most of her adult life. Maybe Russell Zorn was like Jesus was to her now. He was the answer to all of her problems back then, someone she could believe in no matter what.

"He was an amazing man," she recalled. "The first time I ever saw him was in a coffee shop on the boardwalk along the beach in Venice. I was living on the street, broke and desperate. Russell was like a beacon in the night providing me with a safe sanctuary. I don't remember what he said to me or what I said to him. It really didn't matter. He just stared at me with those beautiful blue eyes, and I was drawn to him immediately. I sat down and I stayed with him from that moment on.

"We all lived together in the desert. We cut ourselves off from the rest of the world. We had our own world. Russell's idol was Charles Manson, you know. Manson was in prison, but Russell said he was the embodiment of Charlie's spiritual presence outside that cell. It was almost like Charlie was living with us there too. That song "Helter Skelter"—which is where Charlie got the name for the coming war he said would overthrow the establishment—was always playing in the house. And Russell was constantly quoting from Manson sayings to us. I remember some of them like it was yesterday: 'Total paranoia is just total awareness'; 'Pain is not bad, it's good. It teaches you things'; 'Death is the greatest form of love'; and—my favorite Russell–Charlie Manson quote—'No sense makes sense.' "

No sense makes sense. That phrase had been on one of the threatening notes sent to Abbie before her death.

"Were you Russell Zorn's girl?" I asked.

"We were all his girls." She said it with an obvious sense of pride, even after all these years. "Me. Gail. Clarissa. Any of the women who passed through our collective. Russell wasn't like other men. I was never jealous of the others. I was just gratified to be close to him. He was a very complicated and unique individual."

"He killed people, didn't he?"

"Yes, he did."

I waited to see how she would explain that one away. It could be a thorny kind of moral dilemma, what with her being saved by Jesus and all now.

"Russell explained to me that sometimes killing was necessary for the good of society," she said. "He said it was like in a war. A soldier becomes a hero for killing the enemy because doing so saves a lot of other lives in the long run. That's what we were doing, he said. Fighting a war."

"Against who?"

"The oppressors. The rich. The powerful. He wanted to lead a revolution against the oppressors. When Manson killed Sharon Tate and all those other Hollywood people, it was the first step in the revolution. Russell wanted to carry on that fight."

"Did he specifically say he wanted to kill famous people?" I asked.

"Yes, he said it would make a statement to the people."

"How about movie stars?"

She nodded. "He believed movie stars and all the other celebrities of our culture were the symbols of an evil and corrupt society. He wanted to burn their big houses and distribute their wealth among the poor and the downtrodden. He wanted to punish them, to make them pay for all the damage they had done to our planet."

I took out the list of names Abbie had written down. I showed it to Sally Easton and asked if the names meant anything to her.

"They were famous people," I said. "Celebrities, stars."

"Okay."

"And they're all dead."

"What does that have to do with me?"

"I think they may have been killed by Russell Zorn and the Sign of the Z. Do you recognize any of the names on the list?"

She pointed to the name of Deborah Ditmar, the actress who'd been shot on her doorstep in Los Angeles three years before Laura Marlowe's murder.

"Just that one."

"How do you know her?"

"Sometimes when he got high or had a lot to drink, Russell used to brag to people that he had killed an actress named Deborah Ditmar to teach the pigs of Hollywood a lesson—to scare them, just the way Manson had done with that other actress, Sharon Tate."

I stared at her in amazement. This all seemed too easy.

"I was never sure if I believed him though," Easton said. "Russell sometimes made up stuff like that to impress us or the new recruits in the group. I think he liked to see the look on our faces when he talked about murdering someone famous in cold blood. He thought it was really funny. Russell liked to make jokes like that. I know this is probably difficult for you to understand, but he was an awful lot of fun to be around."

Yeah, that Russell Zorn sure sounds like he was a lot of laughs, I thought to myself.

"So you don't know whether or not he killed Deborah Ditmar?"

"No."

"And you don't recognize any other names on the list or remember Russell ever bragging about killing any of them?"

She shook her head no.

Damn.

"The only people I know we killed was during that holdup at the store," Easton said. "Then Russell and me were arrested. The rest all died. Russell, Bobby Mesa, and me survived. Russell and Bobby are dead now too. The Sign of the Z has been history for a long time."

"Maybe somebody else in the group decided to keep the dream alive."

"Who?"

"There were others over the years, weren't there?"

"Yes, of course."

"So who were they?"

"Most of them were just people that came and went. There was Doug and Clarissa and Jerry and Gail and Billy and Heather, I think. None of them stayed. Clarissa and one of them ran off together after about six months. Or maybe Russell banished them, I don't remember. Billy died of a drug overdose. Jerry got busted for shoplifting and went to jail before the robbery. Heather went back to her parents' house in upstate New York. None of them were dedicated. None of them were true believers. They never would have carried on Russell's mission after he was gone."

I showed her a picture of Ray Janson. I knew now Janson didn't kill Laura Marlowe, but he was stalking her. There had to be some connection between him and Sign of the Z. I was desperate at this point.

"Did you ever see this man before?" I asked her.

"No."

"You're sure."

"Absolutely."

I sighed and took the picture of Janson back. I'd found out some stuff from this woman about the case. I had a potential connection to at least one of the deaths on Abbie's list of victims. But no connection to Laura Marlowe that I could see. Or anyone else on the list.

Sometimes, when you're all out of ideas, it's the simplest thing that works. That's what happened here. I had a picture of Laura Marlowe with me. I showed it to Easton now just to see if it jogged anything in her memory.

"Clarissa," she said.

"Excuse me?"

"That's Clarissa."

I stared down at the picture of Laura Marlowe in my hand.

"She was so beautiful," she said.

Suddenly it all made sense. There'd been a girl named Clarissa, who'd spent six months with the group, Easton had told me. And there was a missing period of about that time in Laura Marlowe's life before she showed up in Hollywood and eventually became a star, according to Sherry DeConde and Jackie Sinclair.

Laura Marlowe wasn't some random target of the Sign of the Z. She'd been a part of the group.

"Clarissa," Sally Easton said again, looking down at the thirty-year-old picture of Laura Marlowe.

"Clarissa," I repeated.

PART FOUR

NO SENSE MAKES SENSE

CHAPTER 30

BEFORE I left Sally Easton's farm, she told me more that she remembered about the girl she knew as Clarissa.

Like most of the people who'd passed through there, Clarissa had been pretty much of a mystery. No past, no future—just the present. That's what Zorn used to preach to them, she said. You seize the day, you live for now. But some details slipped out during the time Clarissa was there. She came from New York, she hated her mother, and she hardly knew her father. She seemed very confused, Easton remembered. She also seemed fragile and delicate and innocent—like a little girl in a woman's body. It was as if she'd never really experienced anything about life until she came to Zorn's ranch.

"One day we were talking about school," Sally Easton had told me. "I said I hated it, because all the other kids made fun of me for being different. I asked her if that happened to her too. She said no, because she never knew any other kids. She'd never gone to school. She said her mother had tutored her at home. Her whole world had been what her mother had planned out for her."

With Zorn's group, Clarissa began making up for lost time. She drank, did drugs, and—most importantly—discovered sex. Easton said Zorn had a no-sex rule among the members of his group. That is they weren't allowed to have sex with anyone besides him—or without his permission.

Clarissa—or Laura—began sneaking off with one of the men in the group. Sally didn't remember his name, because he wasn't there for very long. They went off for long walks together, deep in conversation and almost oblivious to the others in the group. Then one day they were just gone. But people came and went from the ranch like that all the time, Easton said, so she never thought much more about Clarissa.

Until I showed her the picture.

I had a couple of questions about Sally Easton's story. First, how could she not know that the woman she once knew as Clarissa had gone on to become one of American's most famous movie stars a few years later? Her answer was that she never paid attention to popular culture. Movie stars, TV shows—they meant nothing to her. Of course, if Zorn had put out the order to kill Laura, Sally Easton would have known who she was then. But she said nothing like that had ever happened. Zorn never mentioned Clarissa again. She'd only been with them a short time, and so her absence from the group wasn't really missed that much.

She could have been lying to me, of course, but I didn't think so. She'd already told me everything else. Why lie about this?

There was also the question of what happened to the guy Laura ran off with. But finding him would be a nearly impossible task at this point. No name, no real description. I didn't figure he was very significant anyway. He was only in the cult for a few months, according to Sally. He probably just faded off into obscurity.

———

Which brought me back to the five dead celebrities on Abbie's list.

If Zorn really did kill Deborah Ditmar, what about Laura and the other three?

I drove back to my hotel in Los Angeles. I ordered a big pot of coffee from room service to keep me going, took out my laptop, and went to work.

First, I downloaded pictures of all five of the people from the web. Then I went through what I knew about each death. Other than the fact they were all celebrities, I couldn't see any real similarities. Laura Marlowe. Deborah Ditmar. Susan Fairmont. Stephanie Lee. Cheryl Carson. They all died in different places, in different ways, over a span of several years.

The only concrete connection to Sign of the Z—except for the fact that Laura had once been a member—was what Sally Easton had said about Deborah Ditmar.

I went online and read as many articles as I could find about the Ditmar murder. There weren't a lot. Most of the coverage had occurred thirty years ago before newspapers even thought about putting their stories online. But I found one article that had been written just several months earlier as a Sunday piece for the *Los Angeles Times*. The headline was DEBORAH DITMAR: HOLLYWOOD'S FORGOTTEN TRAGEDY. The piece delved into the long-ago murder of the rising young star, all the unanswered questions about the case, and how her rise to stardom had been cut tragically short.

In reading it, I was surprised that—like with Laura Marlowe— many of the so-called "facts" of the case turned out not to be true. The fan who everyone thought at first had killed Ditmar was apprehended by police. But it turned out he'd been arrested on another charge in another state—and was in custody there at the time of the murder. No other suspect was ever found.

The byline on the article was someone named William Crider. I figured he might be a grizzled veteran who covered the original murder. But instead he turned out to be a young guy in his twenties who'd graduated from the University of Missouri journalism school a few years earlier and gotten a job at the *Los Angeles Times*—first on the Style section and now on the news desk.

"I've always been fascinated by unsolved cold cases," he said when I got him on the phone. "So I pitched this idea to my editors for a Sunday piece, they liked it, and now I'm up for some nice awards for it. Hell, one day I might even become as famous as you, Malloy."

He knew all about me. My triumphs and my disasters. I guess my career was pretty much an open book in the journalism world. To be honest, he seemed a bit in awe of me. Which isn't a bad thing when you're trying to get information out of someone.

"Do you think this might be connected to the Laura Marlowe murder?" he asked me at one point.

"Why would you say that?"

"You wrote an article about the Laura Marlowe case for the *Daily News*. Now you're asking me about another unsolved celebrity murder from thirty years ago. I don't have to be Bob Woodward to figure out why you're so interested."

I didn't want to tell him any more than I had to. I didn't want him to steal my story. So I said I was just fishing around, looking for any possible angle.

"What did you find out about the investigation into the Deborah Ditmar murder?" I said, trying to change the subject.

"After the crazy fan thing fell through, they never found another suspect. The most likely scenario is that it was some *other* crazy fan. But they were never able to pinpoint anyone. That's what made it so fascinating for me. A rising star's life is snuffed out and no one has any idea who did it or why."

"So you're saying the cops back then never really had any other leads?"

"Well, they thought they had one at the beginning. But it fizzled out too. Someone speculated that the Ditmar woman had tried to write something in her own blood before she died. But then the ME's office determined she died instantly from the first shot. The authorities decided in the end it didn't mean anything."

"What did they think she wrote?"

"They hoped it was a clue to her killer."

"You mean a name?"

"Actually, it looked like it was just a letter."

"Which letter?"

"The blood was smeared so badly that they couldn't really tell for sure."

"Any guess?"

"Yeah, the cops at the time said it looked like . . . well, it looked sorta like someone had tried to write the letter *Z*."

"A *Z*?" I said.

"Uh-huh. Weird, huh?"

"And the cops never made any sense out of it?"

"Nope. But even if it was a *Z*, and even if Ditmar had somehow tried to write the killer's name or initials, no one could figure it out. I mean how many names start with *Z*? Zeke, Zelda? Zorro? C'mon, now. Anyway, like I said, they determined that Ditmar died instantly and couldn't have written it."

I sat there stunned. Sure, it didn't mean anything to the cops back then. Or even to Crider now. But they didn't know what I knew. They didn't know about Sign of the Z.

"What if the killer left it?" I said.

"Now why would the killer do something like that?"

To leave his signature behind, I thought to myself. So he could brag about it to his followers later.

"You're right, it doesn't make sense at all," was the only thing I said to William Crider though.

CHAPTER 31

AFTER I hung up, I could barely contain my excitement.

All serial killers were different, but there were often some similarities in the cases I'd covered. One of them was that a serial killer always walked a fine line between not wanting to get caught and still having the need to leave something behind to let people know what he had done. That was the high for a serial killer, to leave behind his signature. A note. An object. Some kind of sign to show the world he was there.

The Z could have been that sign.

Plus, writing the letter Z in the victim's blood was similar to what Manson and his followers had done in the murders of Sharon Tate and the others. They wrote *pigs* in large letters on the wall of the actress's home after killing her and four other people there. Later, at the home of the next victims—supermarket executive Leno LaBianca and his wife, Rosemary—they used the victims' blood to write *Death to Pigs*, *Rise*, and *Helter Skelter* on the walls and refrigerator.

"Helter Skelter" was, of course, a reference to the Beatles song of that year. Manson played it constantly and thought it was a signal—a sign for him—of the upcoming war against the establishment that he predicted was coming. The Tate and LaBianca killings were supposed to be the first blows against the rich and famous in this apocalyptic battle.

Okay, the Manson family left their signature behind at these crime scenes.

Russell Zorn idolized Manson and tried to emulate him with his own group of fanatical followers.

So did Russell Zorn write the letter Z in Deborah Ditmar's blood as his signature?

And if he did, was there a sign left behind at any of the other four murders?

———

The biggest problem with my Sign of the Z theory for the five celebrity killings was that the timeline didn't match for any of the victims besides Ditmar. Laura Marlowe was killed in 1985. Russell Zorn couldn't have been responsible for that because he was in jail. Sally Easton too. Most of the other members of the Sign of the Z were either dead or incarcerated by then. And the other three murders—Stephanie Lee, Susan Fairmont, and Cheryl Carson— were carried out in 1988 and 1989. Zorn had already been executed by then.

Then I remembered something. One of the Sign of the Z members had escaped after the convenience store holdup and the shoot- out with police at the ranch where the others died or were arrested.

His name was Bobby Mesa.

Mesa had been Zorn's right-hand man.

I tracked down as much information as I could about Mesa. Like Laura Marlowe, he seemed to be a strange candidate to be a member of a crazy cult like Sign of the Z. Born to wealthy parents in Philadelphia, he graduated from the University of Pennsylvania as a Phi Beta Kappa and then studied political science as a gradu- ate student for a year at Princeton until he dropped out to travel around the country. He landed in Los Angeles where he tried without success to make it first as an actor, then as a musician.

He wound up working off and on as a roadie for different musical groups—but mostly just panhandling on the street and doing drugs.

Eventually he met Zorn and moved to the ranch in the desert with the others. Everyone said he worshipped Zorn and the two were inseparable. I found a picture of Mesa. He was a burly man with big, bushy, dark hair. After the shootout where the others died or were captured, he remained on the run for several years.

I cross-referenced that time period against the other murders on Abbie's list. It matched. All of the other murders on Abbie's list besides Ditmar—including Laura Marlowe—took place during those years when Mesa was still at large. He was finally captured at a New York City hotel in 1989. Several years later, he died in a prison cafeteria brawl.

After Mesa was in custody, there were no more celebrity killings. At least none that I knew about. Also, all of the last three murders—after Ditmar and Laura—had occurred after Russell Zorn was executed in early 1988. I wasn't sure if there was any significance to that, but it seemed intriguing.

There had to be some kind of a link here. If I could just figure out what it was . . .

———

I spent a long time trying to find any possible connection between Mesa and Laura or any of the other killings.

I googled different names in hopes of getting lucky and stumbling across a clue. Mesa's name. The victims' names. There was nothing until I typed *Sign of the Z*. Before I could type another name as a possible link, my screen auto-filled with references to *Sign of the Z*. A lot of them said *sign of the Zodiac*. Of course. That's what Sign of the Z might mean.

Sure enough, I checked and discovered that Russell Zorn had

been a big astrology buff. I had always just assumed Sign of the Z was because of Zorn's last name. But it was really a reference to Sign of the Zodiac according to those who knew him. Zorn had astrology charts everywhere at the ranch. He never made any kind of decision without checking his horoscope first. He truly believed his fate—and the fate of his followers—was predestined in the stars. Everyone on the ranch was expected to believe and embrace astrology and the secrets of the Zodiac the same as he did. I also remembered something Abbie had written in the notes I'd found in her office. "It's all about the stars." I thought she was referring to the fact that all of the victims were celebrities. But maybe she meant stars as in astrology.

That opened up some new possibilities. I started checking each murder again for astrology connections.

I found one with Susan Fairmont, the cable TV talk show host murdered outside her Denver studio. Police at first thought her murder was a robbery gone bad and checked to see if any of her possessions—purse, jewelry—were missing. They weren't. But they did find something very perplexing. There was a necklace around her neck that no one had ever seen her wear. It was a Zodiac necklace with a pendant that had an astrological sign as its centerpiece. It was a bull, the sign of Taurus. The Fairmont woman's birthday was in September, which meant she wasn't a Taurus.

On a hunch, I checked out Russell Zorn's biographical information again. It turned out that Zorn had been born on May 12. He was a Taurus.

Not definitive proof of anything. But interesting. I moved on to the other cases.

Stephanie Lee, the New Mexico TV anchorwoman, was tougher. She'd disappeared right after her newscast, and then her body was found, shot to death and dumped into an animal cage at a local zoo in Santa Fe. I read through an article about it until I found the type of animals that were in the cage. They were lions. It was a bit of a reach, I know. But a lion was the astrological sign of a Leo. I found Bobby Mesa's birth date. August 14. Yep, he was a Leo. Of course, it could have been a coincidence that the victim's body was found in a lion cage, but I didn't think so. I was convinced now that astrology was the Sign of the Z connection to all these murders. And that Mesa, or someone else, had left astrology references at all of the crime scenes as their signature for the bizarre killing spree.

I couldn't find any astrological connection to Cheryl Carson though. Plus, she wasn't shot or even murdered as far as we knew. She died of a heroin overdose. People around her said she'd been battling drug addiction for much of her career. But when I dug deeper into the long-ago accounts of her death, I found that members of her entourage said they'd been concerned about a suspicious man who had turned up at several of her concerts and might have been selling her drugs. He was described as a big, bushy-haired man. Which sounded like Bobby Mesa. And Mesa had done part-time work as a roadie for music groups. Maybe he kept doing that to make money while he was on the run during those years.

So did Mesa sell Cheryl Carson the drugs that killed her?

Were the drugs what he used to murder her, the way I now believed he murdered Stephanie Lee and Susan Fairmont?

It all made a certain kind of logic when you put it together like that.

But if Mesa did kill Cheryl Carson, why didn't he leave an astrological link behind at her death?

I found the possible answer in one of the articles about the drugs that killed her. It described the heroin she took as a powerful new brand of heroin being sold under the street name of Scorpio. There it was. The astrological reference I was looking for. The connection to Sign of the Zodiac.

But why Scorpio? The other two murders had been Zorn and

Mesa's astrological signs. Who in the hell was a Scorpio? That stumped me for a while, until the answer hit me. It was so damn obvious I couldn't believe I hadn't thought of it before.

I looked up Charles Manson's birthday.

Manson was born November 12.

He was a Scorpio.

And he'd been Russell Zorn's idol.

———

Of course, none of this really proved anything. It was all speculation and conjecture.

And there was no astrological connection to Laura Marlowe's murder that I could find. But I was convinced I was onto something. Russell Zorn had killed Deborah Ditmar. Bobby Mesa, maybe to carry on his leader's mission, had killed at least three others—and maybe Laura Marlowe too.

So what about Abbie Kincaid? How did her murder fit into all of this? Or did it? Mesa was dead now. He'd been dead for a long time. Zorn too.

Still, one of those threatening letters to Abbie that Lt. Wohlers showed me contained the phrase "no sense makes sense." That didn't mean anything to me or to him at the time. But Sally Easton had said it to me again during her interview. She said it was Russell Zorn's favorite phrase. He was constantly repeating it; so did all the rest of his followers.

And then it showed up again in a letter to Abbie Kincaid just before she was shot to death.

"No sense makes sense."

Was there still someone out there from Sign of the Z after all these years who murdered Abbie as part of Zorn's twisted vendetta against stars and celebrities?

CHAPTER *32*

O N the flight back home, I excitedly went through my notes on everything I'd found out. It was all coming together now. I didn't know all the answers, but I had a lot of them. This is what I lived for. Breaking the big story. It was the biggest high in the world. And I was riding that high now.

I was on the verge of finally solving the murder of legendary Hollywood movie star Laura Marlowe.

And maybe linking it to a series of other unsolved celebrity murders over the years too.

It all made perfect sense when you put all the pieces together. Russell Zorn wanted to be just like his idol Charles Manson—who'd killed a movie star, Sharon Tate. What better movie star to kill than one who'd abandoned his own flock? Even though he was in jail, maybe he somehow convinced Bobby Mesa, his right-hand man, to carry out Laura Marlowe's murder. It would have been fitting symbolism to Zorn's followers who thought he was a god. And even though I didn't find any astrological reference connected to Laura's murder, that didn't mean there wasn't one somewhere.

For some reason, Mesa then continued to kill celebrities—or at least that was what I now believed—even after Zorn was in jail and following his execution in the gas chamber.

Yep, the more I thought about it, the more I liked that scenario.

I ordered a drink from the flight attendant, took a big sip, leaned back in my seat, and congratulated myself on what a great job I'd done in California. I was still a helluva reporter. I still had the old news instinct. Malloy's the name, scoops are my game.

Of course, I still didn't know exactly how Thomas Rizzo fit into all this, but he had to be involved somehow. He'd had an affair with Laura, he'd helped her become a movie star, and then he'd gone back to his wife and family. Now, thirty years later, his son—all grown up—had begun dating a TV journalist who was investigating what really happened. Then she winds up dead at the same hotel where Laura died.

There were too many coincidences here to ignore.

What I couldn't figure out was how a mob boss like Rizzo and a wacky cult like Sign of the Z could be part of the same story.

Who did what and why?

Was there some connection between all of this that I was missing?

———

When my plane landed at Kennedy Airport, I got some startling news. After being without Wi-Fi for more than five hours on my flight, I turned on my iPad and saw a series of breaking news messages flashing across my screen. They said that a suspect had been arrested for the murder of TV star Abbie Kincaid. He was identified as Bill Remesch of Milwaukee, Wisconsin. The story had broken on the rival *New York Post* website just about the time I was boarding my plane for the flight back.

I checked the *Daily News* site. I saw that our story didn't go up until an hour or two later. It was clear from the way it was written that we'd had to scramble just to match the basic information of the *Post* story. There wasn't a lot of detail. Remesch had been arrested at his home in Milwaukee for the Abbie Kincaid murder. New York

City police had gone there with a search warrant for the house and also for his auto parts and body shop. They discovered a series of threatening letters directed at Abbie Kincaid—similar to the ones she'd been receiving at her studio in the weeks before her death. Even more importantly, they found a gun. A .45 caliber handgun. The same kind of gun that had been used to shoot Abbie. Final ballistics tests were still pending, but a police spokesman said they were confident it would turn out to be the murder weapon.

Her ex-husband. The one she'd humiliated on national television.

It made sense, I guess, and everyone had said the cops were zeroing in on him.

Except I wished it had been somebody else.

I'd wanted to believe all along that Abbie's death really had something to do with Laura Marlowe. That way, by solving the Laura mystery, I would somehow gain some sort of closure on Abbie's death too. It would have been a nice neat little package if it turned out that way. But as I'd found out a long time ago, life doesn't usually work out the way you want it to.

Abbie was gone, and there was nothing I could do about that now.

All I had left was Laura Marlowe.

CHAPTER 33

THERE was a series of emails and text messages to me from Stacy Albright too. They had begun several hours earlier and become increasingly more frantic as they went on. The last one said: *Malloy, I want to talk to you ASAP!!* In addition to the capitalization and exclamation marks, she'd marked the *ASAP!!* in bold-faced letters. She'd also written the word *URGENT* at the top of the message. I had a feeling it might be important.

"What kind of a mood is Stacy in?" I asked Jeff Aronson when I got to the newsroom.

"Regarding?"

"Me."

"Not good."

"How not good?"

"Borderline manic, I'd say. She keeps asking for you. I don't think it's to name you Employee of the Month."

"How can I get in so much trouble when I wasn't even here?"

"It's pretty amazing, when you think about it."

"What did I do?"

"It isn't so much about what you did, it's all about what you didn't do."

"The Remesch arrest?"

Aronson nodded. "We got beat on the story," he said. "The big bosses were very unhappy about that."

"How in the hell was I supposed to know they were going to arrest someone? I was out in California."

"Yeah, well the editor-in-chief wanted to know about that. He said he thought you were supposed to have some kind of an in on this story because you were friends with Abbie and all. He wanted to know who the hell sent you to California and why. Let's just say he made it clear he didn't think it was a particularly good idea."

"Did Stacy happen to mention that she'd approved my trip? That she thought it was a good idea?"

"From what I hear, that wasn't her version of what happened."

"So the editor of this newspaper thinks I just went out there on my own and blew off the story he assumed I was working on."

"That about sums it up."

"And Stacy never said a word in my defense?"

"Did you really think she would?"

"I always believe in the innate goodness of my fellow human beings."

"Stacy's not a human being," Aronson said. "She's an editor."

———

I went to see her. She was sitting at her desk with the *New York Post* website on her computer. The headline said: COPS NAB TV STAR'S KILLER.

"What happened?" she asked.

"My trip to California was very pleasant, thank you for asking."

"What happened?" she repeated.

"Oh, I saw Hollywood and Vine. Went to the Beverly Wilshire where all the big producers hang out. I didn't make it to Disneyland, but maybe next time. I'll be sure to show you all my pictures as soon as I have them developed. There's one of me standing in front of George Clooney's house and . . ."

"You were supposed to be Abbie's friend," Stacy said.

"I was."

"You said you had close connections to the case."

"Yes."

"So why is this story appearing in the opposition's paper?"

"Because I was in California when it happened."

"Which raises the question of why you were in California when the damn story was in New York."

"Wait a minute, Stacy—you sent me there."

"I didn't send you. You asked me to go because you said you could get a big story out there. You said the Laura Marlowe case and Abbie Kincaid were all related. That if you solved one, you solved the other. I believed you. My mistake. While you were three thousand miles away, we got scooped on the real story right here."

"I never said I was certain the two cases were connected."

"Sure you did."

"Stacy, I said I was doing the Laura Marlowe story. I said it was possible that her murder and Abbie's were related. If so, by solving the Laura Marlowe case, I'd solve Abbie's too. That's what I told you. There were no guarantees. You don't get guarantees with a story. You just follow it and see where it leads you. That's how it's done."

She wasn't listening to me.

It was pretty clear to me what was going on here. Stacy had gotten a lot of flack from above about why we got beat on the story. She dumped the blame off on me. Maybe she knew she was lying, maybe she'd actually convinced herself that it was all my fault. You never know how a mind like Stacy's works. I couldn't fathom it.

Just a few days ago, I'd been a big star again at the *Daily News*. Front page stories on Abbie Kincaid and then Laura Marlowe. The paper loved me. The readers loved me. Stacy loved me. And now I was back in the doghouse again. Welcome to my life. You'd think I'd have gotten used to the ups and downs of the newspaper business and how quickly you can become a star and then see it all disappear in an instant. But I never have.

"We need to go into damage control," Stacy said. "The *Post* won round one of the Abbie Kincaid story, but the fight isn't over yet. We still have you and your relationship with Abbie on our side to build readership and web traffic on in a bounce off the arrest. People still remember the way you cried on that webcast after Abbie's death. The video of that went viral and is still all over the net. Okay, there's a police press conference upcoming on Remesch's arrest. We'll have you liveblog it for the website, along with a biography stressing the close relationship you had with Abbie before she died. I want your byline on all of the follow-up stories on Remesch too. Maybe you can even write a first-person piece about your feelings on the ex-husband snuffing out the life of this beautiful, talented woman."

"Why me, Stacy? I mean if you really feel I screwed up the arrest story that badly . . ."

"I need you to be the face of the *Daily News* on the Abbie Kincaid story, Gil. It's just good business."

I stared at her.

"What about Laura Marlowe?" I said.

"What about her?"

"I found out some really interesting stuff."

"What do I care about a thirty-year-old murder?"

"You cared before."

"That's because I thought it was connected to the Abbie Kincaid case."

"It's still a good story."

I told her everything that I'd found out. About Laura's secret life as a young porn star before she made it big. About the details of her love affair with Rizzo. Most of all, about her being part of the Sign of the Z cult out in the California desert. And how there might even be a connection between the Sign of the Z cult and other killings.

But, even as I went through it all, I could tell she wasn't really that interested. Laura Marlowe was yesterday's news to her. No matter how sensational the details were, it was still about a murder that happened thirty years ago. Abbie Kincaid was today. Some editors—not many—have the capacity to see beyond the narrow confines of today's story. Stacy wasn't one of them.

"So go write the friggin' Laura Marlowe thing," she said when I was finished.

"But I don't think it's the whole story."

"What is the whole story?"

"I'm not sure yet."

"So when you find out, write that too. But in the meantime, get me something to put in our paper on the Abbie Kincaid arrest that I haven't already read in the *New York Post*."

CHAPTER **34**

"T ELL me about Bill Remesch," I said to Lt. Wohlers.

We were sitting in a Dunkin' Donuts down the block from the 19th Precinct. This time I'd bought Wohlers a box of assorted glazed, sugar, and jelly donuts as a bribe to get him to talk to me. He was working on one of the sugar donuts at the moment. Some of the powdery sugar had dribbled down onto his chin and the front of his shirt. I thought about telling him he was a sloppy eater, but decided not to.

"They arrested Remesch in Milwaukee," Wohlers said. "He waived extradition, he was flown back to New York, and he's now sitting in the Rikers Island House of Detention. He was arraigned on a charge of first-degree murder, the murder of his ex-wife. The former Abbie Remesch. Who you and I and the rest of America knew, of course, as Abbie Kincaid."

"What makes everyone think that Remesch did it?"

"Don't you read the newspapers?"

"I work for one, remember."

"One of your rival papers had a good story about it the other day."

"Thanks for reminding me."

"You got in trouble for that?"

"Let's just say my editor prefers to read her scoops in the *Daily News* and not the *Post*."

Which is why we were at the Dunkin' Donuts this time. I figured Stacy wouldn't be as generous with me on the expense account in her current mood. So I opted for the budget interview. Jelly and glazed and sugar donuts instead of corned beef. I do whatever it takes to get a story.

"How did you miss the arrest?" Wohlers asked me.

"I was out in California on the Laura Marlowe thing."

"Bad timing for you."

"My editor, Stacy Albright, got in trouble with her bosses for sending me. Stacy is very ambitious. So she blamed me even though she knew all about it beforehand. You know what they say—crap like this always runs downhill."

Wohlers shook his head. "Boy, it does sound like you really managed to get that bitch's tit caught in the wringer on this business about the Kincaid broad."

"Uh, I don't think you're supposed to say stuff like that anymore, lieutenant."

"Not say what?"

"Any of the three somewhat colorful—albeit offensive—comments about women you just packed into that one sentence."

"Why not?"

"It's against the rules."

"What rules?"

"The rules of political correctness."

"There's rules?"

"Oh, there's rules."

"What are they?"

"I'm not sure. They keep changing. But I'm pretty sure it's illegal to say 'tit caught in a wringer,' 'bitch,' or 'broad' about a woman in the twenty-first century."

"So call a cop," he shrugged.

Wohlers took another bite of a donut. This time jelly spurted out onto his face and the front of his shirt. I decided I had to say something. He wiped some of it off his face, but he used his sleeve to do it. Now there was a combination of sugar and jelly on that too. He was rapidly becoming an environmental hazard.

"Anyway, we got a break when one of the bellhops at the Regent remembered seeing Remesch there the night that Abbie was killed. He identified a picture of him, then later picked him out of a lineup too. The bellhop can even put him on the same floor as the room where Abbie was staying. That means Remesch had the opportunity to kill her.

"Then we talked to some of the people from Abbie's show, and they said he'd showed up there too. That's probably why she was carrying a gun. She was afraid of her ex-husband. He told a lot of people that she'd ruined his life, and that someday he'd make her pay for it. He was mad because she'd trashed him on national TV. That's what we call motive.

"Finally, we sent cops to go talk to him in Wisconsin. They got a search warrant and checked out his house and his auto repair shop. There was nothing at the house, but they found a .45 caliber revolver hidden at the bottom of an oil drum in the shop. Ballistics tests confirm it was the same gun used to kill Abbie Kincaid. That's the means. Motive, means, and opportunity. We've got 'em all. End of story."

"That's very good thinking," I said.

"Yeah, it was fine police work."

"Almost too good."

"What do you mean?"

"Doesn't it seem just a little too easy?"

"Huh?"

"Why'd he take the gun back with him to Wisconsin? I mean he presumably had to get it on a plane—which isn't an easy thing—or else drive all the way back with it. He must have known that if he was stopped it would connect him with the murder. And he had to know too that somebody was going to be looking for him. He was her ex-husband, and ex-husbands of a murder victim are always on the list of possible suspects. So why didn't he just dump the gun in New York so it couldn't be used as evidence against him? That would have been the smart thing to do."

"Remesch isn't exactly the smartest guy in the world," Wohlers said.

"And what about this witness who says now he saw him at the hotel? You canvassed that place at the beginning, and no one saw anything. Suddenly this guy remembers Remesch and picks him out of a lineup. That seems awfully convenient, doesn't it?"

"So what are you saying? That cops planted the gun in Remesch's auto shop? That we came up with a phony witness to frame him? C'mon, it was a clean bust."

"I'm just asking some questions," I said.

Wohlers finished off the last of the donuts. He wiped some of the residual sugar and jelly from his mouth onto his sleeve. I took it as a sign that I'd gotten pretty much everything out of him that I was going to get.

"Why are you so interested in figuring out some reason why Remesch didn't do it?"

I wasn't sure about that. I just knew that it somehow didn't feel right to me. I didn't understand a lot about what was going on here, but everything I'd found out still made me believe that there had to be some connection between what happened to Laura Marlowe thirty years ago and Abbie Kincaid. That theory fell apart if Remesch was the killer.

I looked down at the empty box of donuts. I'd only gotten to eat one before Wohlers finished them off. It was very good. And I was still hungry. I looked up at the counter and saw a line of about a dozen people waiting to order. I thought about how much I wanted another donut and weighed that against what a pain in the ass it would be to wait on that line for it. My life is an endless series of hard choices.

"It was a good bust," Wohlers repeated. "We got the gun, we got a witness who puts him at the scene, and we know he'd threatened her in the past because of what she'd done to him. We've got the right guy."

"You're sure about that?"

"Of course we're sure."

I didn't say anything. I just stood up to go back on line for another donut.

"You don't believe me?"

"Yeah, I guess so, except . . ."

"Except what?

"The police were sure about Ray Janson thirty years ago too," I said.

CHAPTER 35

BILL Remesch was one of those guys whose life story you could read the minute you looked at him. The stories about his arrest said he'd been a football star in high school before Abbie married him. He was big, and you could see how he might have once been an athlete. But the years had not been kind to him. He'd put on a lot of weight. He had a huge gut now, and his face looked bloated too. If I didn't know he was the same age as Abbie, I'd have thought he was at least fifteen years older. In high school he'd been voted the most popular guy in the senior class. High school had been the high point of his life. After that it was all downhill.

Sitting there across from him now in the visitors' area of Rikers Island Prison, I couldn't imagine Abbie ever being with him.

"It was a different time," he said, as if he sensed what I was thinking. "Everything was different. Abbie was so young. I met her after a football game. I was an all-conference halfback. She was a cheerleader. She just walked up to me one day after practice and introduced herself. She said she thought I was cute. Well, one thing led to another, and we made out under the bleachers. We started dating when we were juniors, went steady the entire senior year, and got married right after graduation.

"We were the golden couple back then, that's what people used to call us. The high school football star and the beautiful cheerleader. There's all kinds of pictures of us in the yearbook I have at home. Best-Looking Couple. Steady Senior Couple. King and Queen of the Senior Prom.

"Like I said, she was a knockout. I'd never seen anyone so beautiful as Abbie was when she was young. Oh, she was still pretty on TV and all, I know. But there was something so pure and innocent and perfect about her back in Wisconsin. I used to kid her because her mother and father were both very ordinary looking, and a little overweight. I'd say she must have been a mistake that the stork dropped off at the wrong house. She'd laugh and ask me if I'd still love her when she got old and fat. We were really happy there for a while. I thought it would last forever. But it didn't last very long at all. Not after she won that damn contest and went to New York."

Remesch wore a prison uniform that didn't fit him well. It was baggy around the shoulders and tight around his stomach. His hair was greasy, he hadn't shaved, and his eyes looked like he hadn't slept for days.

I'd gotten in to see him by telling the public defender lawyer assigned to his case that I wanted to give him a chance to tell his side of the story to the public. I said the press and police had practically convicted him already. I told the lawyer that an interview with me couldn't do anything but help.

That wasn't strictly true.

But he wasn't a very experienced lawyer, and I think he wanted the publicity anyway. His only concern was that he knew I'd been a friend of Abbie's, and he wanted to make sure I wasn't prejudiced against his client. I said I was an objective reporter, and I had no preconceived notion about his guilt or innocence. The truth was I wasn't sure how I felt about Remesch.

"So what happened to your marriage after Abbie went to New York?" I asked.

He shrugged. "She was different."

"And you didn't like that?"

"I married the old Abbie."

"She was growing as a person."

"I didn't want her to grow. I liked her just the way she was."

"Maybe that was the problem," I said.

He told me more about how she'd won that contest to go to New York City, the one Abbie had said led to her big break. She went without him, and she'd met people in New York who told her she had a big future in show business. She wanted to move to New York. He said no. They argued about it until one day she just left him—and never came back.

"Is that when you started to beat her?" I asked. "When you were arguing about her going to New York?"

"I didn't beat her."

"Okay, you hit her."

"We were fighting a lot. It got physical. She hit me too. She never mentioned that on her TV show, did she?"

"It's hardly the same thing," I pointed out. "You were a football player. She was maybe a hundred and ten pounds. You could have killed her. That's why she went public with the whole thing. She was trying to save other women's lives."

Remesch shook his head no. "It wasn't like that."

"You hit her, didn't you?"

"Yes, and I'm sorry about that. I was mad and I was confused and I didn't understand why she wanted to leave me. But it was never as bad as she said on TV. She made me out to be this terrible person. I still get letters from people calling me all sorts of terrible names. My second wife eventually left me over it, my business is on the verge of bankruptcy—my life is a mess. All because of Abbie."

"That's a pretty good motive for murder," I pointed out.

"I didn't come here to kill her. I just wanted her to tell the truth."

"Is that why you kept trying to see her?"

"Yes, I wanted her to set the record straight."

"What happened when you caused a scene on the set of her show a while back?"

"Things got out of control. I couldn't believe what she'd done to me. I was very upset. I was really hot under the collar. So I tried to force my way into the studio set. The security guys stopped me before I got to her dressing room. One of them put a choke hold on me. I took a swing at him. I'm not in as good a shape as I used to be. He messed me up pretty badly."

"And the incident when you showed up at *The Prime Time Files* studio just before she died?"

"I came here to try and see her again. To try and convince her to clear my name on TV. I was desperate, I didn't know what else to do. But they wouldn't let me see her."

"What did you do then?"

"I sent her a note. I asked one of her people to deliver it to her. I said I was sorry about everything that had happened. I said I just wanted to clear the air. I told her about how screwed up my life was now. I said she could make it better with just a few words on her TV show. I'm not perfect, but I'm no monster. That's all I wanted her to say. I said I loved her once, and I knew she loved me then too. That was a long time ago, of course, and we were different people. She had it all now, and I had nothing. I asked her to help me. For old times' sake. For what we once meant to each other."

"What happened?"

"She called me."

"Really?"

"Yes. I was surprised too. She said I was right. She said there were things that needed to be made right between us. She asked me to come see her."

"And that's why you went to the hotel?"

"That's right."

"Wasn't she afraid to meet you without any bodyguards around?"

"She knew I wasn't going to hurt her."

"So what happened that night?"

"It was nice. We talked about old times. We laughed a bit. She admitted to me that she'd exaggerated some of the stuff for TV ratings. She knew now that was wrong. She said she'd discovered things about herself in the past few weeks that had changed her entire outlook on what was right and wrong about life. She wanted to repair some of the damage she'd done to people. She said she was going to be revealing a lot of things on her next show. That it was going to be a blockbuster show and the entire nation would be talking about it. She said she'd include me in the show too, and that she'd set things right by me. She said she'd set things right by everybody. 'The truth will set us all free,' she told me. I remember her saying that just before I left."

"What did you do the rest of the night?"

"I went to a bar and had a few drinks."

"By yourself?"

"Yes."

"After that?"

"I went back to the hotel where I was staying."

"So you have no alibi?"

"I'm afraid not."

I thought about what he'd just told me. Abbie said she was going to tell the truth about a lot of people on her next show. The show she never got a chance to do. So who was she going to tell the truth about? Laura Marlowe? Remesch? Thomas Rizzo? Or maybe someone else too. Someone who didn't want the truth to come out.

"My lawyer thinks I should plead guilty," Remesch said. "He says I don't have much of a chance. He says they've got all this evidence against me, and the jury is going to know all about my reputation. He thinks I should make a deal for second-degree murder. It's twenty-five years to life, but that way I won't get the death penalty. He says it's my only chance."

"Is that what you're going to do?"

"I didn't kill her."

"Okay."

"I didn't kill her," he repeated.

"Just keep telling them that."

"No one believes me."

"I think I do," I said.

CHAPTER **36**

M Y interview with Remesch became a Page One story for the *Daily News*. The headline was:

I DIDN'T KILL ABBIE . . . I LOVED HER!

Exclusive jailhouse interview
With Abbie Kincaid's ex-husband

I managed to pack a lot of his emotional quotes—as well as his seemingly genuine affection for Abbie and confusion over what happened—into the piece. I also listed all the evidence against him, including my conversation with Wohlers about the case. All in all, it was a pretty compelling article. Stacy and the other editors liked it too. We broke it on the website, made it a two-page spread in the morning editions, and the paper even set me up to do some TV interviews to promote it.

It was pretty amazing the way I'd been able to pull myself out of the mess over getting scooped on the Remesch arrest. But, as they always say in the newspaper business, you're only as good as your last story. And my last story was pretty good.

I also wrote up the Laura Marlowe story. The Sign of the Z stuff, how she was a member of the cult for several months, plus all the new details from Jackie Sinclair about the romance with Thomas

Rizzo. I didn't include any of the serial killer stuff yet though. I needed to pin that down more before I could go with it. That piece got me some attention too after it ran in the *News*. But not nearly as much as the Remesch interview. Maybe Stacy was right after all. The Laura Marlowe story was in the past, and people didn't care as much about the death of a long-dead movie star as about the murder of Abbie Kincaid, a genuine TV star today.

Unless, of course, the two were related. But everyone—from the cops to Stacy—now seemed to have eliminated that possibility. No one thought there was a connection anymore after the arrest of Remesch. Except me. Because if Remesch really was being framed somehow for Abbie's murder, that meant Abbie's real killer was still out there. And maybe—just maybe—that killer was responsible for the murders of both Abbie Kincaid and Laura Marlowe.

———

When I left the *Daily News* building, a car was sitting out front across from the entrance. It was a brown sedan. Looked like a Lincoln to me. The car wasn't doing anything.

I began walking up the street toward the subway station. When I got to the end of the block, I crossed the street. That's when I saw the car again. It was moving now. Slowly. In the same direction I was.

I figured it must be Rizzo's people again. He probably didn't like the fact that I'd mentioned him again in the article about Laura Marlowe, the Sign of the Z, and Jackie Sinclair's movie business. Hell, I'd done more than mention him; I'd talked about their affair. So my new friends from Florentine's might be a tad cranky with me at the moment.

I decided not to go down into the subway. If someone followed me there, I could be trapped. So instead I hailed a taxi. I got in quickly, told the driver to take me to my apartment building, and looked behind me. The brown sedan was following.

I figured telling the cab driver to *lose that car behind us* would sound a bit melodramatic. Besides, the driver was engaged in an animated discussion on his hands-free cell phone, arguing with someone in a language I didn't understand. So I just let him make his way up to my place in Chelsea. The brown car stayed behind us the whole way. But it never got close enough for me to see who was inside.

As we approached my building, it dawned on me that I might not have made the wisest decision coming straight there. Now Rizzo's people would know where I lived. Still, the high-rise gave me a sense of protection I might not have elsewhere. There were several hundred apartments here. Plus a doorman. And even a concierge, for God's sake! The ad for the place when I moved in had stressed the top-notch security and sanctity from crime. Of course, I wasn't sure how a concierge would stand up to a mobster with a gun, but at least it might buy me some time.

I walked through the lobby, got on an elevator, and then— instead of going to my apartment on the thirty-sixth floor—got off at the pool and sundeck on the eighth floor. I knew I could look down from there at the street. Which is what I did. I saw the brown sedan parked in front of the building.

I sat there for about an hour. I didn't move from the spot. The car didn't move either. This was turning into a standoff. I went through my options. I could 1) call the police or 2) go up to my apartment and ignore the car outside or 3) confront whoever was in the car, tell them it was getting late, and ask if they wanted to come up and tuck me in for the night. The problem with going to the police was no one had broken any laws, and the third option seemed a little pushy to me. And so, after another thirty minutes of waiting, I gave up and went up to my place on the thirty-sixth floor.

I realized something was wrong right away. My door was already open. The lock had been broken.

So much for the sanctity of the building.

I pushed the door open slowly and looked inside. The place was a mess. Furniture overturned. Drawers emptied. Pillows ripped open. A lot of my stuff—papers, books, DVDs—lay all over the floor.

I went back into the hall and used my cell phone to dial 911. They said a team of officers would be right over. I probably should have waited for them. I mean whoever did this could have still been in the apartment. But I went in again.

There was no one there anymore.

I walked carefully around to check out all the damage.

First the living room, then down the hall into my bedroom.

That's when I saw it.

Someone had spray-painted a big letter on the wall of my bedroom.

It was the letter Z.

CHAPTER 37

CHECKED my messages when I got to the office in the morning. There were a lot of emails and voicemail messages. Mostly from people wanting to congratulate me about the Remesch exclusive. Nothing from Sign of the Z. Or Thomas Rizzo. I wasn't even sure that it was Rizzo's people in the car anymore after what happened in my apartment.

The cops hadn't been a lot of help the night before. I showed them the big Z spray-painted on the wall when they showed up.

"It looks like someone is trying to send you a message," one of them said.

"Do you have any idea what the Z means?" the other one asked.

"I think it's the symbol of a cult group."

"Why would a cult group be interested in you?"

"I wrote a story about them. I think they might be connected to some murders in the past. Maybe the present too. Abbie Kincaid, the TV star who was murdered, told me she was afraid of them before she died. Maybe they killed her."

The two cops looked at each other and shrugged.

"We'll pass it on to the detectives. Probably just pranksters. If I were you though, I'd get that lock on your door fixed."

"Gee, thanks a lot. Any other crime-stopper advice, guys?"

"Yeah, watch your back."

———

I was about to start answering all my messages when I saw a new one that had just come in. It was from Susan. She asked me to call her.

I did, and she answered on the first ring.

"We really should talk," Susan said.

"Talk is good."

"Can I see you later?"

"Business talk?"

"About you and me."

"Even better."

"I feel badly about our last few conversations."

"Me too."

"That's why I want to see you. Are you free for lunch today?"

"Sure. How about that little place near your office?"

"Closed."

"What about the other one . . ."

"It's now Indian."

"I don't like Indian food."

"Yes, I remember."

"Well, there's still always . . ."

"Absolutely."

"I'll meet you there at twelve thirty."

Well, things were definitely looking up, I decided after I got off the phone. Big stories. Lots of acclaim. So what if Thomas Rizzo and the mob or some crazy Sign of the Z cult member was out to get me? Susan and I were going to have lunch together. I loved the way we anticipated each other's words, finished each other's sentences—like two people who know everything about each other.

I got to the restaurant at 12:15. I didn't want to be late. I didn't want to take a chance on anything going wrong. While I waited, I went over again what I was going to say to her.

The main thing I'd decided was that I was not going to give her a hard time over the new guy in her life. I wasn't happy about him, of course. But Susan had had other men in her life after me. She'd even been engaged to one of them. In the end, she always seemed to come back to me. Because we were meant for each other. I knew that and—somewhere deep down—I was certain Susan knew that too. So I would just play it cool, not make a scene about it, and maintain the best relationship I could with her—then wait for destiny to take its course. Susan and I will be together again, I told myself. It just may take a little longer now than I had hoped.

It was a little after 12:30 when she got there. The first thing I noticed was her hair. It was shorter. A lot shorter. Susan had always worn long, flowing hair that made her look really sexy. Now it was cut in a kind of pageboy style. It gave her a very businesslike look. Probably good for her career. But I still didn't particularly like it.

I gave her a big hug. She hugged me back, but she seemed uncomfortable about it. I had a feeling she had something on her mind. We sat there making small talk for a while.

"It looks like things are going pretty well for you at the paper again," she said.

"Well, it depends on which day you check."

I told her about all the ups and downs I'd had on the Remesch and Laura Marlowe stories. I talked about Stacy Albright, the twenty-six-year-old wunderkind who was more concerned about marketing, promotion, and social media presence than she was about the actual stories. I told her about what happened at my apartment last night. I pretty much opened up to her about everything that had been bothering me. Just like I used to in the old days. It felt good to be having a conversation like this with Susan again.

"Have you had any more . . . incidents?" she asked.

"You mean the anxiety attacks?"

She nodded.

"No, not at all."

That was a lie, of course. I'd had a series of anxiety attacks, the most recent coming after my conversation with Stacy about the Remesch arrest. But not bad enough to send me to a hospital or doctor again, like one of them had in the past. And I sure as hell wasn't going to tell anyone about them. Especially Susan. I wanted her to think I was this strong, indestructible knight in shining armor for her. Not some guy carrying around a lot of emotional baggage.

"Did you ever have them, these anxiety attacks, when we were married?" she asked me at one point.

"Of course not."

I wasn't entirely sure about that. Maybe I had had the beginnings of a few stress-related attacks back then. But even if I did, I didn't realize what they were until later.

"Would you have told me about it if you did?" she said.

"I'm not sure."

"There's a lot of things you and I never talked about when we were married, huh?"

"Like what?"

"Having children. Our future together. We just lived day to day—you chasing after your big stories and me working twelve to fourteen hours at a time to advance my law career. We were both so young and so naive, I guess we just thought it would go on like that forever. Everything seemed so simple."

"We were really great together back then," I said.

"Yes, we were."

"And now?"

"Now things are different, Gil."

"Well, I think we're making some progress in putting our relationship back together again. I mean we're having this nice lunch together, aren't we?"

She smiled, but it was a sad smile. That's when it suddenly dawned on me that this wasn't going to go the way I had hoped.

"I got married yesterday," she said. "Michael and I didn't want a big wedding. So we just went over to City Hall, took our blood tests, and got hitched right there. I didn't want you to find out about this from someone else. I wanted to tell you in person. So that's why I invited you to this lunch. I hope you're not too upset."

I don't remember a lot about what happened after that. I somehow made it through the rest of the lunch, sitting there with a stupid smile pasted on my face as she told me about her new life. I don't know how I survived for an entire hour, but I did. Most of the words were pretty much of a blur. Susan did almost all the talking; I hardly said anything. But there was one question I had to ask her. One thing I needed to know.

"Why did you cut your hair?" I asked.

"I got tired of it being so long."

"How many years did you have it long?"

"Forever."

"And suddenly you just wake up one morning and get it cut short?"

"Michael didn't like it that long."

"I always loved your long hair."

"I remember, but . . ."

Susan didn't finish the thought. She didn't have to. It didn't matter what I thought anymore.

———

After I left Susan, I went back to the newsroom. I spent the rest of the day sitting there at my desk, acting like I was alright. But I knew

I wasn't. I knew I was damn close to having another full-blown anxiety attack. The only thing I could do to avoid it was keep as busy as possible so I didn't have time to be thinking about it or Susan. But what did I do when work was over? If I just sat there all alone in my apartment, I realized that those feelings of stress and anxiety would overwhelm me. I needed to be with someone. But who?

Susan was the person I always turned to for emotional support when I needed it, but she certainly wasn't a viable option here. This time she was the problem, not the solution. I thought about Jeff Aronson; he seemed to like me. But he had a wife and four kids to go home to. I couldn't ask him to babysit me all night.

I rode the subway and then walked around until I came to the building where I knew all along that I was headed. I stood in front of it for a while. Then I rang the doorbell. She must have seen me out front because she was waiting for me. She opened the door almost immediately.

She had a smile on her face and seemed happy to see me.

"I was hoping you'd come back," said Sherry DeConde.

CHAPTER 38

S HE was dressed even more casually than the times I'd seen her before. She had on a long T-shirt, cut-off jeans, and a pair of flip-flops. She clearly wasn't expecting me or anyone else to show up at her door. But she still looked damn good to me. I impulsively reached out and hugged her. This time she didn't resist. She hugged me back.

"I'm sorry about the way I acted last time," she told me. "I was nervous; afraid, I guess, to get too close to you. I wanted to call you afterward. I picked up the phone maybe a hundred times. I just never could think of what to say. I wanted to see you again, Gil. I really did."

"So here I am now," I said.

"Here you are," she smiled.

Then she kissed me.

"So here I am," I repeated.

———

For me, the best sexual encounters have always been an impulsive thing. I either feel right about it at that moment, or I don't. Right now, I wanted to have sex with Sherry DeConde. I'd wanted to from that first day we met. There was something drawing me to her—something so strong, so mesmerizing that I didn't want to fight it anymore. Maybe it was something good like I'd had once with Susan. Or maybe it would end badly like other sexual encounters of mine in the past. But this just felt right.

It had been a long time since I'd made love with anyone, and I think a long time for her too. We devoured each other hungrily, like two desperate alcoholics on a binge after too many months of sobriety. The feeling of her hands exploring my body sent shivers of excitement and arousal through me, and I could see she was feeling it too. There was something wonderfully erotic about our lovemaking. The impulsiveness of it, the long buildup beforehand while we both had struggled with our feelings for each other, the first glimpse of her body that I saw as I undressed her—it all helped create a magical moment as our bodies moved up and down in unison, while the rest of the world seemed far away.

Later, as we lay in bed together, I looked around her bedroom. She had a picture of Laura Marlowe on the wall too. Just like Valentine, although not as big. Laura Marlowe sure had made an impact on a lot of people in her short life. Out the window, I could see the Hudson River—she actually had a real view of the water from the West Village. It was dark now, and the lights of the buildings on the New Jersey shore twinkled in the distance. I could see the lights of boats out on the horizon too. I thought suddenly about my trip on Valentine's boat. What if I chartered that boat from him, and then Sherry and I just sailed off together somewhere and lived happily ever after?

It was a nice dream.

"What made you come back here tonight?" Sherry asked.

"I wanted to be with someone."

"Someone?"

"You."

"Why me?"

"I like you. I think you're sexy as hell. And I needed someone I could trust."

She snuggled her head into my chest and looked up at me. "You hardly know me, Gil, how could you be so sure you can trust me?"

"Laura Marlowe trusted you," I said. "You told me that at our first meeting. At the end, she came to you for help in turning her life around. Not her mother. Not her husband . . ."

"But I couldn't save her," Sherry said sadly.

"Still, there was something that made her trust you, despite all the terrible things her mother had said about you. Maybe whatever it was turned out to be the same reason I turned to you when I needed someone tonight. Maybe it was some kind of karma between Laura's ghost and me. Maybe we connected on some spiritual level because I've been thinking about her so much. Christ, I don't know. It just seemed like the right thing to do. It still does."

I talked about what I'd found out in Hollywood. About Laura and the Sign of the Z cult. About the possibility that cult leader Russell Zorn and some of his members could have been behind the murder of Laura as well as other unsolved celebrity deaths over the years. About all the new details I'd learned about Laura's romance with Thomas Rizzo. About the things Sally Easton had said Laura told Sign of the Z members: her fight with her mother and the estrangement that tore them apart enough for her to flee across country and live with a cult.

"Let's stop talking about Laura Marlowe," she said finally after I'd peppered her with a lot more questions.

"Change of topic?"

"I think that would be a good idea."

"So what do we do instead?"

"Oh, I imagine we'll think of something," she said as she leaned over and kissed me.

As I pulled her close to me, I looked over at the picture of Laura

Marlowe again on the wall of her bedroom. Laura had this smile on her face, like she kept a big secret from the rest of the world. She looked just like a movie star was supposed to look, without a care in the world. Except I knew now that wasn't true.

All the people that were supposed to be bad in her life—Sherry, her father, Thomas Rizzo, maybe even Russell Zorn in his own way—seemed to have tried to help her.

And the woman who was supposed to be the one person looking out for her—her own mother—might have been the biggest villain of all.

Nothing about Laura Marlowe's life was what it seemed.

Maybe the same was true for her death.

CHAPTER 39

G o back to the beginning and start all over again. That's one of the things a reporter needs to do sometimes when he can't figure out all the answers to a story. An old newspaperman told me that a long time ago. "Just forget everything you think you know already about the story, go back to square one, and do it all over again. You'll be amazed at what you missed the first time." This technique had worked for me in the past, and so I decided to try it now.

When I got to the *Daily News* office the next morning, I typed a chronological list of everything that I knew happened to Laura before her death into my computer:

Splits from mother, disappears from New York, and moves
    to California
Spends time living in the desert near Barstow with Russell
    Zorn and his cult. Calls herself Clarissa. Runs away
    again after several months
Works for Jackie Sinclair in soft porn–escort business.
    Gets first legitimate movie role after Sinclair blackmails
    producer. Meets Thomas Rizzo. Has romantic affair
    with him
Lands starring role in *Lucky Lady*

Lucky Lady released. It becomes a smash hit and catapults
   her to stardom.

Begins work on *The Langley Caper*. Production temporarily
   shut down soon afterward when Laura Marlowe is
   hospitalized, ostensibly because of injuries suffered in
   an auto accident. But no details are ever released.

Production on *The Langley Caper* resumes

Meets Edward Holloway

Marries Holloway in lavish Hollywood wedding

The Langley Caper is released and becomes her second
   smash hit. Begins shooting of next film, *Once Upon a
   Time Forever.*

Production shut down briefly because of Laura Marlowe's
   "health problems"

She's hospitalized again, the studio calls it "exhaustion."
   Production shut down indefinitely.

Released from hospital in time to attend Oscars ceremony

Back on set of *Once Upon a Time Forever*. Production
   resumes.

Hospitalized again for unspecified reasons

Finishes *Once Upon a Time Forever*

Wrap party for movie in New York City. Laura Marlowe
   attends. She dies later that night.

I studied the sequence of events. There were a lot of things I still
didn't know. What did she do when she first went out to California? How did she hook up with the cult, and why did she leave it?
What exactly happened on the set of *Once Upon a Time Forever*
that closed down production several times? If I could find out the
answers to those questions, maybe I could find out what had happened to her.

Plus, if Bill Remesch didn't kill Abbie, and I was pretty sure now that he hadn't, then I was back with the theory that Abbie's death was somehow related to what happened to Laura Marlowe. Laura Marlowe's death was the key. The catalyst that somehow set all of this in motion again three decades later. The answers to this story were back there at the beginning somewhere.

I thought about the people I knew that were around Laura back then. There were basically four of them that I knew about. Laura's mother. Her husband. Her father. And, of course, Sherry, her first agent. All I could think to do was go back and talk to all of them again in hopes of uncovering something I'd missed so far. I decided to leave Sherry for last, because that one would be the most fun. The mother and husband weren't as much fun. I really didn't like either of them. But I did like David Valentine, Laura's father. So I called him first.

Valentine said he didn't know anything about the new stuff involving Sign of the Z or Thomas Rizzo that had come to light since our first conversation on his boat. But I told him I had some other questions I wanted to ask him. Especially about what brought him back into Laura's life again at the end.

"When Laura was growing up, I tried to forget about her," Valentine said. "I'm not proud of that, but it's true. The whole thing with Beverly—the marriage, the fights, and especially the divorce— was so ugly that I wanted to just erase it from my memory. I never really was able to do that. I used to think about Laura a lot. About what she was like, what kind of a person she was growing up to be.

"And then one day I turned on the TV, and there she was. Laura Marlowe. My daughter, the movie star. I've got to admit that I was proud. This beautiful woman in Hollywood was the same little girl I'd known all those years ago. I thought about trying to contact her, to tell her how happy I was for her—but I never did. I didn't know how. I didn't know how to just walk into her life as her father again after so much time.

"But then, like I said, she reached out to me. I thought it was going to be awkward, but it wasn't at all. It was as if we'd known each other for a long time. We talked about everything. I guess I told her the things she wanted to hear. She said she wanted me back in her life. She needed someone she could trust. She had all this money and all this adulation, but she seemed sad. I was able to help her, at least for a while. I was her father. There was a bond between us that Beverly couldn't break up with all her lies and manipulation.

"It was very clear to me that she had real problems. I guess that came with all the pressures of being Laura Marlowe. It was me who got her into a hospital before she died. I knew she was headed for disaster if we didn't do something. I tried to help. I really did. But Beverly . . . well, Beverly was never going to let me get away with it. Everything came to a head after I got Laura into the hospital. The movie studio was going crazy about her not being on the set of *Once Upon a Time Forever*. Beverly was terrified that they might try to replace her and also that the press would find out about Laura's problems. I thought my daughter's health was the most important thing. I wanted her to stay in the hospital until she got well. But Beverly and the movie studio and all the other money people around her were too strong for me to fight. They wanted her back working on the movie.

"I guess the only thing I am grateful for is that I did get to spend time with Laura before she died. And I was even there at the end, the night she was murdered. I'd gone to the hotel to try and convince her one more time to let me help her get away from all the things that were making her so unhappy. But I was too late. That image of her—lying mortally wounded on the street—still haunts me. After she died, I had to take care of everything at the hospital. The kid Holloway was a mess and couldn't help at all. Beverly was away on this damn Laura Marlowe cruise. So I did what I had to do, and then I left for good. Let Holloway and Beverly have all her money. I didn't care about the money. All I cared about was Laura.

"I have no idea who killed my daughter or why. But I've always thought that, if I was still around more at the end, maybe I could have prevented it. If I wouldn't have waited so long to come back as Laura's father. Maybe I would have made a difference in her life, maybe things wouldn't have ended up the way they did for her. I'll never know for sure. But it's a question I'm going to have to live with all my life."

———

Laura's mother didn't seem particularly interested in talking to me again.

I tried calling her several times without any success. I finally reached someone who said she was in Palm Beach, Florida, and would get back to me when she returned. I knew they had telephones in Palm Beach, so I asked for a message to be passed on to just give me a quick call back. But she never did.

The more I found out about Beverly Richmond, the more I disliked her. She was too worried about maintaining the Laura Marlowe image to deal with the fact that her daughter had ever been a real person. I didn't even get the feeling when we talked that it mattered to her to find out who really murdered Laura. She seemed happy to just let the memories stay the way they were.

So I went to the next person on my list.

Edward Holloway.

CHAPTER 40

WANT the truth about Laura," I said to Holloway when I found him again at Sardi's. "The one thing that's pretty clear out of all this is that Laura's life was no fairy tale. Especially at the end. She was spinning out of control. She was a mess. Maybe there's a clue there to whoever murdered her—and why. You were there with her back then. You say you loved her. So what the hell was going on?"

You never know how it's going to work out when you play it like that with someone during an interview. I've had people break down in tears and tell me all their secrets. I've also had them clam up, cut off the interview, or storm out of the room. I even had one who tried to take a punch at me. I didn't figure Holloway was going to punch me. I thought he might storm off in anger. But he didn't. He was one of those who talked. He'd probably wanted to talk about it for a long time.

"I loved Laura," he told me. "I really did love her."

"Did Laura love you back?"

"That's a difficult question."

"No, it isn't. The answers are either A) yes or B) no."

Holloway's face was tan, and his hair was groomed neatly. But I knew the hair was false, and the tan probably was too. When he smiled, his teeth looked like they'd been bought and paid for. Then, of course, there was all the plastic surgery he'd told me about. Fake hair, fake teeth, fake face. I wondered if anything about Holloway was real.

"It was never that easy with Laura," Holloway said. "She was a very complicated person. I tried to make Laura happy. I'm not sure she was ever happy in her entire life. It just kept getting worse instead of better. She had everything, yet she acted as if she had nothing."

"So what was happening during those last months of her life?" I asked.

"Well, I was only with her for a year and a half. I knew right from the start that it was going to be a very high-maintenance relationship. She was one of the biggest stars in the world. Me, I was just this lucky guy who crossed paths with her one day and got to marry her. It was never easy. But in the end, it got worse. She was in such bad shape.

"We didn't tell the public any of this, of course. The studio had this image of what a star should be. Laura Marlowe was America's darling. Beautiful, innocent, always smiling for the camera—the girl who had it all. You weren't supposed to do anything that would ever damage that perception of her. So we tried to ignore all the problems. We lied about them, we hid them, and we pretended they didn't even exist. I'm still doing that now, I guess.

"I'm not proud of myself for my actions. I've played it over in my mind so many times. Should I have done things, could I have done more to help Laura? I still think about that a lot. But at the time, I thought I was doing the right thing for her. I really did.

"By the end, the studio was pretty much at the end of its patience with her. *Once Upon a Time Forever* had already been put on hiatus a couple of times because of her problems. The studio executives said she had to finish the picture. She needed rest, she needed help, she belonged in a hospital. But they put all sorts of pressure on us to get her back to work. Beverly was terrified

Laura's career would be over if she didn't do what they wanted. So she came to me and begged me for my help. She said Laura wouldn't listen to her anymore. She asked me to convince her to go back to work.

"That's what I did. She began to cry. She said she never wanted to be a movie star. It was always her mother who had all the ambition. She said we should leave Hollywood, leave her mother, leave them all. I said we could talk about it later. But she had to go back and finish this picture now. There was no choice. Not for any of us.

"Later, after she was killed, I thought back on all of these things. It ate me up with guilt for years. I don't know that it had anything to do with what happened to her. She was killed by someone with a gun. On the one hand, that didn't have anything to do with her state of mind then. But I always wondered what would have happened if I hadn't made her go back and finish that picture. I've never been able to come to grips with that. Those what-might-have-been thoughts, they can tear you up inside. Anyway, that's the real story about Laura Marlowe. That's what happens when you strip away the fairy tale."

I wrote it all down in my notebook. I wondered if he'd ever told this to anyone before.

"Did you know about her being in Russell Zorn's cult?" I asked.

"Not until I read it in your article the other day."

"Laura never told you about it?"

"We had this agreement, me and Laura. On our first date together, she told me she wanted it to be the first day of the rest of our lives. She said she wanted us both to forget all about our pasts. She said she wanted her life to be about the present and the future. So we never talked about what happened before we met. I know that may not seem normal, but Laura was not a normal woman. So all that stuff about her living in the desert with that cult and calling herself Clarissa or whatever—well, that was news to me too. I was as stunned as anyone when I read it."

"What about Thomas Rizzo?" I asked.

"The same. Never heard of him—at least not with her—until I read your article. I still find that hard to believe. I mean what would Laura have been doing with a crime boss like that? They had absolutely nothing in common. He killed people for a living, and Laura was the most nonviolent person I ever met. I just don't see it."

"Well, Laura was young and very beautiful. Rizzo was a man. I don't think it's too hard to figure out what he was looking for."

"And Laura? Why would she do it?"

"For a lot of reasons. The most obvious was it helped her to become a star. I know it's a nice Hollywood fairy tale to say she just got a lucky break when she became famous so fast. But I think it was more than just luck. Rizzo was an important man with a lot of influence in the entertainment industry back then. I think he used his influence to get Laura her big break. Maybe that's why she was sleeping with him."

Holloway shook his head slowly.

"You don't believe it?" I asked.

"Oh, it's probably true."

"What's wrong then?"

"I prefer the fairy tale."

"Yeah, me too," I said.

The restaurant was starting to fill up now. A few B-level celebrities stopped by to say hello to Holloway.

"Can I ask you one more question?" I said. "It's kind of personal."

"Sure, go ahead."

"I've been thinking about what you told me the other day about plastic surgery. I'm considering giving it a shot. I'm pushing forty now, and I'd like to look at least a little bit younger. How exactly does it work?"

He was happy to talk about it. It was a big topic with him. He described the procedure in great detail. I sat there listening and looking like I was really interested.

"Does it really give you an entirely new look?" I said when he was finished.

"A better one."

"But it's still you?"

"Of course, that's the key to a good plastic surgeon. He doesn't change your appearance. He improves it. He takes what you give him to work with, and then he gives you something better from that."

"So in other words, the way you look now—that's kind of the way you looked when you were a lot younger?"

"Exactly."

"Some things are different?"

"Of course."

"But anybody who knew you a long time ago—let's say back when you married Laura—would still recognize you today?"

"That's what good plastic surgery is all about," he smiled.

———

Sometimes it's the things you weren't looking for—not what you go after—that make all the difference.

I'd gone to see Holloway because I was hoping he'd tell me more about what was happening to Laura in those final days before she died.

And he had, whether he realized it or not.

When I'd asked him if she ever talked about being with Russell Zorn and the cult in the desert before they met.

"We had this agreement, me and Laura . . . we never talked about what happened before we met," Holloway said to me. "So all that stuff about her living in the desert with that cult and calling herself Clarissa or whatever—well, that was news to me too. I was as stunned as anyone when I read it."

There was only one problem. I'd never told him her name in the cult was Clarissa. It wasn't in the paper either. I'd put it in the original article I wrote, but somehow it had gotten edited out before publication. So how did Holloway know that her cult name was Clarissa?

There were two possibilities.

One, he was lying when he said she'd never talked about her past or her time in the cult with him. She *had* revealed it after they met. But he never talked about it—and he still wouldn't admit it—because he was concerned it tarnished the image he and everyone else had carefully constructed of her as this American golden girl.

The second possibility was even more intriguing.

I made a phone call when I got back to the office. I asked the person at the other end if she had a computer. She didn't, but said she could get access to one. I said there was a picture I wanted to email her. I asked her to call back when she got to the place with the computer.

I googled Edward Holloway's name, downloaded a picture of him onto my computer, and stared at it.

A good plastic surgeon never changes the features of the person—he just makes them better, Holloway had explained to me at the restaurant. If someone who knew him a long time ago saw him now, they'd just think he looked good. That he hadn't aged very much. That was the key to good plastic surgery.

A few minutes later, my phone rang.

"Are you at a computer?" I asked.

"Yes," Sally Easton said.

I attached the photo of Edward Holloway to an email, typed in the address she'd sent me, and pushed the *send* button.

It didn't take long to get her answer.

"That's him," she said.

"You're sure?"

"Yes, no question about it."

"His name is Edward Holloway."

"That wasn't his name when I knew him back at Russell's farm."

"But you're sure it's him?"

"Yes, he's the one who ran off with Clarissa."

CHAPTER 41

HAD a story. A good story. Edward Holloway—New York social figure, Broadway public relations–man and producer, and husband of the legendary Laura Marlowe—had been a member of the same radical cult as her. The whole story of how they met was all a lie. It was another dramatic development in the debunking of the Laura Marlowe legend.

The problem was I was pretty sure there was an even better story out there. A story I didn't have yet. If I wrote this one now, I might blow my chance to get the rest of the story.

I wished I could talk to my editor about the dilemma. But I knew I wasn't going to get any help from Stacy.

Over the years, I've had some really good editors. My first city editor was a legend in the New York newspaper world, a colorful character named Paul McDermott who talked out of the side of his mouth like Humphrey Bogart and smoked big cigars all day long. He was famous for his boozing and brawling, as well as his journalistic skills. The legend was that once in the days before computers he picked up one of the metal spikes that were used to collect used wire copy and used it like a sword to chase a reporter around the room. Another time a dispute with the copy desk chief over a displaced comma degenerated into a wrestling match, with the two of them rolling around the floor of the newsroom.

But McDermott had a sensitive side too. In my first year at the paper, I blew a crucial stakeout assignment. I was supposed to stand outside a building until a key murder witness came out. I did just that for hours, until the call of nature intervened. I found a nearby coffee shop, used the bathroom, and then ran back to the stakeout location. While I was gone, the witness had come out and another paper got the story. I was devastated and wondered if I would be fired. Especially when McDermott called me into his office the next day. But he didn't fire me. He said bad breaks like that happen to even the best of reporters sometimes. He said I'd get a better story the next day. He said I shouldn't get too down about it, because he thought I was a terrific reporter with a great future in the newspaper business. When I told him that I'd been afraid my gaffe might have cost me my job, he just smiled. "I've never fired a reporter for taking a piss, kid," McDermott said.

Of course, that was a long time ago. There weren't too many editors around like Paul McDermott anymore. They were mostly like Stacy Albright now.

———

I sat at my desk in the newsroom for a long time, trying to figure out what to do next.

Then my telephone rang. It was Lt. Marty Dahlstrom, the cop I'd talked to when I was in Los Angeles. I'd gone to see him again before I left LA and told him about the possible astrology connection I'd found in the four celebrity murders. He told me now that they were still looking into the astrology angle. Nothing definite yet, but it did look like a promising lead, he said. If something did develop, he promised he'd give me the exclusive before it was released to anyone else in the press. I guess he felt he owed me a favor.

"I've got something you might be interested in," Dahlstrom

said. "I checked out all those names you gave me on Laura Marlowe and Rizzo and all the rest. I did find a connection between Rizzo and one guy you mentioned."

I wasn't sure who he was talking about.

"Edward Holloway?"

Of course, that would make perfect sense. Holloway kept popping up everywhere in this story. He'd met Laura in the cult. He'd made up the whole story of how they met. He was also another surviving member from the Sign of the Z cult. Holloway had lied to me and everyone else about a lot of things. Maybe he had a reason. Maybe he was connected to the other deaths, and they all had something to do with what happened to Laura.

"Not Holloway," Dahlstrom said. "The other one."

It took me a second to realize who he meant.

"David Valentine," I said.

"David Valentine," he said, sounding as if he was reading from a file in front of him. "He was discharged from the Marine Corps. A dishonorable discharge, by the way. AWOL, drunk on duty—lots of other complaints like that. One night he had too much to drink and decided he didn't like the way a colonel's face looked. He tried to rearrange it. The colonel wound up in the hospital, and Valentine went to the stockade for six months. When he got out, they booted him out of the Marines. He lost everything—his pension, his benefits, the whole works."

"Valentine told me he was living in part on his Marine pension."

"Well, he lied to you."

"So how did he live?"

"He drifted around the country after that, doing a lot of odd jobs—mostly in private security. He got married for a while, he worked as a bodyguard for a couple of people in Hollywood that he apparently knew through his daughter before she died. None of the jobs lasted very long. He kept going from place to place.

Most of them aren't that interesting. But one of them was. He was a bodyguard for a guy out in Hollywood back in the '80s. Not your typical Hollywood executive. This was a very shady guy. A guy with big connections to the underworld. Those connections got a lot bigger as the years went by. Do you have any idea who I'm talking about?"

"Thomas Rizzo," I said.

"You're a very sharp guy, Malloy."

Valentine had told me he never knew anything about Rizzo. So that was a lie too. I wondered how many other lies he'd told me.

"Oh, one other thing," Dahlstrom said. "When I got the read-out from the FBI computer in Washington, I found out something kind of interesting. It turns out I wasn't the first person to ask for the information. Someone else had done it just a few weeks earlier. They said that's why it was so easy to get it. They had all the information accumulated already. Do you know who made the other request?"

"Abbie Kincaid," I said.

"Weird, huh?"

"No, it makes perfect sense."

There was something else Dahlstrom had said that intrigued me.

"You said Valentine got married. Did you mean the marriage to Beverly, Laura's mother?"

"No, he remarried after her. Right around the time Laura died actually. The marriage only lasted a couple of years. Divorced in '87."

That might be another lead. If I could find Valentine's ex-wife, the one he married after Beverly, she might be able to give me the real story about him. Especially if the marriage happened near the time of Laura's death.

"Do you happen to know the name of the woman?" I asked.

I heard him rustling through papers on his desk.

Like I said before, a good newspaper reporter pulls on all the loose threads of a story—without knowing what they might mean or what he might find out from them or where they might take him.

Doing that can take you to a lot of strange places.

And sometimes you wind up wishing you hadn't pulled on that thread at all.

"Her name was Sherry DeConde," Dahlstrom said.

PART FIVE

TELL LAURA I LOVE HER

CHAPTER 42

NEED your help," I said to Susan.

"Wow, I sure didn't expect to hear from you so soon."

"Why not?"

"I know you, Gil. You were hurt by what I told you. When that happens, you go off and sulk and brood and try to be angry with me. Some people can be mature about this kind of situation. Be friendly with their ex even after that person has moved on to someone else, be happy for them. You're not one of those kind of people. So this must be about something pretty important. What is it?"

Susan was right. I sure as hell didn't want to make this phone call. In fact, I had to summon up all my strength and resolve to do it. But, like Susan always said about me, I'll do anything for a story. Well, this was proof of that.

"I want you to do a background check on a woman named Sherry DeConde. She's a theatrical agent in Greenwich Village. She lives there too. I need to know if she has any kind of criminal history or anything else in her past that might have put her on law enforcement's radar over the past thirty years or so."

I gave her as much specific information about Sherry as I could.

"Why do you want to know about this woman?" Susan asked when I was finished.

"I can't tell you."

"That's not good enough, Gil."

"I've been seeing Sherry DeConde, okay? We had a couple of dates. I slept with her too. I like her, Susan. I like her better than anyone I've been with since you. Do you need more details than that?"

"I'm glad you found someone you like. But I sure as hell am not going to use the DA's office to do background checks on women you have the hots for."

"I think she's involved in the Laura Marlowe story," I said.

"How?"

"I'm not sure. But I think she knows a lot more than she's telling me."

I laid out everything I'd found out about Sherry and Valentine and Rizzo and the mysterious connections between all three of them.

"Will you help me, Susan?" I asked.

There was a long pause at the other end of the line.

"Let me see what I can find out and get back to you," she said finally.

———

Some of what Sherry DeConde had told me turned out to be true. Some wasn't. And she'd left out a lot of stuff according to the results of the investigation that Susan ran for me.

Sherry had been a struggling young agent in New York City—one of many trying to get a toehold in a tough business—when Laura Marlowe walked into her life. She nurtured the young actress, got her a start in show business with some small parts, but then lost out on the big prize when Laura Marlowe hit it big.

That was the way she had told it to me.

What she didn't say was that her agent business failed after that, she filed for bankruptcy, and wound up working a string of secretarial jobs on the side to make ends meet.

Then, not long after Laura Marlowe's death, her agency business got a fresh influx of capital from a new investor that put her back on her feet. The agency began signing clients, making deals with big people in the entertainment world, and turned Sherry DeConde into a bit of a player in the show business world.

The new investor was never publicly named, but law enforcement authorities determined it was Thomas Rizzo.

Sherry DeConde was quietly put on a "known associates" list of Rizzo by a federal–New York joint task force investigation monitoring Rizzo and his underworld connections. On several occasions, she was called before secret grand juries and other investigative bodies looking into Rizzo's criminal empire. In all of the cases, she refused to testify, pleading the Fifth Amendment against self-incrimination.

The last entry on Sherry DeConde said that—as far as law enforcement sources could determine—Rizzo remained a silent partner in her agency.

The marriage with Valentine appeared to have taken place at around the same time she got the money from Rizzo for the agency. That seemed significant to me, but I had no idea how or why. As Dahlstrom had said, the marriage ended a few years later. There were no further details. But the background report did point out that Valentine had worked for Rizzo as a bodyguard and described him as another "known associate" of the mobster.

———

I barged into Sherry's office unannounced. She looked up, startled, and happy at first to see me. But then she saw the look on my face.

"What's wrong?"

"Do you still keep in close touch with Thomas Rizzo?"

"What are you talking about?"

"You and Rizzo worked together."

"I've worked with a lot of people over the years."

"He gave you the money to set up this agency."

"Who told you that?"

"Are you working with Rizzo now?"

"No, I'm not working with Rizzo now."

"Still exchange Christmas cards with him?"

"Look, I'm sorry . . ."

"And what about Davy Valentine?"

"Gil . . ."

"You neglected to mention him to me when you were running through your list of ex-husbands. Why didn't you tell me about any of this?"

"Some of the things I've done in my past I'm not proud of."

"How in the hell did you ever hook up with someone like Rizzo in the first place?"

"I got to know him through Valentine because Rizzo was seeing Laura."

"So you knew first-hand about the affair with Rizzo?"

"Well . . ."

"And you lied to me about it."

"I told you I was sorry."

"Are you lying to me about other things too?"

She didn't answer.

"I'll take that as a yes."

I whirled around and started to storm out of her office. She followed after me and tried to get me to stay.

"Can't we just get past this?" she pleaded.

"I have to know the truth first."

"I told you the truth now."

"All of it."

"That's all there is to tell."

"I don't believe you."

———

I drove down to Barnegat on the Jersey Shore to find Valentine again. I wanted to confront him with all this. Maybe he'd tell me the truth.

But when I got there, his trailer was gone. Someone nearby told me Valentine had driven off with the trailer an hour earlier. Sherry must have called him after I left and told him what happened.

I tried her on the phone, but just got an out-of-office message saying the Sherry DeConde Agency was closed until further notice.

Sherry.

Valentine.

Rizzo.

The answer to the Laura Marlowe mystery was there somewhere if I could just figure out how to connect the dots.

I drove back to New York, went into the office, and read as many past stories as I could find that had been done about Rizzo. There were a lot of them. Murders, bribery, bookmaking, drug dealing—you name it. He'd sure become a mob superstar in the years since Laura's death. The media talked about him the way they used to talk about John Gotti or Al Capone. He seemed to like the publicity too. There were stories and pictures of him showing up at parties, movie premieres, and fine restaurants. He was a celebrity— just like a movie star or a Super Bowl quarterback or a rock idol.

It took me quite a while to go through all the stuff on him. I actually thought it would take me longer, except coverage suddenly stopped. About a year ago. There were only a few mentions of him after that, and even those were about his new low profile around town. There were no more movie openings, no more restaurant appearances—it was as if he'd become shy after years and years of being an underworld celebrity. One article speculated that it might mean some sort of mob war was about to break out, and that Rizzo didn't want to make himself too easy of a target. There were even rumors that he might have left the country.

I wasn't sure what any of this meant, but I was sure about one thing. Rizzo was the only clear-cut connection between both Laura and Abbie's murders. And when you linked those two murders up—when you made the leap to the assumption that Abbie died because of something she'd found out about Laura's murder—then everything started to fall into place. I'd been nibbling around that idea ever since the story started, but now it was time to embrace it wholeheartedly.

Whoever killed Laura Marlowe thirty years ago also killed Abbie.

Thomas Rizzo seemed to be the most likely candidate. Rizzo was a killer, we all knew that. He had a motive—he'd had an affair with Laura that went bad. And, most damning of all, he was the only one directly linked to both cases. His son was dating Abbie at the same time she was uncovering new evidence that reopened the Marlowe murder case. Thomas Rizzo's fingerprints were all over this, and it was hard to ignore that fact.

Davy Valentine was gone, in the wind now.

Maybe Sherry too.

I knew one thing for certain though. Thomas Rizzo was the key to this entire story. Rizzo was somehow at the center of everything that had happened. Rizzo had all the answers.

All I had to do was find him.

CHAPTER 43

FLORENTINE'S was more crowded this time. Most of the tables in the front room were filled. There were also people in the back room—the Thomas Rizzo enclave. I could hear them laughing and shouting to each other all over the restaurant.

I walked past the back room on my way to the bar and glanced in. The guy with the heavy cigarette habit who'd picked me up the other day was there. So was the young guy who drove the car. And the one who questioned me at the bar the last time I was here. There was no sign of Rizzo though. I kept going to the bar.

The same bartender was on duty.

"Oh, you again," he said, as I sat down.

"Good to see you too."

"What do you want?"

"A little civility would be nice."

He was wearing a nametag on the front of his bartender vest. It said: *Sid*.

"How's it going, Sid," I said. "My name is Gil Malloy. I'm with the *New York Daily News*." I took out a business card and handed it to him. "I'm looking for Thomas Rizzo."

The bartender glanced at the card, then put it on top of the cash register behind the bar.

"Who?" he asked.

"Didn't we go through this same charade last time? Thomas Rizzo. Gray hair. Dresses in fancy suits. Kind of a tough guy from what I hear. He kills people for a living. Those are some of his pals in the back room over there acting boisterous."

"Okay, let's say I do know who Thomas Rizzo is. You're still not going to find him here tonight."

"Maybe I'll just hang out here every night then until he comes in. Maybe I'll bring some of my friends along. You know, a lot of my friends are cops. That ought to be good for business. Police in and out of the place all night long. They'll make sure you don't have any undesirable elements finding their way in here."

Sid disappeared from behind the bar. I watched him go into the back room. When he came back, he had some people with him. The guy with the cigarette—I decided to call him Marlboro Man—and the other two I'd met before. They came straight over to the bar.

"We seem to be having some communication problems," Marlboro Man said.

He sat down next to me on an empty stool. The young one sat down on the other side. The third guy stood in front of me, blocking my path toward the door in case I decided to make a run for it. But I was right where I wanted to be.

"We talked about this the other day, Malloy. We explained to you that Mr. Rizzo was not a part of your story. But you don't seem to be getting the message, so I'll give it to you one more time. Leave Mr. Rizzo out of whatever you're doing."

He took a big drag on his cigarette. A big cloud of smoke blew into my face. Maybe that was his plan to get rid of me. He wasn't going to shoot me. He was just going to kill me slowly with second-hand cigarette smoke.

"What happens if I don't stop trying to talk to Rizzo?"

He shook his head. "I like you, Malloy. I really do. And I know exactly where you're coming from. You've got a job to do, and I respect that. But I've got a job to do too. I want you to respect that."

"The Laura Marlowe story keeps leading me back to Thomas Rizzo," I told him.

"Yes, Mr. Rizzo had a romance with her a long time ago. You've already written about that. But that's all there is. None of the rest of it has anything to do with Mr. Rizzo."

"I think it does. I think there's more. I think Rizzo knows something about her murder."

"He had nothing to do with that."

"His name keeps popping up everywhere I look."

"He didn't kill her, Malloy."

"Why should I believe that?"

"Because he loved her."

I stared at him.

"I was with him back then. I was just a young guy starting out. But I saw him with her. He loved her, believe me about that. Everybody always has somebody who's the true love of their life. Well, she was his. I know it didn't work out and he went back to his wife and they lived a happy life together. But I don't think he ever got over Laura. If her name ever came up or one of her movies was showing on television—well, he got this really sad look on his face. She was the one thing he wanted that he never could have. But he didn't kill her. You're wasting your time."

"I'd still like to talk to him," I said. "Tell him that."

"It isn't going to do any good."

"Tell him anyway."

I took out some more of my business cards and passed them out to all three of them.

"I'm not going to stop working on this story," I said.

"Yeah, I know," Marlboro Man sighed.

"Like you said, it's my job."

"I have my job too."

"All I want to do is talk to him."

I stood up from the bar stool and started for the door. But, before I got there, I turned around to say one more thing to Marlboro Man and his buddies.

"By the way, guys, if you want to mess with me in the future, try something else besides following me around in that damn brown car and sitting in front of my apartment house all night. It's really kind of annoying."

"I don't know what you're talking about," Marlboro Man said.

"I suppose you don't know anything about the break-in at my apartment or the graffiti on my wall either, huh?"

Marlboro Man shook his head.

"If we wanted to mess with you, Malloy, believe me—you'd know it was us doing the messing."

———

Outside, I hailed a cab and paid the driver to wait with me there for a while. We parked on the street across from the restaurant so I could see who came in and out the front door. I'd made sure I got myself noticed by everyone in there. Now I just had to see what they were going to do about it.

About thirty minutes later, Marlboro Man came out of the restaurant, went into a parking garage, and came out driving a green Buick. I made a mental note that it wasn't a brown sedan. And he had seemed genuinely mystified when I asked him about following me or breaking into my apartment. Okay, so if it wasn't Rizzo's people, who in the hell was in the brown sedan?

I told the cab driver to follow the car. The driver gave me a quizzical look, but I promised him a big tip and he did it. Marlboro Man drove downtown, then made a left toward the Brooklyn Bridge. We kept a few car lengths behind him as he went across the bridge, then headed south into Brooklyn. The cab driver asked me where we were headed. I said I wasn't sure. I was just going wherever Marlboro Man was going.

That turned out to be a small medical complex in Red Hook. He got out of his car and went inside. I paid off the taxi driver and followed him. The building was only a few stories tall, and it didn't look like it could admit a large number of patients. But there was a nurse at the reception desk inside the front door. I stood outside and watched as Marlboro Man got on the elevator. Then I went in, walked past the nurse station before she could stop me, and checked the floor. He'd gone to the fourth floor. By now the nurse was standing there next to me.

"Can I help you?" she asked.

"Is this the veterans' hospital?"

"No, this is a private facility."

"My father's in the cardiac care unit at the veterans' hospital. They just called me, but I was so upset I forgot the address. Do you know where it is?"

"There's a veterans' hospital about ten blocks from here. That might be the one you're looking for. Just make a left when you leave here. There's a sign at one of the traffic lights. You can't miss it."

"Thanks a lot," I said.

I went back outside, stood on a street corner, and waited. A little while later, he came back out and got in the green Buick. I waited until the nurse turned her back on the door to do some filing. Then I slipped past her onto the elevator and took it up to the fourth floor.

It was a hospital ward, alright, but most of the rooms seemed to be empty. Except one with a closed door. The number on it was 409. Like Sherlock Holmes, I quickly deduced that Room 409 was probably the one I was looking for. Then I smelled something. Cigarette smoke. I turned around, and there he was. Marlboro Man.

"You spotted me tailing you here from the restaurant, huh?" I said.

"Not on the way. I don't know how I missed that."

"When you came out of the hospital?"

"Yeah, you were standing underneath a street light. I could make out enough to see it was you. So I waited to see what you were up to."

"I'm impressed."

He shrugged. "I've been doing this job for a long time."

"So what happens now?"

"Now," he said, "it looks like you're going to get a chance to meet Mr. Rizzo after all."

CHAPTER 44

ROOM 409 turned out to be a suite. In the first room, there were four men playing cards and watching TV. Some of them wore guns you could see, some didn't. But they were all armed, I knew that. They were Rizzo's soldiers. It was a good thing Marlboro Man had caught me. If I'd tried to crash in unannounced, I probably would have been dead by now.

Marlboro Man gestured to the four bodyguards that we were going through. He opened another door where there were two more guards. They had guns too, and seemed ready to use them when they saw me. But they relaxed as soon as they realized who I was with.

All this protection meant something pretty important—or more precisely, someone—must be here.

I didn't have much doubt who was that important.

He was lying in a bed in a corner of the spacious room.

Thomas Rizzo.

There were tubes hooked up to his arms and a heart monitoring device recorded his pulse and breathing. On the table next to him was a stack of pills. A large color TV was in front of him, showing a rerun of *Mannix*—the cop show from the '70s. Rizzo wasn't watching though. His eyes were closed, and he seemed to be sleeping peacefully.

"It's cancer," Marlboro Man said to me. "Started in his lungs about a year and a half ago. They thought they caught it in time, but they were wrong. Now it's spread to his throat, his spine—all over his body. It's a helluva thing to see someone so strong wasting away like that."

I looked down at Rizzo. He stirred gently in the bed now, as if he knew we were talking about him.

"We've tried to keep it quiet, mostly for practical business reasons. If a man like Thomas Rizzo appears weak, other people get ideas about trying to take advantage of the situation. Move in on his territory. You can't appear vulnerable in the line of work we're in. So we've never told anybody. He's stayed out of sight, and people think he's just reclusive. That's why I couldn't let you see him. But you showed up anyway. If you write a story about this, it will make life very difficult for us. So now that you know, it means we gotta"—he made a slitting gesture with his finger across his throat—"do something to keep you quiet."

He was kidding, I think.

"The thing is I had to make a decision quickly when I realized you'd followed me here. Like I told you before, I understand you're just doing your job. I'm doing mine too. Part of that job is reading people's intentions. I'm pretty good at that. And you—well, you read to me like a guy with a terminal case of stubbornness. You're going to try to keep getting to Mr. Rizzo no matter how many times we try to make you stop. I realize this is very important to you. Believe it or not, it is to Mr. Rizzo too. He wanted to talk to you. It was the rest of us who told him it wasn't a good idea. But now here you are. So this is the deal: you don't write about Mr. Rizzo's condition, and I let you talk to him about the other thing. What do you say?"

I didn't really have much of a choice. Underworld boss dying of cancer was a good story, but it wasn't the one I was after. I'd never made a deal with the mob before, but there's a first time for everything. Besides, I knew there was no way I was voluntarily leaving the room at this point without getting some answers from the old man in the bed.

Rizzo opened his eyes as I moved toward him. Probably slept lightly like that all his life for self-protection. He had a lot of enemies. Old habits die hard, I guess.

"This is the reporter I told you about, Mr. Rizzo," Marlboro Man said. "Gil Malloy."

He looked up at me from the bed with surprisingly clear eyes. Whatever ravages the disease had done to his body, it didn't seem to have affected his mind. He still seemed to be a formidable presence, even lying in that bed hooked up to all the machines.

"How are you, Mr. Rizzo?"

"Oh, I've been better," he smiled.

He reached out his hand to me. He was withered and frail, but his handshake was strong.

He gestured to Marlboro Man and the two bodyguards to leave the room. They didn't think that was such a good idea.

"We don't want to leave you alone, Mr. Rizzo," one of them said.

"I'll be fine. The only person here is Mr. Malloy. He's not going to harm me. That's not why he's here."

When they left and we were alone, Rizzo picked up the remote and turned off the sound of the TV.

"I watch a lot of these old shows now." He smiled, gesturing toward the screen. "Never watched much TV before. I find I don't care for most of the new shows that are on today. But the old programs, they bring memories of a different time for me. A simpler time. A better time." He shrugged. "Anyway, it helps pass the time for me."

He gestured for me to pull up a chair next to his bed. I sat down.

"You were a friend of that TV reporter Abbie Kincaid, weren't you?" he asked.

"Yes, I was."

"She came here to see me a while ago. Just like you. With a lot of questions."

"She's dead now."

"I know."

"Did you kill her?"

I said it matter-of-factly, as if I were asking him what he'd had for breakfast.

"No," he said softly, "I didn't kill her."

"Do you know who did?"

"No, I'm sorry."

"Why did Abbie come to see you?"

"For the same reason you're here."

"Laura Marlowe."

"Yes, everyone wants to talk about me and Laura."

He told me the story then. An old man lying in a hospital bed talking about his romance with a glamorous movie star that had taken place more than three decades ago. At first, I thought it might be more lies. But he was beyond that now. He was telling the story for himself, more than for me.

"I met her at a party in Hollywood," he said. "I was spending a lot of time out there then, getting very involved in the movie business. Part of the job of fitting in out there is being part of the social scene. So I was at this bash at a mansion in the Hollywood Hills, and someone introduced me to Laura.

"I'd already been married for a few years then. I had a wife and a young baby back in New York. I was always a faithful husband. Never a skirt chaser. I believe that adultery is a sin. That a man should not cheat on his wife. Like it says in the marriage vows, you're with this one woman until death do you part. That's how I always felt anyway. Until I met Laura. There were never any women besides my wife before Laura, and never after her either. She was the only one.

"Laura was a working girl that night at the party. She was working for an X-rated film company that also provided some of the actresses as escorts for important people in Hollywood. I suppose that made it easier for me. It wasn't so much like just cheating on my wife, this was more like a business proposition. I began paying her to have sex with me.

"Of course, it quickly developed beyond that. I fell in love with her. I'd never felt like that about anybody before. Nothing else mattered to me—my business, my career, even my family. I just wanted to be with her. She loved me too. Or at least she saw something in me that she needed. She told me that she was happy for the first time in her life.

"Eventually, I helped her get her big break in Hollywood. I used all my influence out there—which was considerable then—to get her the role in *Lucky Lady*. Of course, no one knew how big *Lucky Lady* would turn out to be. It made her a star. And that, as it turned out, was the death knell for our relationship. Not because of her. Because of me. She was in the public eye now, and—sooner or later—the press would find out we were together. I had to protect her from that kind of scandal. So that's what I did.

"I sat her down one night and told her how much I loved her. I said I would always love her. I said I'd keep on doing everything I could to help her career. But I needed to go back to my wife. I'd taken holy vows to be with her as long as we lived. I had to honor those vows. 'Thou shalt not commit adultery' is one of the Ten Commandments. I was violating that every second I spent with her. I couldn't keep living a lie like that for the rest of my life.

"I came back to New York and sold off most of my business interests in Hollywood. I didn't want to keep going back there and be tempted. A little while later, I read that Laura had married that Edward Holloway fellow. I was happy for her. But I was sad too. Sad for both of us. After that, I just got on with my life. I thought she would too, but she didn't have much more life left. Such a tragedy.

"I hoped people would never have to know about any of this. My wife is dead now, and I wanted the secret to go to the grave with me. I didn't want to tarnish Laura's memory in any way. But you've already printed some of it. And I suspected you would keep on digging. In the end, I decided it was best for you to hear the truth."

The story was really pretty ludicrous, if you thought about it. I mean here's Thomas Rizzo, a guy who's stomped all over the Ten Commandments for most of his life with a career of murder and robbery and God knows what else. But he's upset about cheating on his wife. That somehow violates his moral code.

On the other hand, it did make sense to me in a crazy way. We all have our own rules we live by. I did, and—it appeared—so did Thomas Rizzo. Now Rizzo was dying, and he was trying to make peace with God—and with himself—as best he could. He couldn't do anything about all those he'd killed and committed crimes against during his lifetime. But he wanted to set the record straight on Laura.

"That night you said goodbye to Laura," I said, "was that the last time you ever saw her?"

"No."

"What happened?"

"I couldn't forget about her. I tried, but she was always in my mind."

"So you went back to her?"

"She came back to me."

"After she was with Holloway?"

"Yes."

He looked over at the television screen. The *Mannix* rerun was still on. There was a car chase with the good guys after the bad guys, or maybe it was the other way around. Rizzo watched the flickering images from the old show, but I imagined he was seeing something else. I think he was watching his own life flash before his eyes. Trying to make some sense of it in the little time he had left. Like everybody in this story, Rizzo hadn't turned out to be what I expected. I thought I'd hate him, but I didn't. He'd told me a lot of things about Laura. But no matter how much I found out about her, none of it was helping me find out the answer to who killed her.

"I slipped away for a weekend with Laura," Rizzo said. "This was in the early summer of 1984, and she was really famous now. But she wasn't happy. She told me that. She said she wanted me to hold her and make her feel better and tell her how much I still loved her. The two of us checked into this out-of-the-way hotel, and we never left it the entire weekend. We talked. We ordered room service. And, most of all, we made love. I knew then that I'd made a terrible mistake. So did she. We belonged together. So we came up with this big plan. We were going to run off together. She was going to break her contract with the studio, and walk away from this next picture. I was going to try and become a legitimate businessman, because she said she didn't want to always be looking for policemen behind every door. I know it sounds crazy. We knew it was crazy even as we were talking about it. But I still think about that dream of ours all the time. If we'd done it, who knows how things would have turned out . . ."

He let his words drift off. But I knew what he was going to say. She'd probably still be alive.

"And that was the last time I ever saw Laura," he said.

"Why was it the last time?"

"Her mother contacted me later. She told me some things. Then she said that if I ever tried to contact Laura again, she would make sure that I regretted it for the rest of my life. She would go public with everything. She warned me that she had left a letter about me in a secret safe deposit box just in case I got any ideas about trying to shut her up. If she wound up dead, the letter would be opened. I couldn't stand that kind of a scandal. Not for my wife. Not for my family. Not for my standing in the—well, the business organization I was in."

"So you walked away to make sure no one ever found out about the affair with Laura?"

"It wasn't just our affair that I needed to keep secret."

"What else was there?"

There were tears in Rizzo's eyes now. The same man who had cold-bloodedly killed a lot of people in his life—most of the estimates I'd seen ranged somewhere from fifty to one hundred victims—was crying.

"I loved Laura," he sobbed. "I loved her so much. I would have done anything for her. You have to believe me."

"I understand."

"But after her mother told me . . ."

"Told you what?"

"She said that Laura's relationship with Edward Holloway was just a sham. That she had arranged the whole thing to make sure Laura stayed away from me. Even made up a phony story about how they met like out of some Hollywood fairy tale. It was all part of her grand design for her daughter. She told me that Holloway and Laura . . . well, they'd never actually had sex together. He adored Laura like she was some princess or goddess, but he never touched her. He was completely impotent."

"Why did she tell you all this?"

"Because Laura was pregnant."

It suddenly all made sense.

"She was having our baby," Rizzo said.

CHAPTER 45

R IZZO told me the rest of the story then.

Laura Marlowe was the epitome of everything good and wholesome and unspoiled to the American public. Her fans would have been shocked to learn she was having a baby as the result of an affair not just with a married man, but with one of the country's most infamous underworld leaders. There was no way Laura Marlowe could have survived that kind of scandal with her career intact.

Rizzo knew that. And so, like a modern-day *Tale of Two Cities* story, the mob boss did a far, far better thing than he had ever done before. He walked away from the woman he loved. He made the ultimate sacrifice to make sure no one ever learned that Laura Marlowe, America's sweetheart, was pregnant with his baby.

That's how he related it to me as he lay there in his hospital bed with the life seeping away from him.

Laura was supposed to get an abortion; that was her mother's plan. But then Laura decided she couldn't go through with the abortion. She said she could never kill their baby, Rizzo told me. It was the only thing she had left of their love, of their relationship. Later, he found out she'd had the baby—and given it up for adoption. That happened right before she died, he said.

Sitting there next to this dying old man, I put the rest of the pieces of the puzzle together. Laura had disappeared several times from the set of *Once Upon a Time Forever*, her last film. The longest period was for a few months at the beginning of 1985. Everyone thought it was drugs she'd been getting treated for. Or booze. Or a mental breakdown. Maybe she was. But there was something else too. She had disappeared from the public eye to have a baby. Rizzo's baby.

I talked to Rizzo for maybe an hour. Rizzo finally fell asleep, looking exhausted and spent from the emotional ordeal of reliving it all one more time for me. I sat there for a while longer, watching him breathe heavily and wondering what he might be dreaming about at that moment. Then I got up, walked to the door, and told Marlboro Man I was ready to leave. If there were any more secrets Rizzo was going to reveal, they would have to wait for another time. And I didn't think he had too much time left.

———

So what happened to the baby?

Rizzo never told me that, but I was pretty sure he knew the answer to that question. A man like Rizzo would have made it his business to find out.

I had a crazy hunch about it too.

Or maybe it wasn't so crazy.

There was something I picked up on when Rizzo talked about Abbie Kincaid coming to see him for an interview too before she died. He didn't talk about her as if she was just another reporter. His voice had a sadness to it that fell right in line with my theory about what happened to Laura Marlowe's secret baby.

Bill Remesch had said to me during his jailhouse interview that Abbie's mother was a very plain-looking person, nothing like Abbie's natural beauty. He said he used to kid her that the stork had made a mistake and dropped her off at the wrong house.

Of course, there was another possible explanation for why Abbie didn't look at all like her mother or father.

I went through the phone listings for the name Kincaid in the Wisconsin town where she grew up and tracked down Abbie's mother. She confirmed to me that my speculation was dead on target. Abbie had been adopted. Mrs. Kincaid said she had been unable to have children and she and her husband had tried for a long time to adopt a baby until they found Abbie.

"Did Abbie know she was adopted?" I asked.

"Yes, we told her when she was very young."

"Did you tell her who her birth mother was?"

"We couldn't—we never knew."

"How did you get Abbie?"

"We adopted her through an agency here in Wisconsin."

"So the mother was from that area?"

"No, she was from California."

"California," I repeated.

"Yes, that's where the adoption actually took place."

"Where in California?"

"From a hospital in Santa Barbara," she said.

She gave me the name of the hospital.

It turned out to be the same place where Laura had been a patient in those months at the beginning of 1985 when she left the set of *Once Upon a Time Forever*.

I've got a big story I'm going to break, Abbie told me. I thought she was talking about the serial killer angle. No, this is even bigger, she said. I didn't understand what she was talking about then. But now I did. I knew the big exclusive she was going to break on her next show if she hadn't died.

Abbie was the illegitimate daughter of Laura Marlowe and Thomas Rizzo.

And now she was dead.

I'd gone looking for Laura Marlowe's killer, not sure exactly what I would find—but my instincts kept telling me to find out whatever really happened to her.

Now it had brought me back to where I knew it would all along. I was looking for Abbie Kincaid's killer too.

———

I went back to the *Daily News*, sat down at my desk, turned on the computer, and typed in everything I'd found out. I needed to do this while it was still fresh in my mind. I hadn't wanted to take notes while I was talking to Rizzo, because I was afraid it might freak him out. So I memorized the things he said, then jotted it all down in my notebook as soon as I got outside the hospital. I had a lot of stuff. It took me a while to decipher my hastily scrawled notes and put them into the computer.

It was late by the time I finished, and all the top editors were long gone from the office. I had a big story here. Mob boss had secret love child with murdered movie star. And that love child turned out to be murdered TV star Abbie Kincaid—who was investigating her mother's long-ago murder.

I could have called Stacy at home and told her all about it to get a story up on the website as quickly as possible. But I didn't.

For one thing, there was no real urgency with this story. It was completely exclusive, so no one was going to beat me on it. The story could easily wait until tomorrow when Stacy and the other editors were here to figure out the best way to break it.

But there was something else too. Sure, it was a good story. A great story. But it wasn't the whole story. I still didn't know who murdered Laura Marlowe. Or Abbie Kincaid. Or the answers to a lot of other questions. I wanted to know it all. And I wasn't going to let go of this story, no matter what Stacy or anyone else at the paper decided. I was going to tell Stacy that in the morning. Yep, tomorrow should be a really interesting day, I thought to myself as I shut off the computer and left the office.

On the way out of the *Daily News* building, I was so excited about all of it that I didn't even notice the brown sedan outside this time.

Not until I was walking across the street, heard the roar of an engine, and saw the car barreling toward me.

I leaped out of the way and landed on the curb.

I was shaken up but not hurt.

The car raced away without stopping.

"If we wanted to mess with you, Malloy—believe me, you'd know it was us doing the messing," Marlboro Man had said to me.

No, it wasn't Rizzo's people I had to worry about.

I didn't think they were the bad guys anymore.

This time I'd seen who was driving the brown sedan.

CHAPTER 46

THINK I know who killed Laura," I told Edward Holloway.

"Who?"

"You."

Holloway looked stunned.

"Why would I do that?" he asked.

"For the money."

"I loved Laura."

"You loved the money even more. I figure Laura—or more probably her mother, Beverly—made sure you signed a pretty strict pre-nuptial agreement before the marriage. I think Laura was getting ready to dump you. So you'd have been left with nothing. Unless she died, of course. If she died, you got the money. Even more important, you got the Laura legend. You became one of the caretakers of the Laura Marlowe legend. You made a career out of being the grieving husband. And you earned a fortune from it. That's why you killed your wife thirty years ago and that's why you killed Abbie when she got too close to figuring out the truth."

We were sitting at the same table at Sardi's, where I'd met him before. Holloway had come a long way since Laura Marlowe's murder. He'd gotten his fifteen minutes of fame, and he'd parlayed it into a lifetime of big money and quasi-celebrity status. And now I was about to take it all away from him.

"I know it was you who tried to run me down on the street," I said. "I checked and found out you drive a brown Lincoln sedan. And I caught a glimpse of you behind the wheel. Which means you were the one who was following me the other day. And the one who trashed my apartment and spray painted the letter Z on the wall. Why did you do that, Eddie?"

"I wasn't going to hurt you," Holloway said meekly. "I just wanted to scare you."

"I also know that you were a member of the Sign of the Z. That's where you met Laura, long before that supposed 'traffic accident' on Rodeo Drive. Both of you had been in that crazy cult together. A cult whose leader wanted to emulate Charles Manson with his own bloody murders of famous people."

I took out a sheet of paper with the four dead celebrity names on it—Deborah Ditmar, Susan Fairmont, Stephanie Lee, and Cheryl Carson—then slid it across the table to Holloway.

"I think all four of these people were killed by someone in the Sign of the Z cult, and you knew that," I said. "You gave these names to Abbie, didn't you? Sent them to her in an anonymous letter after she came to you with questions about Laura's death. Along with a lot of other threatening notes and emails. That's why she was so scared and had all that security. You wanted to make her suspect that the Sign of the Z cult had been behind Laura's murder too. That way this crazy cult—with most of its members dead— could be blamed for all of the deaths, including Laura, and no one would ever look at you as a suspect. You made Abbie terrified that the Sign of the Z was out to get her. That's why she was in such a frazzled emotional state until right before she died.

"Then, when I started asking the same questions about Laura, you did it again with me. Painted that big Z on the wall of my apartment. Followed me down the street. Pretended to try and run me over. All so that I would believe that the Sign of the Z was after me too. So I would go off in the wrong direction, just like you sent Abbie, rather than finding Laura's real killer. Blame it all on the big bad Sign of the Z. Except there is no Sign of the Z anymore, Eddie. Just you.

"I think Abbie figured that out at some point, just like I eventually did. She realized just before she died that she wasn't really in danger from any crazy Sign of the Z cult. And that they weren't the ones who killed Laura Marlowe either. It was all a misdirection orchestrated by you. You were the one who killed Laura thirty years ago, and now you were trying to cover that up. She was going to reveal that—along with a lot of other secrets—on her TV show. That's why you had to kill Abbie. Once I tell the cops about this, they'll put it together pretty quickly. There are all sorts of new crime detection and DNA techniques they didn't have back then. Even after all this time, maybe they'll find something to directly link you to Laura's murder. And Abbie, well that should be easier. As soon as they zero in on you as the main suspect, they'll track down someone who saw you at the Regent that night. The night you killed her because she knew what you did to Laura."

Holloway sat there with a deer-in-the-headlights look of fear on his face. He'd built his whole life on a lie, and now it was finally over.

"That's not the way it happened," he said softly.

"Sure it is."

"I didn't kill Abbie Kincaid and I didn't kill Laura."

"I don't believe you."

"No, no, you have to believe me . . ."

"I know about the baby, Eddie. Thomas Rizzo's baby."

Holloway nodded.

"Beverly told Laura she had to get an abortion," he said.

"But she never had the abortion, did she?"

"No, it was the only time Laura ever stood up to her mother.

They finally worked out a deal. Laura would have the baby, but then give it up for adoption afterward. In the meantime, they'd come up with some sort of cover story about her being in the hospital for another reason to explain why she was missing time on the set. Fortunately, Laura never really began to show she was pregnant until the last few months. There were a few gossip items about her putting on a little weight, but no one ever figured out the real reason. By the time she came back to finish the movie she looked normal again. And the baby was gone. Beverly thought they'd weathered the crisis, but she was wrong. It wasn't over."

"Why not?"

"Laura never got over giving up the baby. While she was pregnant, she seemed okay with the idea. But after the baby was born—well, everything really fell apart for her. They let her hold her daughter in her arms for a just few minutes after the birth before they took her away. She never saw the baby again. That really upset Laura. She believed she was supposed to be the mother of that baby. That giving birth to that human life was the only worthwhile thing she'd ever done. She was never the same after that. And then she died."

"Which brings us back to you," I said. "She had a baby with another man, Thomas Rizzo. She wanted to run off with him. You were jealous, you were angry, you were convinced she was going to leave you with nothing. That's when you got the idea, isn't it? If she was dead, all your problems would be over. You'd be Mr. Laura Marlowe for the rest of your life."

"I didn't kill Laura."

"Why not? You had the motive. And the opportunity too. You left the party and went back to the hotel that night where she was shot. You're the one who claims to have seen the killer running out of that alley. You're the only witness who saw him standing over her with the gun. I think that's because you were the only one there. There was no other gunman. You were the one who shot her."

"I didn't kill anyone," he said. "I couldn't kill anyone."

"Okay," I sighed, "if you didn't murder your wife, who did?"

"Nobody killed her," Holloway said.

"Are you going to try to tell me she's still alive?"

"No, Laura died," he said sadly. "She died on July 17, 1985, just like everyone thinks."

"So who killed her? If it wasn't you, someone else had to do it. Do you know who shot her?"

"Yes."

"Who?"

"Laura Marlowe."

That's when I realized I was still missing something. I thought I was so smart, I thought I'd figured it all out. But there was something else going on back there that night thirty years ago when Laura Marlowe died. Something I didn't count on.

"Laura killed herself," Holloway said.

CHAPTER 47

He told me the whole story then.

"That night, Laura didn't want to go to the party," he said. "She was in pretty bad shape. She hadn't been sleeping, she was tired, she was depressed. I tried to talk to her. But nothing really helped. She'd been going downhill for a long time, and now she'd hit rock bottom.

"The only time she ever really seemed happy was back when I first met her at Zorn's ranch in the desert. It was as if she'd gotten this giant load off her by breaking from her mother and running away to California. She was free for the first time in her life, she said. I guess we were both pretty confused back then, looking for something that Zorn provided—at least for a little while. But eventually the two of us realized we didn't belong there. You have to understand something: Laura and I, we were never really lovers—not in the traditional sense. But we connected on some sort of spiritual level. So we ran off together.

"Laura never could get completely free of her mother's influence though. Beverly had told her all her life she was destined to become a movie star, and so she wound up in Hollywood. She started out making those porn movies, then got into the legitimate kind. That's when Beverly took control of her career again.

"It was Beverly who brought me back into the picture. I was

hanging around Los Angeles—panhandling on street corners, doing odd jobs and just trying to figure out what to do with my life. I guess Laura told her mother about me, and Beverly thought I was a safe alternative to Thomas Rizzo. Someone she could control, just like she controlled her daughter. So she made up this romantic story of us meeting in a car accident, and fed it to the gossip columns. I was Laura Marlowe's new love interest.

"But Laura was such a troubled person. She kept talking about killing herself. One night she took too many sleeping pills and had to have her stomach pumped. Another time she made a halfhearted attempt to cut her wrists, but didn't do any real damage. I was never sure if these suicide attempts were for real or just dramatic calls for help. Then, she was hospitalized for wounds to her face. We said it was from a car crash, but the truth is the wounds were self-inflicted. Laura had cut her own face. She told me afterward that maybe if she wasn't so beautiful, then everybody would just leave her alone.

"Beverly was terrified the truth would come out, but the secret held. Everyone bought the cover story about an accident. Eventually Laura's scars healed, and she went back to work. But Laura was an emotional wreck. Then Rizzo saw her again, and we found out she was pregnant with his baby. No matter how hard Beverly tried, she couldn't convince Laura to have an abortion. So Beverly decided I would marry Laura in a big Hollywood ceremony. That way, if anyone did find out about the baby, they could say it was mine. Laura had the baby in early March of 1985, we turned it over for adoption right away, and then we even dragged Laura to the Oscars a few weeks later so that no one would suspect anything was wrong. But it was the beginning of the end. She never got over giving up that baby.

"That last day in New York, she started drinking and doing God knows what else very early. By the time she got to the party, she was pretty wiped. But she always put on a good show. She was an actress. And she played her part to the hilt that night. Greeting people, acting charming—being the Laura Marlowe all her fans expected. It must have been very difficult for her. But she pulled it off.

"At some point though, she slipped away from the party. I didn't realize she was gone. Once I found out, I went back to the hotel. That's the only place I could think of to look for her. That's where I found her."

Holloway said he saw her coming out the front door of the hotel.

"She said she was going back to the party," he said. "Then she showed me the gun she was carrying in her purse. She said she was going to shoot herself in front of everyone there. She said she wanted the world to see the real Laura Marlowe one time before she died. She said it would be her greatest performance ever. Her final curtain, she called it.

"I tried to stop her. I told her not to do this. She started to run away, and I ran after her. That's when she went into the alley. Finally, she stopped running, turned to face me, and put the gun to her head. I told her I loved her; I told her I'd help her do anything she wanted. But it was too late. She said all she wanted to do was die. Then she pulled the trigger.

"I'm not sure exactly what happened after that. I guess I panicked. There was blood all over. I didn't know what to do, I didn't know how to help her. I finally remember running into the hotel. By the time I got back outside the police were already there. Then the ambulance came. The rest of it's all kind of a blur. I just stood there and watched it all happen like it was a nightmare. Then the cops asked me if I'd seen the gunman and that other people thought they saw this guy Janson running away."

"And you never told anyone it was a suicide?"

"Everyone assumed it was Janson. By the time I realized that assumption—well, I just let them keep believing it. And later, when I told Beverly, she told me to keep my mouth shut about what really happened. She thought it was better for Laura's memory if she died tragically at the hands of an obsessed fan instead of people finding out it was a suicide. I wasn't sure what to do. I just did what Beverly told me to do. I've always done what Beverly told me to do. I never planned for it to turn out the way it did. It just happened."

"What happened to the gun Laura shot herself with?"

"I took it."

"You took it?"

"I don't really remember doing it. Like I said, I don't remember much about what happened afterward. But later I found it in my pocket. I must have picked it up in my confusion and panic. When I realized what it was, I threw the gun into the East River."

"So Laura's death wouldn't look like a suicide?"

"Yes."

"What about Janson?" I asked. "You knew he didn't do it. Were you going to let him take the fall for it?"

"It never got to that point. Janson killed himself in that hotel room, and so it just seemed easier to let everything play out the way it was going. Beverly insisted it was all for the best. Everyone believed the legend, she said. And I guess the legend was much nicer than the truth. Hell, after a while, I even began to believe it myself. All of this happened such a long time ago. We didn't hurt anybody. And no one ever found out the truth."

"Until Abbie showed up one day and started asking questions?"

"Yes."

"She figured out some of it. That's when she came to you, and you panicked. So you came up with this celebrity serial killer connection. You gave her the list of the four other celebrity deaths in hopes that would take her in the wrong direction on Laura. You knew there was a link between those four other deaths because you were in the Sign of the Z, and Sign of the Z killed them. I'm pretty sure Zorn killed Deborah Ditmar himself. But who did the killings after Ditmar. Bobby Mesa?"

Holloway nodded.

"Zorn killed the first one. The Ditmar woman. He told me about it on the ranch, bragging about how it was just the first blow in this war he was going to wage against the evils of Hollywood and all the rich and famous people there—just like Charles Manson had done with Sharon Tate back in the '60s. It scared the hell out of me. That's the reason I ran away from the ranch. And I took Laura with me."

"What about the other three killings?"

"That was Mesa. He had this crazy idea of carrying out Zorn's mission after Zorn was executed. Mesa said it came to him when he read about Zorn dying in the gas chamber that this would be a fitting memorial to him. They were all so scary. I still can't believe I ever got mixed up with them in the first place."

"But you left Sign of the Z years before those last three murders in 1988 and 1989, after the Zorn execution. So how did you find out that it was Mesa who had killed Fairmont, Lee, and Carson? And why he did it?"

"Mesa came to me one day. After he'd been on the run for years. Showed up right here in New York City. Said he had been hiding ever since the others got killed or nabbed after the botched store holdup. He told me about the three new celebrity killings. He said he did them. He was proud of them. Mesa said he wanted to make some kind of violent statement on behalf of the Sign of the Z and his hero Russell Zorn."

I told Holloway about the astrology clues left at each of the murders. He said he knew about that.

"Mesa boasted to me about leaving the clues; he said one day he planned to reveal to the world what he'd done. But not until he killed more. He wanted me to help him. I saw how crazy he was, how crazy that whole cult had been. So I put him up at a hotel near here. Then I made an anonymous phone call to police and told them where he was. They were after him for the holdup killings. No one knew anything about the other deaths. And, after he died in prison, I was the only person left who knew what he had done."

"What did Mesa say about Laura?"

"He thought it was hilarious that Laura—or Clarissa as he knew her—had become such a big movie star and that she'd wound up being killed. He said it was what she deserved for selling out to the establishment. He said he would have killed her himself if he'd had the chance, but she died before he started on his mission for Zorn. He said it was good that she died just like the other four celebrities had."

"So when Abbie started asking questions about Laura's death, you tried to divert her by giving enough information to link the four celebrity deaths to Laura's. A way to think that Laura died at the hands of a crazy cult. And to make sure that no one found out the truth—that Laura killed herself. But eventually Abbie figured out what was real and what wasn't about Laura. I think in the end she knew everything. She knew that Laura was a suicide, not a murder. And she was going to put that on the air."

He nodded. "That's what she told me."

"How did she find out?"

"I have no idea."

I did. I was pretty sure it came from Thomas Rizzo Sr. I didn't know how Rizzo found out the truth, but he must have known. Probably from Valentine and Sherry, who were there that night when it all happened. They all knew. And never told anyone all these years. Then when Rizzo is sick and close to dying, he finds out his son is dating Abbie—who's really his daughter. I talked to that other reporter too, Abbie Kincaid, Rizzo had said to me at the hospital. He told her about Laura's suicide and that Janson couldn't have killed her. That was Abbie's secret source for the story. But then Rizzo told Abbie something even more startling: that she was Laura's secret daughter. And he was her father.

"You met her that last night at the Regent, didn't you?" I said to Holloway.

"I begged her not to run the story. I said it would ruin me and Beverly once people knew we'd made up the whole story about the murder."

"What did she say?"

"That it was time for the truth to come out."

"So you killed Abbie?"

"No," he said, shaking his vehemently from side to side. "I told you, I didn't kill her . . . I didn't kill anyone . . . I couldn't kill anyone. Look at me. Do I really seem like a murderer to you?"

The damn thing was I believed him. He wasn't a murderer. He didn't have the guts to kill anybody thirty years ago, and he didn't now either. He was a weasel and a liar and an operator and not a very admirable human being. But he wasn't a killer.

"Did you tell anybody else that Abbie was going to reveal all this on her television show?"

"Just one person."

"Who?"

I already knew the answer, of course.

"I told Beverly," he said.

CHAPTER 48

BEVERLY Makofsky—now Beverly Richmond—had even more to lose than Holloway if Abbie's story had come out.

She had a penthouse apartment on Fifth Avenue, a summer place in the Hamptons, she traveled around the world, and she served on the boards of several museums and charitable organizations. Her entire life had been built upon the legend of her dead daughter. Which turned out now to be a lie. If Abbie had ever made that public, her entire life would fall apart. She couldn't stand that, not with her self-inflated ego. There was only one way to stop it. By killing Abbie before she could put it on the air.

"That's absolutely ridiculous," she said as I laid it out for her in the living room of her apartment. The lights of the Manhattan skyline twinkled from a picture window behind her. It was late, almost 10 p.m. I'd tried to reach her all day after my meeting with Holloway, but she was unavailable. Meetings, a charity dinner—she lived a busy life. Finally, I was just about ready to leave the office and go home when I tried to call her one more time. This time she was there. I told her I needed to see her right away. Now here I was sitting across from the woman I believed had murdered Abbie in order to keep her own secrets buried.

"Did Holloway tell you at some point that Abbie had found out about your daughter's suicide?"

"You know he did."

"What was your reaction?"

"I was upset."

"How upset?"

"I was upset because this—the circumstances of Laura's death and her last days—was something we'd tried to keep out of the public eye for a very long time. I didn't want this kind of a scandal to become my daughter's legacy. People loved her, they idolized her—I didn't want that to change. I mean I was out on that Laura Marlowe cruise ship when my daughter died. I was trying to help her career, to promote her image at the very moment she killed herself. All I cared about was Laura. I flew back right away and made sure Edward didn't tell anyone the real story of what happened. Especially after that crazy Janson guy killed himself. Why not just let people continue to think he did it?"

"Is that why her body was cremated so quickly?"

She nodded.

"I didn't want to take any chances that there might be more of an investigation into her death. Nothing that might reveal it was a suicide. I said it was because I didn't want any kind of public spectacle over her body. And no one ever questioned that. I just tried to protect her memory. Is that such a terrible thing for a mother to do?"

"I don't think Laura's memory was all you were worried about. I think you were worried about what it meant for you. This was never about Laura. It was always about you. You got rich off of your daughter's memory. So did Holloway. In the end, her suicide worked out really well for both of you. Except your daughter was dead. Doesn't that ever bother you just a little bit?"

She stood up. I thought for a second that she might physically attack me. But she walked out of the room instead. I sat there wondering what to do next. A few minutes later, she returned with a piece of paper in her hand. The paper looked very old and yellowed by age. She handed it to me.

It was from Laura. A suicide note.

Dear Mother,

If you are reading this, then I finally got the courage to do what I've been wanting to do every day for as long as I can remember. Maybe if you were here, I wouldn't be able to do this. But the fact that you're so far away right now . . . well, it just seems like saying goodbye to everyone this way was meant to be.

I know now there is no hope for me anymore. I thought for a few brief, fleeting moments not so long ago that maybe I still had a chance at living a life that I wanted. Those were the moments that I held my newborn baby daughter in my arms. But now even that momentary happiness has been taken from me.

My baby is my only comfort, my only solace, as I prepare to leave this world. Wherever she is, I pray she will get a chance to live the kind of life that I never did. That she will be loved and nurtured and be allowed to grow into the kind of person she wants to be. I want her to have everything I never did. I want her to be happy.

I'm not blaming you completely for what I'm about to do, Mother. I'm not blaming Eddie either or anyone else. I've always been able to walk away. I've had the power to make my own decisions. I realize that now. It's just that I never made any decisions. I've always allowed other people to decide for me. Now I'm making this one last decision for myself.

I'm just too tired to go on. I want it all to end. I want to go to sleep and never wake up. Or—when I do wake up—I want to be in a better place, somewhere far, far away. I know I'm living the life you always wanted for me. The problem is I never wanted it. Or, if I ever did, I don't anymore. Be careful what you wish for, they always say, because the wish might just come true. It did for me, and now I simply can't bear it for another day. I'm sorry if I let you down. I'm sorry about everything.

Goodbye,

Laura

"Eddie found this in Laura's hotel room after the shooting," she said. "I suppose I should have given it to the police and made it public. But, like Eddie told you, it just seemed easier to go with the flow after everyone assumed it was that stalker who did it. I'm sure I would have come forward and told the truth if he'd been arrested. But once he killed himself, it didn't seem so important anymore. Laura was being idolized as this heroic star cut down in the prime of her life. All that would have ended if the truth came out. She would have become an object of pity and maybe even ridicule. I didn't want that for her."

"For her or for you?"

"You don't believe me, do you?"

"Which part?"

"That I did all this for Laura?"

I shrugged. "You never seemed to care that much for her before. You weren't much of a mother."

"Do you think I don't know that? Do you think I don't still regret after thirty years that I wasn't there with my daughter at the end? That maybe if I'd been there she wouldn't have done it? I was always at Laura's side until that last cruise. I thought it was important at the time because of Laura's fashion line. But now I would give anything to go back in time and not have been on that boat so far away from my daughter.

"And there probably hasn't been a single day that's gone by when I haven't taken out this letter and read it, wishing I could go back and do it all over again. That's why I've kept it all these years. I wanted to remind myself always of what had happened. I guess I always knew this day would come. I could put it off, but sooner or later I was going to have to deal with the past. I'm ready for that now."

She handed Laura's suicide note back to me.

"I want you to print this," she said.

"In the *Daily News*?"

"Yes. You're going to write a story about this anyway. You're going to tell the world how my daughter really died. They might as well have the entire story. It's time for the whole truth to come out. It's been buried for too many years. You can quote me on that, if you want. It doesn't matter anymore. All that matters is that Laura is dead. She's been dead for thirty years, and nothing's ever going to change that. But I can do this one last thing for her. I can tell the world what really happened to her."

Then she began to cry.

It was a helluva performance, but I wasn't 100 percent sure I was buying it. This woman had never cared about her daughter before. She'd used her daughter all her life to attain her own goals. I figured she was still doing it one last time.

She knew I was going to write this article about Laura's death . . . one way or another. She couldn't stop that. So she was going to turn it around and make it work for her. Maybe even cash in on it one more time. Thirty years ago, she'd been afraid that if the public knew that Laura killed herself after having a mobster's baby her daughter's memory would have been tarnished forever. But it was a different time now, and a different set of rules. A scandal like that about a celebrity—whether dead or alive—could be good. There was no such thing as bad publicity anymore. This would pique public interest in her long-dead daughter all over again. Her mother could read that letter on *The View* and *Dr. Phil.* Even in death, Laura could never be free of her.

There was nothing I could do about this, of course.

But I needed to find out about Abbie.

"Did you go to see Abbie Kincaid on the night she died at the Regent Hotel?" I asked.

"Yes," she said.

They were all there that night. Laura's mother. Holloway. Abbie's ex-husband. Abbie was seeing everybody connected with this case and with her own life too at the same spot where Laura Marlowe had died three decades ago. Why? Was she seeking some kind of closure? Maybe that was it. She'd just discovered the truth about Laura and about herself too and she was bringing it all together at the place where Laura died. She was going to tell the whole story on her next TV show, and this was all part of it. Except someone killed her first.

"She told it all to me, just like the way you did earlier," Beverly Richmond said. "About the suicide, the affair with Rizzo, and the baby we put up for adoption. I was stunned, but there was nothing I could do about it. I think there was almost a sense of relief on my part that all the years of lying and hiding the truth were finally over. She asked me if I would come on her next show for an interview. I said I would. We talked some more. And then I left."

"What time was that?"

"About seven thirty."

"Can you prove it?"

"I'm not sure what you mean. But I was at a fundraiser for the Metropolitan Museum that began at eight. I can give you a list of people who saw me there. Does that help at all?"

Abbie had been alive at 8. She called down for room service after that. She was killed sometime between 10 and midnight. Of course, Beverly could have gone back for a second time and done it, I suppose. But I didn't think that was what happened anymore. Just talking to her, I realized that wasn't her style. The only person she'd ever killed was her own daughter. Maybe not literally killed her, but she was the reason Laura wound up in that alley outside the Regent and pulled the trigger of the gun to her head. The law couldn't do anything about that, of course. Still, the woman would have to answer to a higher authority someday.

There was one more thing though.

Something I was pretty sure she still didn't know.

She said Abbie had told her everything, the same way I had—about the suicide, the affair with Rizzo, and putting the baby they had up for adoption. But I'd left one thing out. I realized now Abbie must have too. She'd asked Beverly to be on her next show. That's when she was going to spring it on her. It would have been a complete surprise. The ultimate confrontational moment in reality TV.

"When you met Abbie," I asked, "was there anything about her that seemed familiar to you?"

"What do you mean?"

"Did she remind you of anybody?"

"She was very beautiful."

"Abbie should have been beautiful. Her mother was beautiful too."

She looked confused.

"After you gave up Laura's baby for adoption, it wound up with a family in Wisconsin. A plain-looking couple, nothing like Laura, but they were good parents. Their names were Ronald and Elizabeth Kincaid."

She still didn't get it.

"Abbie was your granddaughter," I said.

I left her like that. I don't know what happened afterward. Maybe she was overcome by grief as she realized that her last living link to her daughter—her own granddaughter—was dead now too. More likely, she was already figuring out how to make it work for her. Abbie was her granddaughter. Abbie was famous too. Not as famous as Laura had been, but maybe she would be before it was all over. She died tragically trying to unravel the mysteries of her movie star mother's legend. I could already imagine the wheels turning in Beverly's head as she tried to figure out all the ways she could make money off of this death too.

By the time I walked out the door her building, it was nearly 11 p.m. I stood there for a few minutes trying to figure out what to do next. I'd found out a lot of things, including the truth about what happened to Laura Marlowe. But the story wasn't over yet. I still didn't know who killed Abbie. If Bill Remesch, Edward Holloway, or Beverly Makofsky weren't Abbie's killer, then who was? I was at a dead end. I was all out of suspects.

Except I'd forgotten about one.

"You're never going to write this story," a voice said from behind me.

I turned around.

It was Tommy Rizzo Jr.

He had that same look of fury on his face as he did that first time I'd seen him at Abbie's studio.

Only this time he was holding a gun.

PART SIX

ONCE UPON A TIME FOREVER

CHAPTER 49

ABBIE always thought you were harmless," I said.

"Everyone thinks I'm harmless."

"She was your sister."

"I know."

"Did you know she was your sister when you killed her?"

"That's why I killed her."

There was no one around us. It was late, and the street on Fifth Avenue outside the apartment house of Laura's mother was pretty much empty. Rizzo moved close to me and I felt the barrel of the gun in my side. He laid a newspaper over it so that no one could see what was going on even if someone did pass by us. He told me to start walking. I couldn't think of anything else to do, so I did.

"Why?" I asked him as we moved south down Fifth Avenue. "You at least owe me an explanation."

"Do you have any idea what it's like being Thomas Rizzo's son? All my life, I tried to distance myself from his world. But it never did any good. Everybody still thought of me as the mobster's kid. No matter what I did, that label was always with me. And, by not following him into the family business, if you want to call it that, I alienated myself from him. I was still his son. But that was it. There was no love there, no respect—he had disdain for me and everything I tried to do. I was a joke to everybody.

"I tried, I really tried to do something to impress him. But everything always went wrong. I went to a good college. I made the Dean's List. Later, I found out I got accepted at the school because my father had paid off people on the admissions board. He paid off professors too; that's why I got such good grades. He wanted everyone to think I was this great scholar. Even my real estate business was built on his money. He never let me forget any of that. My son is so noble, he used to say—he doesn't want to dirty his hands in my business—but he'll take my money. I just wanted to do something right once in my life. To make him proud of me.

"That's why I started seeing Abbie. My father seemed fascinated with her. He was always talking about this beautiful and talented woman on TV. If I had someone like that as my girlfriend, I thought maybe he would see me in a different way. Maybe he'd finally respect me. So I figured out a way to meet her, and we hit it off pretty well at the beginning. We went out on a few dates, and she seemed to like me. But then it all ended. Abbie broke it off. She said I was a nice guy, but she couldn't see me anymore. I didn't understand what had happened to change her so much overnight."

It wasn't hard to figure out what had happened. Thomas Rizzo Sr. had told her the truth. Rizzo was her real father. That meant Tommy Jr. was her half-brother. She didn't tell him that right away, of course. She was probably saving it for her show. But she knew she couldn't keep seeing him anymore. So she made up some excuse to break up with him.

"My father finally told me," Rizzo said. "I'd gone to him out of desperation and said I didn't understand why Abbie had stopped seeing me. He just started to laugh. He was laughing at me. He told me I couldn't do anything right. Of all the women in the world, I fell head over heels in love with my own sister, he said. He said I'd always been a loser. That he was embarrassed to have someone like me as his son.

"He said as soon as he found out I was seeing Abbie, he reached out to her and told her the truth. He even asked me if I had slept with her, can you believe that? I said no, we hadn't gotten to that point in the relationship yet. He seemed very relieved about that. He said he was just glad he found out in time so he could put a stop to it.

"He told me Abbie was the kind of child that should have been his. That she was smart and tough and he could see her mother in her. He told me he should have stayed with Laura Marlowe, but he didn't because of me. He said he'd given up the love of his life out of some stupid feeling of loyalty and duty to his family. Now his family was Abbie, he said. He was going to make her an even bigger star than she was now, even bigger than her mother had been. He said she was everything that I wasn't. And here I was mooning over her pathetically like some lovesick puppy. All the anger, all the frustration that had been building between us over the years seemed to come bursting out at that moment.

"Then Abbie called and said she was at the hotel. She said she was going to put the whole thing on the air. She wanted me to come on the show for an interview too. I didn't know what to do. All I kept thinking about was that I couldn't let our relationship become public knowledge. If people knew I'd fallen in love with my own sister, I would be a laughingstock for the rest of my life. Not just with my father. With the whole world. I just couldn't live with that kind of humiliation.

"I didn't mean to kill her. I just wanted to scare her. I begged her not to do this. But she laughed. She laughed at me, the same way my father had laughed at me. The way people have always laughed at me. Something just snapped inside of me. I pointed the gun at her. She was scared now, and I liked that. It made me feel good that she was afraid of me. She asked me to put the gun down. She promised not to run the story. But I didn't believe her. I knew she would. I knew her well enough to know that she could never not go through with a story that good. That's when I killed her."

Rizzo told me to stop walking, that we were where we were going. I looked around. We were standing in front of the Regent Hotel, which was only a few blocks from Beverly Richmond's building. Laura Marlowe had died at this hotel. So did her daughter Abbie. I had a pretty good idea what Rizzo had in mind next.

"You don't have to do this," I said.

"I'm afraid I do. Once I found out you'd been to see my father, I realized it was just a matter of time until you'd figured it all out. Now that you know, you have to die too. Just like Abbie. I couldn't let her run this story, and I can't let you do it either."

"Why here?" I asked, stalling for time in hope someone would see him holding the gun on me and call the cops.

"It provides a nice sense of closure. Besides, people will say it had something to do with Laura Marlowe's death and Abbie's. You'll be part of the legend. The reporter who died trying to solve the mystery. There's sort of a Bermuda Triangle aspect to the whole thing, don't you think? They'll be talking about you for years. Laura Marlowe, Abbie Kincaid, and Gil Malloy. But no one will ever link it to me."

He motioned for me to walk down the alley next to the Regent. The same alley where Laura had died. We went about thirty feet into the alley. Now, even if someone passed by, there was no way anyone could see us. Just to make sure, he had me walk down some steps toward a basement door. We were completely out of sight now.

"What about Remesch?" I asked him. "How did all that evidence of Abbie's murder wind up in his place in Wisconsin? Did you set him up?"

"I learned from the best," he smiled. "My father. It wasn't hard to fly up there, plant the gun, and then wait for the law to show up.

It gave me a real sense of accomplishment when he was arrested for the murder."

He wanted to tell the story. He wanted someone to listen to him. Even if it was someone who would be dead in a few minutes. All his life no one had listened to him. I heard a police siren in the distance. For a second, it gave me a surge of hope. But then it quickly passed. There was no other sound. We were alone, and I needed a miracle if I was ever going to get out of this alive. I didn't want to become part of the Laura Marlowe legend. This wasn't the way it was supposed to be for me.

"Tommy, you're not really a killer," I said.

"The thing is I kind of liked it," he smiled. "All those years growing up with my father, I guess I always wondered what it was like to kill someone. Now I know. It gave me a feeling of power that I never had before. My father's dying, and I will get everything from him. The money, the business, and the power—if I want it. I never thought I did. But now I realize that everything's working out perfectly for me. I'm not going to be a joke anymore. I'm going to be the man, just like my father. Killing Abbie was the best thing I ever did. Now there's just this one more little thing I have to finish."

He pointed the gun at my chest.

"Drop the weapon," a voice said.

I looked up and saw him standing there at the top of the stairs.

I'd been hoping for a miracle.

Waiting for someone to show up and rescue me.

This wasn't the person I expected.

But I was sure glad to see him.

"Just put the gun down now, Tommy," Marlboro Man said, except he wasn't smoking a cigarette this time. He was all business. "I've known you for a long time, and I'm trying to give you a break. But you're making it damn hard for me. You screwed up, kid. You screwed up real bad."

"This has nothing to do with you," Rizzo said.

He still had the gun pointed at me.

"Yes, it does."

"Why are you here anyway?"

"Your father sent me."

"To do what?"

"Clean up your mess, kid. He's always cleaning up your messes. Now I gotta do it one more time."

"You're not going to shoot me. I'm Thomas Rizzo's son."

"Abbie was his daughter."

"I know, but . . ."

"He's very upset about her death."

"The old man is dying. He'll be gone soon. I'll take over everything then. I'll be your boss. We can make a deal."

"No deal, kid."

"All we have to do is get rid of this reporter. Then no one will ever know. I'll have my father's money, my father's power. I'll be the man."

"Drop the gun, Tommy."

Suddenly, Rizzo whirled around and started firing.

I dived for cover behind a trash canister just as the first shots rang out.

It was really no contest. Rizzo was scared; he'd never been in a spot like this before. But not Marlboro Man. He wasn't scared at all. This was his profession.

He killed Tommy Rizzo with a single shot to the head.

CHAPTER 50

HIS name is James Kilgore," I said.

"Who?" Dr. Barbara Landis asked.

"The Marlboro Man."

"How did you find that out?"

"I asked him."

"After he shot Tommy Rizzo to death?"

"Yes, I just thought it was important to know."

Dr. Landis was the psychiatrist I'd seen in the past to help me deal with my anxiety attacks and the underlying problems in my life—as she put it—that caused me to have the anxiety. I hadn't been to see her in weeks. Well, actually it was more like months. I figured she'd be upset about my long absence. Maybe yell at me or lecture me for not keeping up with my treatment. But she just started talking with me as if we'd left off at a previous session the day before.

"What else did you say to this Kilgore person?"

"I asked him why he did it. He said Thomas Rizzo's last wish, the one thing he wanted to happen before he died, was to find out who murdered his daughter, Abbie, and kill them. So that's what Kilgore did."

"Even if it turned out to be Rizzo's own son?"

"I think maybe Rizzo knew it was going to turn out that way, but he kept hoping against hope he was wrong. Anyway, Kilgore followed me on the theory that I might eventually lead him to the killer. I never had a clue he was right there behind me. Unlike me, he really knew how to follow somebody. Once he heard Tommy's confession to me, that was all he needed. I don't know if he faced any kind of a moral dilemma over killing his boss's son. I don't think he did. I think he had his orders, and he followed them. I understand that. I respect that."

"You respect the principles of a man who probably has killed a great number of people?"

"Yes."

"More than you respect the principles of Edward Holloway or Laura's mother—neither of whom, as it turned out, ever killed anybody?"

"I have a very complicated set of principles," I said.

———

After Kilgore shot Tommy Rizzo that night outside the Regent, I wasn't sure what he was going to do next. The easy thing would have been to kill me too. That way there was no witness to tie him to the crime. I had no doubt he would have done that if Rizzo had ordered it. But that wasn't part of the deal.

He'd asked me—not told me—if I would leave him out of it when the cops came and got my story. If I would tell them I'd never seen the shooter before.

"And that's what you did?" Dr. Landis asked.

"Yes, I said Rizzo had confessed Abbie's killing to me. I said someone shot him afterward and then fled. I said I had no idea who that was. Just to throw the police off the trail a little more, I speculated that it was one of Thomas Rizzo's mob rivals who took out his anger on Rizzo's son. I said I assumed it had nothing to do with the Abbie or Laura Marlowe stories. The cops weren't that upset. They had my testimony about Rizzo's confession, which was enough. Plus more evidence they found once they went back and rechecked everything about Tommy and his movements that night. Anyway, they'd never have to prove it in a court of law since Rizzo was dead. They could close the books on Abbie's murder. Remesch was released from prison, and everybody's going to live happily ever after."

"And you never wrote about Kilgore or Thomas Rizzo Sr.'s role in saving your life in any of your stories?"

"No."

"Or told anyone about this—even your editor at the paper?"

I shook my head no.

"So why are you telling me now?"

"I have to talk to someone about it."

"Still there must be other people you know . . ."

"Someone I could trust."

"Are you saying that I'm the only person in your life right now that you feel you can completely trust?"

"Yeah, whatever . . ."

———

I told her about all the personal stuff that had been going on with me since my last visit there. About Susan suddenly getting married to someone else. About Abbie Kincaid and the short time we'd spent together before she was killed. And about my just-ended relationship with Sherry DeConde.

"Three relationship crises like that is a very traumatic series of events to go through," Landis said when I finished.

"Tell me about it."

"How are you handling the shock of your wife's remarriage?"

"I'm fine with it."

"No, you're not."

"You're right, I'm not."

"Sometimes things change and we just have to move on with our lives."

"That's what Susan said too."

"We've talked about your marriage in the past. You seem to have built that up as a magical time—a Camelot or a utopia—where everything was perfect. But you and I know that wasn't true. There were always problems in your marriage, and you told me that a number of times. And your wife didn't just walk away from the marriage without warning or provocation. It was the culmination of a series of crises—including some infidelity on your part—that you made no effort to deal with at the time."

I sighed. This damn woman knew me too well.

"Look, I know the marriage wasn't perfect," I said. "I know a lot of that was my fault too. But I always assumed—I mean I never really doubted until now—that one day Susan and I would get back together again. In the end, despite everything bad that had happened between us, she would come back to me. That was my dream. So much for that dream, huh?"

"It might be beneficial for you to seek out a new relationship at this point," Landis said. "To move on the same way she has moved on."

"I'm feeling a little pessimistic about me and the dating scene these days."

"Based on what happened between you and the DeConde woman?"

"Uh-huh."

"Perhaps if you went back and gave her another chance . . ."

"Sherry DeConde is dead to me," I said.

She asked me about working on the Laura Marlowe story. What my reaction had been when I discovered that Laura had killed herself, not been murdered by anyone. I told Landis the truth. I was shocked, just like everyone else. But I also felt an almost over-whelming sense of grief and loss for the poor woman.

"Why was she so important to you?" Landis asked.

"I'm not sure. I mean she's been dead for thirty years, but she just felt so real to me. The more I found out about Laura Marlowe, the more fascinated I became with her. I felt her pain, I felt her des-peration, I felt her loneliness. She was America's sweetheart, and she was supposed to be living this fairy-tale life. Except her life was more like a Greek tragedy. But she still clung to the hope that she could somehow find the fairy tale. That's why she tried everything from Sign of the Z to Jackie Sinclair's X-rated movies to the affair with Thomas Rizzo. And then, when she realized the fairy tale was never going to come true, she killed herself. All of it—her entire life, then her death—was so sad."

"It sounds like you relate to her on some level—that you've experienced some of those same types of feeling that she did."

"Well, I'm not going to kill myself, if that's what you're worried about."

"But you dream about a fairy-tale outcome—for your mar-riage, for your entire life—that you're terrified will never happen for you."

"I think we all dream about that," I said. "But that's all it is. Just a fairy tale. For me. For Laura Marlowe. For everyone. Fairy tales don't come true."

It was toward the end of the session when Landis finally brought up my long absence from the sessions with her. She asked if I planned to make another appointment soon.

"Well, that depends," I said.

"Depends on what?"

"Do you think you can cure me, doc?"

"I think we can continue to make progress with the issues in your life."

"C'mon, that's psych-speak."

"I can't guarantee a cure for all your problems."

"I'd really like to get cured."

"Let's just be satisfied with making progress at the moment."

"Do you guys ever actually cure anybody?"

She smiled.

"Okay, so am I making progress?"

"Do you remember when you first came to me? I told you that one of the biggest problems you had was that you measured yourself as a person by your success as a newspaper reporter. When you were on Page One, you felt good about yourself. When your reporting career wasn't doing well, you were unhappy with your entire life. As I recall, you even stopped seeing me at one point back then when you were riding high on Page One. Told me you didn't need me anymore. And yet here you are back in my office again. Even though you're all over the front page and a big media star right now. Despite all that success and adulation, you sought me out for some answers. You didn't bury your problems in the persona of star reporter Gil Malloy. You made a real attempt to deal with them, to confront them, as Gil Malloy the real person. Do you understand what that means?"

I thought about it for a second.

"That we're making progress?" I asked.

"We're making progress," Landis said.

CHAPTER 51

I T was nearly a week after the Rizzo shooting, and I'd written a number of front page articles. About Laura's suicide. About how Abbie was really Laura and Rizzo's daughter. About how Tommy Rizzo Jr. killed Abbie when he found out she was going to talk about that on her TV show. About the astrological links between the four other celebrity killings from the 1980s that police now believed had all been carried out by the Sign of the Z cult.

And, of course, I wrote about witnessing the death of Tommy Rizzo Jr. in the same alley where Laura had died thirty years earlier. This was the biggest story of my life. Hell, it was a whole series of the biggest stories I'd ever done. One Gil Malloy exclusive after another. It was like I hit the trifecta of journalism.

Stacy had a few questions and concerns about the way it all played out.

She complained I didn't keep her in the loop all the time while I was working on the story, which was true.

She complained the Rizzo killing didn't turn out to be a *Daily News* exclusive because all the media had showed up at the scene along with the police, which was inevitable.

And she even complained that there weren't enough good multimedia elements to go along with my story, which was ridiculous.

"Gee," I told her, "if I'd known you needed more video, I could have just taken out my iPhone and shot some footage of Rizzo pointing the gun at me. Sorry about that, Stacy. But, in my defense, I would like to point out that I was a little bit busy at the time worrying about *HOW TO SAVE MY LIFE!*"

Nevertheless, she was more than happy to share in my success and, of course, make sure she got some of the credit.

On the day after it all broke on Page One of the *Daily News*, Stacy gathered the staff into the middle of the newsroom.

"We've been working on this Laura Marlowe and Abbie Kincaid story for weeks," Stacy said to everyone with one arm around me and the other holding up a copy of Page One. "We never gave up. We never quit. We exhibited the kind of doggedness and dedication that this newspaper is famous for. We got the story that no one else could ever get. We got the story that everyone else wanted."

Informal counts later showed that Stacy used the word "we" at least eighteen times during the speech.

When it was over, I just smiled and whispered something in her ear.

"What did you say anyway?" someone asked me afterward.

"I told Stacy I could have never done it without her," I said.

———

Meanwhile, the fallout continued from all the revelations that had come out.

Thomas Rizzo died a few days after his son. There was a battle going on for control of the mob between Rizzo's forces and some other family from Queens. No one was sure how it was going to turn out, but there would be a lot of blood spilled before it was settled. I hoped it worked out okay for James Kilgore. I tend to get sentimental about people who've saved my life.

Beverly and Holloway were in negotiations for a new TV movie about Laura's life and death. As I'd predicted, the revelations about her suicide didn't hurt the image—they'd put her back in the public spotlight more than ever before. The executive producer of the new movie was going to be Gary Lang, the producer of Abbie's TV show. Beautiful, I thought to myself. He and Holloway and Beverly deserve each other. Beverly was also trying to cut herself in for a piece of Rizzo's estate. Since Tommy Jr. died, there were no other clear-cut heirs. Beverly argued that some of it should go to her because she was the grandmother of Rizzo's daughter—which, of course, had turned out to be Abbie. It was an interesting legal point that some experts predicted would take years for the courts to settle. I figured Beverly would figure out a way to win. She always did.

Bill Remesch was released from prison after it became clear Tommy Rizzo had killed Abbie. He didn't go right back to Wisconsin though. He hung around New York for a while, appearing on TV and radio talk shows—talking about Abbie and Laura Marlowe and his connection to the case. It was his fifteen minutes of fame, and he was enjoying every minute of it. He told me it was great publicity for his auto repair business back in Milwaukee. Hell, he might have a chain of them throughout the Midwest by the time he was finished.

Even Jackie Sinclair got in on the act. She said she was writing a book about her life in Hollywood—including the time with Laura Marlowe and running the escort agency. She promised to name names and expose secrets. She said it would blow the lid off of Hollywood.

I shook my head.

Everybody was still making money off of Laura Marlowe, just the way they did when she was alive.

On another front, authorities had been able to determine with a pretty high degree of certainty that the long-forgotten Sign of the

Z cult was indeed responsible for four celebrity deaths—Deborah Ditmar, Stephanie Lee, Susan Fairmont, and Cheryl Carson.

Going back over all four cold cases with a fresh look, police and other law enforcement officials discovered more astrological references linked to each of the killings. Plus, Bobby Mesa had apparently bragged to another inmate before his death that Sign of the Z left their calling card at a series of celebrity murders—and compared it to the way Charles Manson and his followers killed Sharon Tate. This, along with Holloway's account of what Mesa told him, pretty much closed the book on these cases.

There was some concern that there might other celebrity deaths out there too attributable to Sign of the Z—but a search of open case files turned up no similarities. From what Mesa had told Holloway, he planned to commit more murders—but fortunately was taken into custody before he could continue his bizarre killing spree to honor the memory of Russell Zorn.

It was amazing that all of this—the discovery of the celebrity serial killings, the truth about Laura's death, Abbie Kincaid's murder, all the things about Thomas Rizzo and the death of his son—resulted from Abbie trying to do a story about what really happened to Laura Marlowe. The woman who turned out to be Abbie's biological mother. That had set a lot of things in motion, as buried secrets from the past came to the surface and more people wound up dead. It was a helluva story, and I was glad I'd been able to finish it for Abbie.

Yep, after all this time, Laura Marlowe was big news again.

———

I heard from a lot of people. Old friends. Other reporters. TV, magazines, websites. There were plenty of TV appearances, both local and national. The best was Abbie's old show, *The Prime Time Files*. I got to go on that and do the story Abbie would have broken if she'd lived. It even gave me a chance to hang out again with my old pal Lang—who was very nice to me this time. He actually asked me about moving over to network television as an on-air reporter. It made me remember that day Abbie told me she thought I should try TV. Funny how things worked out. But I doubt that I will ever do that. I don't ever want to stop being a newspaper reporter. There's just something pure and noble and unique about the newspaper business for me. God help me, I still love it.

"Can I have your autograph?" Jeff Aronson asked after I hung up from another in a long series of complimentary phone calls.

"This is all pretty amazing, isn't it?" I said.

"I've never seen anyone have as many ups and downs in their career as you. I remember back when you were on the verge of getting fired by this paper. Now you're getting interviewed by *People* magazine and television crews."

"I am pretty much the biggest media star in town right now!" I said.

"And modest too," he smiled.

"Yes, modesty is one of my best qualities, of which I have many."

———

I tried to answer pretty much everyone who reached out to me in the aftermath of the story.

Except one.

Sherry DeConde.

After my article wrapping up the Laura Marlowe death appeared, she left me a message on my voicemail.

The message said: "Yes, I knew about Laura's suicide. I knew about Rizzo. I knew about everything that happened. I know you probably hate me. I know you probably never want to talk to me again. But I want to talk to you. I want to try and explain. I just want to see you again. I miss you, Gil."

She said she was back at work now. Back in the West Village townhouse. She left numbers for both places, but I didn't call her.

A few days later, I got an email from Sherry that said: "I warned you at the beginning not to get involved with me. I never wanted to hurt you. When we did start seeing each other, I thought maybe I could somehow put my past behind me. But I know now that can never happen. You wanted the truth from me. I couldn't give you that. I'm sorry. I know saying that can never undo the damage that I've done, but I am truly sorry for everything."

I ignored that too. I had trusted Sherry DeConde. And she lied to me. So the hell with her. There were plenty of other women out there for me.

Like Sherry had said, she was too old for me anyway.

CHAPTER 52

'VE thought a lot about the way everything came together at the end. How the truth about Laura Marlowe's life, her death, and all those long-buried secrets about the people around her came bubbling to the surface. Was it just chance? Coincidence? A conflux of random events that set all of these things into motion at the same time?

I'm not so sure it wasn't more than that.

I guess a part of me will always believe there was some kind of karma at work here. That this was always meant to be. That there was a reason for everything. And that fate somehow—like a current moving relentlessly through the eddies of time—had inexorably brought Abbie and Thomas Rizzo and Tommy Jr. and everything else together at the end. I just happened to be there to see it all happen.

The bottom line, though, was the story was finally over now.

I'd solved the mystery of how Laura Marlowe really died. I'd found Abbie's murderer. I'd solved a series of other celebrity cold case killings along the way. I'd accomplished everything I set out to do—and more.

And so, after another ego-inflating day of having people tell me how wonderful and how great a journalist I was, I put everything away in my desk and took the subway home. Back to the empty apartment I'd left that morning. Which was the part of my life that wasn't so wonderful and so great.

Still no wife, no kids, no dog waiting for me when I walked in. But that was okay. I was just fine by myself. I had plenty to keep me occupied through the night.

You see, I was working on a new—and still highly secret—theory of mine. I called it the "two Lois Lanes" theory. Phyllis Coates played Lois in the original black-and-white Superman TV series. Then, when it went to color, she mysteriously became someone in the credits called Noel Neill. Only both Lois Lanes looked, walked, and talked almost exactly alike. I feared something sinister was afoot. I hadn't worked out all the details yet but I suspected aliens from outer space and some kind of body transference might be involved.

I was not quite ready to reveal the details of this to the world yet, but I wondered if it was time to share it with someone else. On a need-to-know basis, of course. But who?

I could call Susan, of course, like I always did when I wanted someone to talk to. Except she was married now. And I wasn't sure how her new husband might feel about her getting calls from her ex-husband. Even for something as important as this.

I considered and rejected a series of other possible people to call until I came back to the one person I'd been thinking about the entire time: Sherry DeConde.

But I couldn't call Sherry because I was mad at her. I was done with her. She had lied to me about Rizzo.

I went into the kitchen, took a beer out of the refrigerator, and walked with it into the living room. I tried to think of any possible innocent reasons Sherry might have had for not telling me the truth about her involvement with Rizzo.

I came up with these possible scenarios:

1. She actually worked for another Thomas Rizzo. It was all a mistake, and this Rizzo was a bank president or a lawyer or someone else that had nothing to do with organized crime.
2. It simply slipped her mind that she had ever worked for and gotten money from Thomas Rizzo. She just forgot to tell me; it wasn't deliberate.
3. She did tell me about Rizzo at some point. But I didn't hear her. I was so intent on jumping her bones that my sexual desires had dulled my reporting instincts—and I missed it.

None of these, of course, seemed very plausible.

But maybe I could give Sherry the benefit of the doubt on this.

I clicked on the TV and began to scroll through the channels, looking for something mindless to watch so I could stop thinking about Sherry DeConde. I eventually settled on a rerun of *Bewitched*. One of the later ones with Dick Sargent playing Samantha's husband, Darrin. Not Dick York, who was the husband in the first several seasons of *Bewitched* episodes, which inspired me to come up with another theory that might or might not be related to the "two Lois Lanes" theory.

There were two actors who played Darrin Stephens in *Bewitched*. They were both named Dick and—again—they both walked, talked, and looked amazingly alike. Even weirder was that they both died in real life only a few years apart from each other. Coincidence or conspiracy?

I pondered that for a while and drank some more beer.

While I was doing that, I also thought more about the Laura Marlowe story. Fragments of it kept running through my head, like they did with any big story when it was over. Only this time I played some of them back in my mind over and over again. I had a nagging feeling that I was still missing something. I went through the chronology again of everything I knew, and—more important—what I still wasn't sure had happened.

Of course, some of these questions would never be completely resolved, but I thought I had come up with some pretty good answers for them. Such as:

Why did Abbie start investigating the Laura Marlowe case in the first place? Why was Tommy Rizzo going out with Abbie at pretty much the same time she started working on the story? Why didn't Thomas Rizzo Sr. step in to end the relationship earlier when he realized his son was unwittingly dating his other child?

I was convinced that Thomas Rizzo had secretly kept tabs on Abbie over the years. I think the connection to his long lost daughter became even more important to him as he realized he was dying. And so he reached out to Abbie directly in some way and made a deathbed confession to her. That's how she got onto the entire Laura Marlowe story.

Tommy had told me in the alley that he pursued Abbie because he wanted to impress his father. "He was always talking about this beautiful and talented woman on TV," Tommy said. Rizzo Sr. was probably doing this even more after he met Abbie in his hospital room. Tommy just didn't know why his father was so fascinated with her until it was too late. When he told his father he had gone out with Abbie and now didn't understand why she'd suddenly broken it off, the result wasn't what he expected. His father wasn't impressed with him for dating Abbie, he ridiculed him. Then Thomas Rizzo told him the truth.

Abbie already knew because of Rizzo, which was why she broke off the relationship with Tommy. She just didn't want to tell him the reason before the TV show. The journalist in her wanted to break it as an exclusive on the air. I could understand that. I was somehow happy that Abbie had found out the truth in time to avoid ever having sex with Tommy. That would have been kinda creepy.

Of course, it might not have all happened exactly that way. Some of the facts and the timing and the details could have been a bit different. But I was pretty sure the scenario must have played out something like that.

So then why wasn't I satisfied with all the answers?

What else was I still missing?

Maybe it was the combination of drinking beer and watching mindless TV shows that did it. People say you can lose brain cells from that sort of thing, but I always thought it made me think clearer. Or maybe the doubts had always been there, percolating in my subconscious—and just waiting for the right moment to burst out into full-blown paranoia.

Whatever the reason, sitting there alone in my apartment, I finally admitted to myself that something had been bothering me ever since I wrote my story about how Laura Marlowe really died that night thirty years ago.

The details of the shooting. I went back and read through them all over again.

Laura Marlowe was shot at 10:15 on the night of July 17, 1985. The first ambulance arrived on the scene within minutes and took her to the hospital. They said her wounds were serious, but they thought they might save her. She arrived at Roosevelt Hospital an hour later at 11:15, where she was pronounced dead.

But why did she die? If the first medical personnel at the scene thought she might survive, then what went wrong? Of course, things like that do happen in ambulances and hospitals. Mistakes are made, misdiagnoses happen—and sometimes people just take a turn for the worse for no specific reason.

But what if something else happened in that ambulance? The ambulance didn't arrive at the hospital until 11:15, a full hour after it left the Regent. Why? The hospital was a short distance away. And Erlich, the first detective on the scene, said the ambulance had already left by the time he got there. It should have been a much shorter ride to the hospital even in the worst of traffic—and it was late enough that the streets should have been fairly empty. So what happened during that unaccounted for time?

I'd discovered a lot of people who had possible motives for killing Laura thirty years ago while I was doing the story. I'd eliminated them all one by one—and then forgot about it after I found out she'd shot herself. But what if one of them wanted to make sure she was dead? What if they realized she might live through the suicide attempt, and made sure that didn't happen? It was the perfect cover for a murder. She was already fighting for her life. All they had to do was help it along somewhere along the line.

But how? And who?

Not Holloway. He told me he was still back at the scene. He was too shaken up to go with Laura in the ambulance. He didn't get to the hospital until after she was dead.

Not Laura's mother either. She was on a cruise ship thousands of miles away and didn't even know about Laura's suicide try yet.

I went back and checked the notes I'd made from the original police report on the night of Laura Marlowe's murder. Just to make sure. The facts were just the way I had remembered them.

There were two people who were there with Laura when she was put in the ambulance.

I knew both of them.

David Valentine, her father.

And Sherry DeConde.

CHAPTER 53

FOUND her at the West Village townhouse. She didn't seem surprised to see me. Maybe she was expecting me to come after her, sooner or later. We had unfinished business together, Sherry and me, and I think we both knew that.

I went over there with the intent of confronting her with all my questions about Laura Marlowe and Rizzo and Valentine and all the rest of the tangled web of lies and deceit that I'd uncovered about her.

But it didn't work out that way.

Because the first thing she did was throw herself in my arms, press her head against my chest, and begin crying about how sorry she was.

Then she reached up and kissed me.

I kissed her back.

After that, I decided there would be plenty of time to talk to her later.

We started making out right there in the hallway, moved into the living room and then up the stairs—taking off each other's clothing and dropping it piece by piece along the way—until we got to the bedroom. She pulled me down onto the bed next to her.

I was feeling so many things at that moment. I was mad at this woman, I cared about her, and—I suppose most of all—I was desperately happy and turned on to be with her like this again. All of this—the anger, the desperation, the sexual excitement—turned it into probably the most intense sexual experience I'd ever had. I think she felt the same way too. We went after each other like two animals, as if this kind of primal lust could somehow blot out everything else that had come between us. And, for a while anyway, that's exactly what happened.

Later, as we lay in each other's arms, I looked up and saw the picture of Laura Marlowe on the wall.

Like she was watching us.

Which I guess was kind of appropriate.

———

There was a balcony outside the window of Sherry's bedroom. When I thought she was asleep, I walked out onto it, sat down, and looked out over the Hudson River in the distance. It was dark and I could see the lights from boats out there. I thought again about Davy Valentine's fishing boat. I wondered how far it could take Sherry and me. What if we just sailed off somewhere and lived happily ever after? Except I knew we could never do that. And I also knew that I was just killing time to avoid figuring out how to confront Sherry with the questions I needed to ask her.

I heard a noise and turned around. It was Sherry. She wasn't sleeping any more than I was. She sat down beside me, put her arm around me, and pulled me close to her. She made me feel warm and comfortable and safe, just the way Laura Marlowe must have felt about her when she came looking for help at the end.

"I think there's something you're still not telling me," I said.

"What are you talking about?"

"Laura. There's a big chunk of unaccounted for time right after the shooting. Enough time for someone to make sure Laura Marlowe didn't survive, if they really wanted her to die. You were there with her during that crucial time period. You and Valentine. What the hell were the two of you doing there anyway? Did you really leave when they put her in the ambulance or did you go with her? What happened on that ride to the hospital, Sherry?"

I felt her hand tighten on my shoulder.

"Are you asking if I killed Laura?" she asked.

"No," I said, "I think maybe you tried to save her."

CHAPTER 54

L AURA wanted to die," Sherry said.

She talked about the emotional wreck Laura Marlowe had been when she showed up unexpectedly in Sherry's office in the days leading up to the shooting. Laura was the big star that Sherry lost out on, the missed opportunity that had seemingly doomed her agency business. But she wasn't acting like a big star that day, Sherry said. More like a scared little girl.

Laura told Sherry how sorry she was that her mother had cut Sherry out of her life. How Sherry had always been her friend, someone she could trust, someone who truly cared about her as a person—not just as a show business commodity. That's why she was there now, she said. She had nowhere else to turn. She began to cry then and clung to Sherry, hugging her so hard and for so long that Sherry said it felt like a drowning person clinging to a life raft as the only thing keeping them afloat.

"She said she wanted to kill herself. She said she couldn't live one more day with all the responsibilities, all the pressure of being Laura Marlowe. She said all of them—her studio, her fans, her mother, her husband—wanted her to be someone she wasn't. All she ever wanted was to live her own life, she said. If she couldn't have that, she didn't want any life at all."

When Laura finally left, Sherry called Davy Valentine. They

decided they needed to do something to get her away from Beverly and Holloway and all the rest of the insanity in her life.

"Davy and I, we really just wanted to help her," Sherry said. "But we didn't know how. And so we reached out to Rizzo."

Thomas Rizzo. Of course. He'd been at the center of the Laura Marlowe mystery all along. He was the one who discovered her. He made her a star. He was the father of her baby. And at the end, he was still there.

"Rizzo said we needed to come up with a plan," Sherry said. "A way to make Laura Marlowe disappear forever and allow her to live her life on her own terms. Rizzo said he and Laura had even talked about doing this together in the past. Running off with each other and starting all over again. But in order to do that, they had to leave the past behind. Laura had to run away from her stardom, Rizzo from his past in the mob.

"They'd already devised this elaborate plan to fake one another's deaths at one point. But Rizzo decided he couldn't do it. He felt an obligation to his wife and young son. He had this weird set of values. It was alright to kill people, but he drew a moral line at abandoning his family. He still loved Laura though. He wanted to give her a chance, even if he couldn't be with her.

"And so the three of us talked about all sorts of possible ways to fake Laura's death. A drowning at sea. A fire where her supposed body was burned beyond recognition. It had to be something like that where there was no recognizable body, we decided. I mean how do you fake the death of someone as famous as Laura Marlowe if there's a body? There'd have to be an autopsy—which would reveal the real identity. In the end, it seemed like a fake drowning was the best way to go. At least, that's what the three of us were thinking at the time."

They'd made a deal about what would happen after Laura "died" and disappeared, she said. Her. Valentine. And Rizzo. None of them would ever see Laura or contact her again. The only way Laura could live a new life safely was to put every piece of the old one behind her. It would be like disappearing into the witness protection program, Rizzo had told them. There could be no trace of Laura Marlowe and no links to the people she left behind. She would just disappear forever. He would make sure she was well taken care of. Before she changed identities, she'd get a big sum of money from Rizzo. Enough to live on for the rest of her life, if she needed to. Enough that she'd never have to come back looking for more.

Maybe it would have happened that way if Laura hadn't killed herself.

Maybe Rizzo would have let her go on to live a new life on her own without looking over her shoulder.

"The idea was that Laura Marlowe had to die before Laura Makofsky could live," Sherry said to me now. "The world—especially Beverly and Holloway and the people in Hollywood—would never leave her alone otherwise. It was a crazy idea, I know, but Rizzo really thought we could pull it off."

"Then the shooting happened," I said. "And it was too late for you and Rizzo and Valentine to put your plan into action. Did you know it was a suicide? That Laura shot herself that night?"

She nodded.

"Davy and I had showed up at the hotel to try to talk to her. The ambulance had just arrived there. We even got into the ambulance while the medical people were trying to save Laura's life. I held her hand. She was weak but she could still talk. She said she'd tried to commit suicide, but Holloway showed up unexpectedly and she hadn't counted on that. She was crying. She squeezed my hand and I held on to it as tightly as I could to somehow try to will her to stay alive. But then the medical people made Davy and me get out of the ambulance so they could work on her."

"What happened on that ambulance ride?" I asked. "Why did it take so long to get Laura to the hospital?"

"I have no idea. Like I said, they wouldn't let us stay with her. Maybe there was just a lot of traffic that night."

"Did you ever talk to Thomas Rizzo after the shooting about the details of Laura's death?"

"No."

"Why not?"

"Because he's Thomas Rizzo. You don't talk to Rizzo. He talks to you."

Then I asked her the real question that had been on my mind ever since I came over to see her.

"Do you think Laura Marlowe is still alive?"

Sherry stared at me.

"I'm serious," I told her. "Is there any way at all that Rizzo might have put the plan to make Laura disappear forever in action on his own that night? Without telling you. Did that thought ever cross your mind?"

"C'mon, Gil," she said finally, "it would be nearly impossible to fake the death of someone that famous when there's a body. That's why we had talked about the other scenarios with Rizzo like a fake drowning. But once Laura shot herself, it was too late. I mean with a body—especially a celebrity body—there's going to be too many questions. She had to be identified before the body was cremated. There had to be some sort of medical investigation or autopsy to confirm the cause of death."

———

I nodded. It all made sense except for one thing. Sherry still hadn't really answered my question about whether she thought Laura Marlowe might still be alive. Was there any possibility at all Rizzo could have put his plan in action to fake her death that night without telling them? I asked her the question again.

"Let's be real here," she said, "there's no logical way that could have happened. The evidence is overwhelming that Laura Marlowe died that night during the ambulance ride to the hospital. To pull off a fake death like that, Rizzo would have had to bribe and pay off and threaten everybody—doctors, ambulance attendants, people in the coroner's office, the funeral home, the cops too for God's sake. I mean I know he's a very powerful guy, but it's hard to believe even Rizzo could do something like that."

"Virtually impossible," I said.

"No way at all it could ever happen," she agreed.

Then she looked at me and smiled.

"Did you ever read about all the people who still think Elvis and Jim Morrison are alive?" she said. "I mean there's simply no way that could be true either. Elvis died at Graceland and there's even a picture of him laid out at the funeral home. Morrison may or may not have really died of a heart attack in his bathtub as the official version goes, but they identified his body and buried him in Paris in 1971. And yet there are still people who ignore all of these facts and insist that Elvis or Jim Morrison are really still alive somewhere. That they just decided they didn't want to be stars anymore. So they faked their deaths and fooled the world.

"You want to know something? I sometimes still have those same crazy doubts that Laura is really dead. Why did that ambulance ride take so long? Why couldn't those doctors save Laura? Did Davy really have her body cremated so quickly to avoid a public spectacle or did someone tell him to do that? And then I think about Rizzo. And I think about how if there was anyone who could ever pull off something like that—no matter how farfetched it seemed—Rizzo was the one person with the power, the money, and intimidation to be able to do it."

I didn't say anything. I just wanted her to keep talking. I knew she'd held this in for a long time.

"After Laura shot herself," Sherry told me, "Rizzo offered to invest in my business. I wasn't sure if he did this out of gratitude for what I'd done for Laura or to buy my silence about all the secrets I knew about the suicide and the rest of it. But I took his money. I even worked with him for a while when he operated as a silent partner in my agency. He was never around or anything though. It was just another investment to him.

"He gave money to Davy too. The two of us wound up getting married after all this happened. I guess the whole Laura business brought us together so closely that it seemed like a good idea at the time. Well, it wasn't. Davy's a nice guy, but we really had nothing in common except for our love for Laura. The marriage only lasted a couple of years.

"I never heard much from Rizzo after a while. But I knew he was out there. And I made sure never to do anything that might make him feel threatened by me. That's why whenever some law enforcement agency came around on a Rizzo investigation, I clammed up and said nothing. I wanted him to know that he could trust me to keep my mouth shut.

"As it turned out, he never bothered either me or Davy. Maybe because he knew we wanted to keep the truth about Laura a secret as much as he did. Me, I made peace with it all. As the years went by, I just tried to pretend that none of it had ever happened. I almost did that too. Until you showed up at my door."

Another boat passed by on the horizon, its lights twinkling in the evening sky. I thought again about sailing away on a boat and starting over again with Sherry DeConde—just like Laura Marlowe and Thomas Rizzo had once dreamed of doing.

It was an impossible dream, of course.

Sherry and I weren't going to live happily ever after. We were just two ships passing in the night. We both had too much emotional baggage and too many secrets and too many demons from our past to put this all behind us and start our lives all over again together. It was just a crazy dream. Sherry and I both knew that. Those kinds of dreams only happen in fairy tales.

But what if—no matter how crazy and impossible it seemed—Laura Marlowe really had made her own fairy tale come true thirty years ago.

Just disappeared out there somewhere.

To a new life.

And no one had ever found her.

I think I wanted to believe in that almost as much as Sherry did.

Sherry reached over and pulled me closer to her now. She kissed me again, and I kissed her back. No, this would not last forever, I knew that. Tomorrow or the next day or the day after that, Sherry DeConde would be gone. She was not the one for me. Any more than Susan had turned out to be. But Sherry was here with me now. And so I held on to her tightly for as long as I could, just like Laura Marlowe had done a long time ago.

CHAPTER 55

STILL think about the Laura Marlowe story. A lot.

And wonder what really did happen on that long-ago night.

Like I said, there's a part of me that wants to believe—just like Sherry DeConde—that Laura Marlowe really is still alive out there somewhere. That she didn't die in the ambulance on the way to the hospital. That Thomas Rizzo somehow pulled off the impossible and came up with his own plan to make Laura disappear into a new and better life after the shooting.

What a story that would be, huh? I mean just imagine if I amazingly tracked down this legendary actress thirty years after she supposedly died, wrote about how she faked her death all this time, and told the world about her new life. That would be the exclusive of a lifetime. I'd be famous all over again.

But I know that will never happen.

Whatever secrets Thomas Rizzo still had about Laura . . . well, he took them to the grave with him.

In the end, it really didn't matter though. Because even if I did discover that Laura had somehow lived that night, I don't think I'd go looking for her. Not because I'd be afraid I might fail to find her. Because I'm afraid I might succeed.

I fear there is no happy ending to the Laura Marlowe story. Even if she had managed to run away to a new life, there was no reason to think she wouldn't have made many of the same mistakes all over again that she made in those first twenty-two years of her life. Wherever she went, she probably would have wound up with someone just like her mother or Edward Holloway or Thomas Rizzo. No matter how far you run, you can't run away from yourself. I knew this better than anyone. Eugene O'Neill said it best a long time ago: "There is no present or future. Only the past, happening over and over again."

Laura Marlowe may have been America's sweetheart, but she was inexorably doomed to a life of unhappiness.

Sometimes late at night, when I'm sitting alone in my apartment, I go on Netflix and watch Laura Marlowe's final movie, *Once Upon a Time Forever*. The one about a beautiful princess who runs away from all her fame and power and riches—and lives happily ever after with the man she loves.

She looks so young on the screen.

So beautiful.

So full of hope.

This is the way I want to remember Laura Marlowe.

I still want to believe in the fairy tale.

ACKNOWLEDGMENTS

I've spent a lot of time as a celebrity journalist. I was news editor of *Star* magazine during the '90s. Managing editor for features/entertainment at the *New York Daily News* in between news desk jobs there. City editor at the *New York Post* when we launched Page Six as a must-read gossip column. And I've covered all the big celebrity news stories like O. J., John Lennon, and the death of Princess Diana.

So for a follow-up to *The Kennedy Connection*—which is about the most famous unsolved murder of all time—I decided to make Gil Malloy's next front-page story about the death of a famous celebrity. Because so many people—and I'm one of them—care passionately about the lives and deaths of celebrities just like they do about the JFK assassination. Laura Marlowe is fiction. But I touch upon some true celebrity crime in the book—notably the murders of John Lennon and movie actress Sharon Tate. And I draw on my real-life journalistic experience to paint a picture of Laura Marlowe as a tragic celebrity who had it all for too short a time.

Most of this book was written at The Writers Room in New York City. This is a wonderful workplace located in the East Village—my new office, as I call it since I left daily journalism at NBC News—that is home to more than 200 writers of all types. Thanks to Donna Brodie and the staff there for providing such a creative environment that makes it almost impossible to find an excuse not to write.

I'd also like to express my gratitude to all the terrific booksellers at stores around the country I've met over the past year who prove that reading is still alive and well; fans of the first two Gil Malloy books—*The Kennedy Connection* and *The Midnight Hour*—that have given me so much encouragement; Todd Hunter at Atria Books, who made Gil Malloy come alive in the series; and Nalini Akolekar, my agent who has believed in Gil (and me) from the beginning.

Finally, they always say writers should write about what they know, and I couldn't have written these books without the knowledge and inspiration I've gotten from working in newsrooms for so many years. The front pages, the circulation wars, and—most of all—the colorful characters. I love it—and I've tried to put that same passion for the news business in my Gil Malloy character. My favorite newspaper movie of all time is *Deadline—U.S.A* with Humphrey Bogart as a newspaper editor. At one point, he tells a kid looking for a job at the paper: "About this wanting to be a reporter, don't ever change your mind. It may not be the oldest profession, but it's the best." Gil Malloy couldn't have said it better.